THE
Governess

THE
Governess

Sometimes What You Find Is
Better Than What You Seek

KRISTEN McKENDRY

Covenant Communications, Inc.

Cover image: *Historical Woman Reading on Terrace* © Elena Alferova / Trevillion Images

Cover design copyright © 2016 by Covenant Communications, Inc.

Published by Covenant Communications, Inc.
American Fork, Utah

Printed in the United States of America
First Printing: October 2016

22 21 20 19 18 17 16   10 9 8 7 6 5 4 3 2 1

ISBN 978-1-52440-038-5

To Jon and Tracey Firth

Acknowledgments

THANK YOU TO SAMANTHA MILLBURN for nudging and challenging me so patiently and to the rest of the Covenant team for helping bring this book to life. Thank you to the anonymous reviewers who caught the discrepancies and anachronisms that managed to sneak in while I was busy elsewhere.

Thank you to Sandy McCulloch for understanding when the story in my head was more real to me than whatever work I was meant to be doing and for giving me the time and space to let it out.

Thank you to Bill McCauley for the generous loan of the cottage to get away and think in. The timing of your offer was perfect, and I still believe that staring at an open expanse of water is the most conducive thing to creativity on the planet.

Thank you to my family for your patience and support when I came up for air, glassy-eyed and grouchy from being immersed in the manuscript too long.

Thank you to my friend Tracey for letting me soak in the warmth of your woodstove in silence without making any demands of me whatsoever. You were immensely good at making people feel wanted and welcomed. I am just beginning to realize the size of the hole you have left in my life. If I knew a piobaireachd, I would play it for you.

Thank you to Jon. Even in the midst of your loss, you were so graciously kind. I am glad I have gained another friend.

And, as always, the biggest thank-you to my husband for keeping the home fires burning and handling everything with grace and efficiency while I lingered late over the computer. I couldn't do any of this without you, nor would I want to try.

Chapter One

"It is obvious to me that you cannot be trusted."

Katherine clasped her hands tightly together to keep them from trembling as she faced the man behind the desk. "Mr. Colworthy, I assure you it will not happen again."

He waved a beefy hand and leaned forward until his breakfast-stained waistcoat strained at its buttons. "It will certainly not because you are no longer in my employ."

"But—"

"My daughter could have been seriously wounded, even killed. She missed that pitchfork by mere inches."

Katherine winced. "It's not as if I told Alice to climb up to the hayloft and jump," she protested. "I was trying to get her to come down. She wouldn't obey me."

"Which just reinforces my opinion that you have lost all control over the nursery," he said brutally. "That will be all. Hadley will drive you to the station."

Katherine's nails bit into her palms. She forced her voice to remain steady as she said, "I feel it is unjust to dismiss me without hearing me out, sir."

She watched his mouth sag in astonishment and his face turn an ugly mottled red. She shouldn't have spoken, but the injustice of her dismissal made her bold. She drew a shaky breath, but before she could say anything more, he turned away from her abruptly, picked up his pipe, and began to push the tobacco in with his fat thumb.

"That will be all, nurse." His clipped tone was final.

Katherine felt her stomach constrict. "Am I to receive a character?" she asked stiffly.

"You nearly killed my daughter," he said flatly. "What insane kind of question is that?"

* * *

It was unspeakably humiliating. Katherine stood, hands on hips, in the room she had inhabited for such a short time. Her trunk stood at the back of the dressing room, where it had been placed only weeks before. She wanted to weep at the thought of packing it again. She had hoped—planned—to remain at the Colworthys' beautiful estate for a long time.

"It isn't fair," she mourned, lifting her hand to touch the curved wood of the bedpost. Its dark oak was echoed in the frame around the window, which overlooked the paved drive that ran down to the wrought-iron gates. She was about to go through those gates . . . to what? Her eyes swept the smooth green expanse of Caledon's fields as if seeking the answer. She saw only pasture and maple trees and a wandering cow, of no help to her at all.

She had no other employment prospects and, indeed, had run through several positions in a discouragingly short time already. The idea of having to find yet another place for herself was daunting. She knew most young women her age were married, but though the thriving Dominion of Canada had no shortage of well-connected young men available, she was becoming increasingly aware of her fading chances of catching one of them. The daughter of a Toronto dry-goods merchant, she'd known from a young age that she was solidly middle class, nothing to be done about it, and in addition, she knew she was rather plain. And then to top it off, her father had made her thrice unmarriageable by providing her with a strong education. She had known the dangers of it, but she had so enjoyed learning that she'd applied herself at school and had absorbed all of the classical subjects, along with the usual domestic skills and social graces. Her friends had warned her that men did not want wives who were smarter or more educated than they, particularly the wealthy ones who had gained their position through commerce and often were not very educated themselves. But Katherine, being a practical sort of girl, knew her odds of marrying a wealthy man were low anyway. She'd resigned herself to the prospect of marrying someone middle class like herself, someone hardworking and reliable and financially sound, if not spectacularly so—a factory foreman, perhaps, or a junior solicitor on Bay Street. She had imagined herself in a modest but gracious home with three or four children and a pianoforte and, if not a full staff, at least a cook and housekeeper. There would be social teas and evenings at the theater and a position on the flower committee at church and drives along the lakeshore in a well-appointed carriage. Surely there was no reason why life shouldn't go exactly as she'd planned.

But it hadn't. And now, with Edgar Colworthy's scathing remarks still burning her ears, she told herself that perhaps she'd been a bit too confident.

* * *

Hadley, the coachman, did not try to hide his sneer as he deposited her at the train station, and he left her there as soon as her trunk was unloaded from the carriage. Nannies were difficult, being neither among the lower servants nor the lady's maids, and they tended not to make friends among the others in the house, not that Katherine had been in the household long enough to have made friends anyway. And she had found the other women in service at the Colworthy home to be as disagreeable and pompous as their master. Sighing, Katherine told herself it no longer mattered, then bought a ticket for Toronto with the last pay Mr. Colworthy had given her. She sat on the platform bench to wait for the train.

The air had an early-fall chill to it, and the sky above the station was growing dull with clouds. She hoped it wouldn't rain; that would be unbearable in the mood she was in. There were few other people about, only an elderly couple farther down the platform and a harried-looking woman with two small children. Katherine shuddered. The sight of any child after her latest charge was enough to make her squeamish. She hoped she would not be seated near them on the train. The thought came to her that anyone who felt as she did about Alice Colworthy, age seven, really had no business being a governess in the first place.

She had not set out to be a nanny, of course. Her mother had died in 1869, when Katherine was thirteen years old, and her father had not adapted well. David Porter's wife had been his anchor, the sole impetus behind his energies, and with her died all his will and ambition. Katherine had once admired her father's devotion to her mother, seeing it as terribly romantic, but she had learned to resent it, for her mother's passing had crippled her father. His business interests waned; his already limited resources began to trickle away. As he slid into decline, his wife's cousin's husband, Hugh Fitzgerald, owner of a burgeoning textile mill, came forward and offered to lend him money to stay afloat.

David refused to play the poor relation, and Katherine unexpectedly found herself having to live frugally, watching even her reasonable, modest ambitions trickle through her fingers like water while she played nursemaid to a suddenly old and ailing father. A middle-class husband might settle for a merchant's daughter, but no one would want a penniless orphan. David had died when Katherine was seventeen, and tall, portly Hugh Fitzgerald had stepped in like a steadily chugging train and taken charge.

She still cringed, remembering the morning he'd called her into her father's empty office, sat in the chair behind the desk, and briskly informed her that she couldn't live long on what her father had left.

"I've already arranged to sell the house and shop," he'd told her bluntly. "It will barely cover your father's remaining debts."

Katherine recalled every word raining down on her like shards of glass. She'd stood staring at the sunlight glancing off the bald spot on his head, which he had tried to cover with a sweep of his graying red hair, and hadn't been able to think of a single reply. Hugh hadn't waited for her to respond in any case. He'd gone on unperturbedly to inform her she was henceforth to live with him and his wife, Martha.

At first Katherine had been grateful. Here was a solution to her financial dilemma. She was given the chance to live as she'd always dreamed of living, with a lovely bedroom and occasional use of the carriage and abundant meals served in the opulent dining room. She was allowed to sit with Martha in the parlor when Martha's friends came to call. She accompanied Hugh and Martha when they were invited to visit Hugh's brother, Reginald, and his wife, Elizabeth, at their stately home in Rosemount. But it had soon become clear to her that she would always be a guest and that her role was to play the poor relation through whom Hugh and Martha could display to others how generous they were—exactly the role her father had refused to play. They'd managed to offer Katherine a place in their home while daily reminding her that the luxury and beauty surrounding her was not and never would be truly hers and that with one word they could shatter the stability of her life if she failed to please them. Her enjoyment had quickly soured into humiliation.

The train rushed into the station, jarring Katherine from her gloomy reverie, and she gathered her belongings and stepped forward, her boots thumping on the wooden boards of the platform. An elderly porter stowed her trunk and helped her find a seat. She had ridden the train several times before, but she still found it exciting, and she gripped her hands together tightly in her lap as the train pulled out of the station and gathered speed. In the breeze coming through the partially open window, her dark hair started to stray from its bun in feathery coils about her ears.

"Are you going all the way to Toronto?" the middle-aged woman across the aisle asked her conversationally. She was plump and contented-looking and wore a felted brown dress that made her resemble a horsehair sofa. She appeared to be traveling alone, as Katherine was.

"Yes," Katherine replied. "And you?"

"Just as far as Streetsville. My brother and his wife have bought a new house there, and I am on my way to see it."

"That's exciting for them," Katherine said politely.

"Their first home in Toronto grew too small, you see. They have seven children."

"My goodness!"

"I only have four myself. But I'm younger than Josephine. And you?"

Katherine blinked a moment, wondering if the woman was asking her age, and then she realized what she was really asking. "I have no children. I'm not married," she told her.

"Oh! I'm sorry. I assumed . . ."

Katherine completed the sentence in her head. *At your age you'd be married.* She forced a smile she didn't feel. "A reasonable assumption," she said. "But no, I've never married. I'm a career woman."

She tasted these words in her mouth, trying to find the flavor of them, but they were flat, and she gulped inaudibly. *Some career woman. I have no work. What am I to do?* For an insane moment, she wondered if she should inquire whether this woman's sister-in-law needed a nanny, but the thought of seven children made her mouth go dry. Surely she could find something else, something less terrifying, once she got to Toronto.

The friendly woman turned her attention to the golden, harvest-ready fields they were traveling through, the opportunity passed, and Katherine, with the guilty relief of having narrowly averted a catastrophe, closed her eyes and leaned her head back on the leather seat.

She felt wrung out from the strain of the past twenty-four hours and thought she might do well to sleep while she had the chance, but the woman's words played over and over in her mind. *I assumed . . .*

It cut her more deeply than she cared to admit. She had always made the same assumption herself, that by this age she would be married and settled. There had once been some brief talk about Hugh Fitzgerald settling a small sum on Katherine to enhance her chances of marrying, and thus increasing the chances of removing her from the household, but Hugh had not followed through, and Katherine had not raised the matter again.

Martha had made it perfectly clear how indebted to her relatives Katherine already was, and Katherine was loath to increase that sense of obligation. She remembered Martha clucking over her outdated clothes, assuring her with sweet smiles that she wasn't to worry; she and Hugh would always see that she had a roof over her head, no matter the inconvenience to themselves.

Katherine fought down the tightness in her throat at the stinging memory. Martha's condescending attitude ensured Katherine was always well aware of the dangling carrot of gracious living all around her, close enough to touch but not fully grasp.

Martha's henchman in every little action, every cutting word, had been her horse-faced sister-in-law, Elizabeth Fitzgerald. In hundreds of small ways, with subtle comments and arched eyebrows, the two women had managed to make it clear they held out little hope for their plain, penniless cousin's marriage prospects, even among the working class. Katherine had refused to believe it and nursed her hopes in spite of them, all the while trying to ignore the niggling feeling that they were probably right.

* * *

The train reached Streetsville, and the woman across the aisle disembarked as she gave Katherine a cheerful wave good-bye. Katherine rubbed her cheeks vigorously and told herself to shake off her gloom and think of a solution to her situation. She would be in Toronto soon, and she needed to have a plan when she arrived.

She considered going to her mother's cousin's but immediately dismissed the idea. She'd endured the Fitzgerald house for four years, sitting on her simmering pride until she had reached an age when she could humiliate them all in the best way she could contrive: by rejecting their cold kindness and escaping into service.

She had known at the time that it was a desperate leap to make and probably a foolish one, but she hadn't wanted to remain in the house a moment longer than necessary, and she could still feel the secret shiver of satisfaction that had shot through her when she had announced her intentions at the dinner table one night. Hugh's face had sagged in dismay, and Martha had been livid.

"What on earth are you thinking?" Martha spat. "People will think we've turned you out. All our friends will find out and think we've been heartless. How can you be so heedless of Hugh's reputation?"

"It's something I must do," Katherine replied, trying to sound more confident than she felt. "I've been a burden to you long enough. My father didn't want to accept your help, and I don't think he would want me to, either, now that I'm twenty-one."

"A burden!" Hugh blustered, the word finally penetrating his slow-moving brain. He turned red-faced and started to speak, but Martha rode over him.

"You, earn a living? Ha! What can *you* do to support yourself?"

Katherine had not told them at the time. She had considered her options and had decided to groom herself secretly to be a lady's companion. She had spent much of the six months prior studying the manners of the fine ladies who had visited the Fitzgerald home and the fashions she had seen in the shops on Queen Street. She had listened in on the conversations Martha had had with her friends. She had felt her graces and talents—and yes, even her knowledge of French and Latin—would secure her a place with a discerning and appreciative patroness. Such a position would have allowed her some of the luxuries and delights of the upper social circle she admired, even if those luxuries came to her second hand. The life of a lady's companion could have still afforded her some prestige. She was capable and qualified. But she had not wanted to spread this hopeful plan in front of her relatives for them to walk over. So she had only repeated firmly, "It's time I supported myself."

But it hadn't gone as planned. It seemed the lady's companion positions she had prepared herself for were difficult to come by, and she had instead, desperate and impetuous as always, snatched at the first employment to come along after her dinnertime announcement—that of governess. This had not been a success and had been followed by a series of increasingly dismal positions in rapid succession. Now, three years later, she could not stomach the idea of requesting that Martha and Hugh take her back, repulsed by the idea of admitting, after all her defiance, that she was an abject failure as an employee. If she couldn't have wealth of her own, she didn't want to beg the benefit of others'. This was Canada, a place of expansion and opportunity. If a woman alone could succeed anywhere, it was here.

On the other hand, she had no character from her previous employers, and with the inglorious track record of four positions in three years, she doubted anyone else would hire her.

She had enough money saved to rent a room somewhere for a week or two. She would look for another position as a lady's companion or a tutor. She wouldn't take on such a young child again, though, for Miss Alice Colworthy had convinced her she wasn't meant to care for young children. If she found nothing, she would work in a laundry before she'd consider throwing herself back on Hugh and Martha's cold mercy.

She hoped again that it wouldn't come to that.

The train began to pull out of the Streetsville station at last, and Katherine pulled her cloak more tightly about her shoulders, fixed her eyes on the gentle countryside outside her window, and tried not to think about her unstable circumstances.

Chapter Two

KATHERINE ARRIVED IN TORONTO ON Monday and found a shared apartment to rent on Hickory Street. It was on the top floor of a dilapidated yellow clapboard house, reached by way of a narrow, windowless staircase. She had her own bedroom, with a narrow cot and a clean but threadbare blanket, and she shared the kitchen with a dumpy-looking woman in her forties introduced by the landlady as Gail O'Rourke.

"A bit hard of hearing, Gail is," the landlady whispered to Katherine. "But that means she won't be complaining about any noise you make. Her husband left her, poor creature, and took their two children with him, so she isn't particularly happy company right now, but she won't give you any trouble."

Katherine gave her roommate a tentative smile, but Mrs. O'Rourke only went into her room and shut the door.

"She doesn't come out much, so it's almost like having the place to yourself," the landlady said cheerily. "Let me show you the bath. It's down the hall, and you share it with the other tenants on this floor, so you mustn't linger in it long."

It was not an ideal situation, but it was all Katherine could find. The room cost more than she'd anticipated, so she had only seven days to find work. She tried to forget the humiliation and injustice she'd endured as nanny to Alice and told herself the next position would be better. She would be more selective. She should have recognized Edgar Colworthy's overindulgence of his child immediately and surmised what a spoiled beast his offspring would be. Katherine would be wiser next time.

By the following Sunday afternoon, she decided she couldn't deceive herself any longer. The city was overrun with immigrants eager for work, and there was simply nothing available for someone of her background, not even in a laundry. She had no choice. She was prepared to go through a lot for the sake of her pride but not outright starvation. She decided to treat herself to a good meal at a fashionable teahouse on Yonge Street not far from her room. It would strengthen her to face writing the letter to Hugh. The only good thing about admitting defeat was that she could at least escape the gloomy and silent Gail O'Rourke.

It wasn't proper to go to the teahouse unescorted, but she had no one to escort her, and she wanted to indulge in this one thing for herself, so she put on her good brown dress—outdated, but at least it had a decent bustle—piled her hair artfully on her head, and took herself off with a feeling of reckless daring.

The room was crowded, and she sat at the only available table. She ordered tea, smoked salmon, fruit, and—the ultimate indulgence—an éclair, and sat back to wait. The sunlight sparkled off the crystal vase and dew-wet pink rose on the pristine white cloth. The room hummed with genteel conversation. Most people who frequented this tearoom were patrons of the Museum of Natural History or the adjacent La Fleur Art Gallery. They were, therefore, of the upper middle class of society, usually well educated in Europe or Britain, and slightly bohemian.

Katherine vowed that one day she would belong to a place like this. She would have *les petites duchesses* every day and take part in the glittering conversation. Just how she would accomplish this, she did not dwell on. It was fascinating just to sit and observe the dress, mannerisms, and speech of those around her. The snatches of conversation she overheard were tantalizing. People spoke of artists and new schools of painting and anthropological treks to exotic places. She tried to look as if she weren't eavesdropping, but even her sense of propriety couldn't smother her curiosity, her thirst to belong to this elegant world.

Her food was delivered just as she glimpsed another patron entering the tearoom. Katherine was distracted by the waiter and didn't get a good look at the newcomer at first. When she had been served and the waiter was gone, she glanced again at the man who had paused near the door, and her interest was immediately arrested.

He must have come from the art gallery; perhaps he was a student or an artist himself. He wore a proper dark suit of good make and an appropriate hat, but he had an outlandish crimson shirt underneath his coat. He wore his collar open, with no tie or stock or even a decent button to cover his throat. The kerchief protruding from his breast pocket was a matching crimson, and Katherine's eyes widened at the finely made boots he wore shamelessly specked with mud.

While she watched, he scanned the room until his gaze came to rest on her. Katherine felt as if she'd been caught spying. She lowered her gaze and, a moment later, was astonished to see the outrageous crimson shirt stop beside her table. She looked up into a pair of blue eyes so dark they appeared indigo, fringed in black. The man removed his hat to reveal an unruly shock of dark hair that curled over his ears and the back of his collar. He was unfashionably clean-shaven. The skin of his face and throat was swarthy, the color of milky coffee. He was handsome but not classically so. His face had sharp, pleasant planes, and there were laugh lines at the corners of his eyes. A likeable face.

"Excuse me, there doesn't seem to be an available table." He had a mellow baritone and a slight accent she couldn't place. "I couldn't help noticing you were alone. Would you mind if I shared your table?"

She felt her mouth drop in surprise and quickly amended it into a smile. "You're quite welcome."

He set down the hat and newspaper he held under his arm, sat in the chair opposite hers, and motioned for the waiter. "Tea and scones, please," he said, and the waiter hurried away with an elegantly murmured, "Very good, sir."

"I'm afraid there's no one to introduce us," the man said to Katherine. His smile transformed his face, making it less angular. She guessed him to be about thirty. "My name is Alonzo Colaco."

"Katherine Porter," Katherine replied. *Italian*, she thought to herself. That must be the accent. It would explain his coloring.

"Please, don't let me keep you from your meal," the man said politely.

She was saved from having to decide whether to wait until he'd been served or to go ahead, for his order arrived promptly.

"Have you come from the art gallery?" he asked after a pause.

"No, I only came for tea," she said. "I live near here."

"Ah. If you haven't seen the exhibits, you're missing a very pleasant experience."

"I'll have to go, then," she said, knowing she never would. "Are you an artist, Mr. Colaco?"

"Of sorts," he replied with a shrug. "But my pitiful talents do not extend to painting. You'll never see anything of mine in La Fleur. And yourself? If you live in this area, you're either an artist or a student of natural history."

A little tingle of pleasure went through her. He thought she belonged here. "Neither, actually," Katherine said. She couldn't help responding to his smile with one of her own.

"Ah, the mystery deepens."

"There's nothing mysterious about me. I'm a private tutor." She felt this sounded scholarly, more so than a lady's companion, whose role was more social than intellectual. And far better than nanny.

"I see. Where do you teach?"

"I'm currently . . . between positions." She was pleased with herself for the neat phrase.

"Unemployed?" He seemed to perk with interest. "What do you teach?"

"All general subjects and Latin," Katherine told him, a touch proudly. "My last charge was only seven years old, so, of course, the subject matter was somewhat limited."

He studied her thoughtfully with his blue-violet eyes. "How remarkable. So you teach children."

"Well, I have, yes, but I'm considering looking for something altogether different for my next position."

"Do you have another position arranged yet?"

"Oh. Not yet, but I expect to shortly," Katherine said airily. "I've been enjoying a short hiatus." This was a good phrase too. She congratulated herself on how deftly she was managing the awkward conversation.

"This is incredible luck," Mr. Colaco said. "I am a firm believer in luck. Are you, Miss Porter? Only three days ago, I myself placed an advertisement in the *Toronto Tribune* for just such a person to tutor my children."

He whipped out the newspaper he'd placed on the table and thrust a page under her nose. She saw, wedged between an advertisement for ladies' hats and a testimonial regarding the virtue of sarsaparilla, a block of square, bold letters.

REQUIRED: RELIABLE, WELL-EDUCATED PERSON TO TEACH TWO CHILDREN, IMMEDIATELY. MUST HAVE STRONG LANGUAGE SKILLS AND SENSE OF HUMOR. MUST BE FLEXIBLE, HEALTHY, WILLING TO TRAVEL. SOME LIGHT HOUSEKEEPING REQUIRED.

COMPENSATION COMMENSURATE WITH EXPERIENCE. INQUIRE A. COLACO, CARE OF THE TRIBUNE.

She blinked at the man before her, trying to imagine him as the father of two. He regarded her in return with frank interest. She was more than a little flattered by the approval she read in his expression.

"I just met with a candidate this morning, but I wasn't impressed with her," he said bluntly. "Would you be interested in being considered for the job? We could call this the interview."

"I-I don't—this is highly irregular," Katherine stammered.

"Low score on the language skills," Mr. Colaco said, folding the newspaper, but he was smiling.

She laughed in spite of herself. "What are the ages of your children?" she asked. "I've told you I recently tutored a seven-year-old, but I didn't mention that I didn't particularly enjoy the experience."

"Ah. My children are seven and six, but I assure you they're well behaved and obedient. They're eager to learn. I spend a lot of time with them, and discipline has never been a large problem."

"Ah," Katherine echoed the word. "Do you live here in Toronto, Mr. Colaco?"

"Near Springfield, just to the west," he said. "We remove up north in the spring to Collingwood. I require someone to keep a general eye on the children, feed them lunch, and instruct them a few hours a day, so I suppose it's a nurse position as well as a tutor. I'm very anxious that they receive a proper education, and it's never too early to start. They seem very bright," he added proudly. "I want to encourage that."

Katherine found herself warming to the idea of working for this unusual, enthusiastic man. She wasn't thrilled at the idea of such young charges, heaven knew, but he seemed to be a reasonable sort whom she could approach should difficulty arise—unlike Mr. Colworthy.

"Tell me about yourself, Miss Porter," he said. "What is your background?"

"Well, I attended Fort York Ladies' Academy here in Toronto," she said. "I received high marks and came first in Latin and third in French. My first position was as governess to the Donald White family of York three years ago."

"And the ages of their children?"

"Nine, eight, six, three, and two."

"My goodness!"

"I was with them five months. And then I left." She hesitated, wondering if she was expected to elaborate, but he only said, "I should think so."

Katherine moved on smoothly. "And then I was lady's companion to Mrs. Agatha Wilde in Forest Hill for nine months—taking down letters, reading to her, that kind of thing."

"Just nine months?" he asked, watching her over the rim of his cup.

"Yes, well, the lady passed on suddenly in her sleep," she explained.

"How unfortunate."

"Yes." Katherine swallowed, remembering the shock of finding the kindly old woman stiff in her bed. She'd made the mistake of going blubbering to Martha about it, having no one else to turn to. Martha had called her a silly child. Hugh had told her to stop her foolishness and come home. But Katherine had decided by then that earning wages from strangers was less distasteful than receiving grudging handouts from condescending relatives. "After that I was governess to a young woman by the name of Miss Theresa Mansell-Waring. Perhaps you've heard of the family? They're in Rosedale."

"I'm afraid not. And how long were you with her?"

Katherine swallowed again. "A year and a half. Miss Mansell-Waring eloped to Montreal with her voice instructor, and my services were no longer required."

"Ah. Have you held any other positions?"

She hesitated, but under his steady gaze she couldn't be dishonest. "My latest position was as nurse to the seven-year-old."

"Mmm-hmm. Yes, you said. How long were you there?"

"I-I was there about two months."

He arched one dark eyebrow and waited patiently. There was nothing she could do to avoid answering the unspoken question.

"She was willful and . . . well, I had difficulty getting her to be obedient. She climbed into the hayloft against my express direction one day, and when I went up after her, she ran away from me and—and fell. She wasn't hurt badly," she added quickly. "Fortunately she landed in a large pile of . . . um . . . soft substance."

She thought she saw his lips quirk at this, and she tried not to break into a grin herself at the memory of Alice's outraged, filthy face rising from the compost heap. Katherine hastily brought her own face under control. It would hardly do to laugh about it. Death *had* been narrowly avoided, after all. Drawing a deep breath, she said, "Mr. Colworthy felt I had lost control of the nursery and dismissed me. I-I was unable to procure a character . . ."

"I see." He thought for a moment, and then, to her relief, he moved away from the subject, instead quizzing her about her education. He listened attentively and seemed pleased with her answers.

For her own part, Katherine thought working for him would be agreeable. Mr. Colaco seemed a bit unusual—that crimson shirt really was *too* much—but from his dress and demeanor, she saw he was well off. No doubt his house would be impeccably kept and bright. Surely such an animated man wouldn't live in a dim and overstuffed house like the Colworthys'. She was filled with a sense of relief that her dilemma had apparently been presented with such a simple, serendipitous solution. She wouldn't have to write to Hugh after all! Hope surged within her.

Finally Alonzo Colaco settled back in his chair and nodded in satisfaction. "I believe you are just what I'm looking for," he declared. "I'd like to offer you the position, if you're interested. I can offer you ten dollars a month with every Sunday free. In return, I would ask you to commit to at least one year in my employ. The children need consistency."

This arrangement seemed impossibly good.

"I gladly accept," she said with embarrassing speed.

"Excellent! That's done, then, and I could have saved myself a dollar for the advertisement," he said happily and surprised her by shaking her hand as he would a man's. His palm felt rough against her own, as if he worked frequently with his hands. "What luck I chanced to come in here today."

"My luck as well," Katherine said.

They arranged that she would meet him the following evening at six at the station. He departed, newspaper under his arm, hat once more on his head, and—to her astonishment—his uneaten scones in his handkerchief.

Katherine watched until he'd disappeared into the crowd on the street, then rose and returned to her room. It was with a feeling of deep satisfaction that she went to bed that night. Her life was settled for at least the next year, and the prospect looked joyful, not dreary.

"Furthermore," she murmured as she lay half asleep, "I doubt any child of such a charming man will behave like Miss Alice Colworthy."

Chapter Three

MONDAY KATHERINE SPLURGED A GREAT deal of her remaining funds at the Golden Griffen for some new black stockings and a white apron. She justified the expense by telling herself she needed to be properly turned out for her new position at the home of the unusual Mr. Colaco. Besides, she'd soon have plenty of funds.

She also wondered how she would manage to train and entertain two young children. Her experience was admittedly limited. As a gesture of goodwill, she purchased two illustrated storybooks and ten cents' worth of gumdrops as a gift for her future pupils. She wasn't above bribery if they would behave for her.

Monday evening she took a hired carriage to the train station and stood on the platform, her trunk at her feet, her hat firmly skewered to her head. The platform was crowded with businessmen, and although she was tall, she couldn't see more than ten feet in any direction. The air was growing cool. The jostling people and the prospect of embarking on her new adventure made her stomach jumpy. She began to wonder if she'd mistaken the day or if Mr. Colaco had changed his mind. If he failed to come, what would she do? She could hear Martha's laughter when she showed up on the doorstep with her belongings in hand.

She was musing over the dramatic but more appealing idea of begging in the street when suddenly Alonzo Colaco appeared at her side, his smile warm and reassuring.

"Good evening! All ready, then?" he greeted her, bending to pick up her trunk.

"Oh, please, have a porter carry that. There's no need—"

"Nonsense. It's quite light," her employer said and lifted the trunk, which she knew to be quite heavy, onto his shoulder. This knocked his hat slightly awry, but he didn't appear concerned about it.

"Follow me, please," he said and strode off at a fast clip.

Musing at this eccentricity, Katherine followed. She had difficulty keeping up despite the heavy load he carried.

They boarded a waiting train, and he deposited the trunk in the baggage car. He ushered Katherine into an empty compartment and closed the door after them. Katherine hesitated, not knowing what to think. She'd expected him to come for her in his carriage. But Alonzo Colaco threw himself down on one of the seats and gestured for her to sit opposite him, facing forward.

"Excuse me, but where are we going, sir?" she ventured. "I didn't expect . . ."

"I told you I'm just outside Toronto at the moment," her employer said cheerfully. "It's a village called Springfield. I find it easier to take the train down than to drive in myself. I hope you don't mind."

"Not at all," Katherine replied, wondering what he meant by "at the moment." Oh, but he had mentioned moving north in the spring, hadn't he? That must be what he meant.

At that instant, the train whistle screamed, and they began to move off, gathering speed as they left the station. Katherine watched the platform slide away and tried to relax her grip on her handbag.

"The children are looking forward to meeting you," he told her, stretching his long, lean legs out before him. "I told them they were getting a teacher of their very own, and Lilia's first question was, 'Is she pretty?' Of course I answered in the affirmative."

Katherine blinked at him. She'd never been told she was pretty by anyone but her mother, and mothers were obliged to say such things. Her years in school among girls of a higher class than herself, followed by four years with the Fitzgeralds, had given her rather the opposite impression of herself. With biting little remarks delivered in false, cloying sweetness, Martha and Elizabeth had made it clear they considered Katherine plain. *Are you really going to wear that? Well, perhaps no one will notice how sallow it makes you look." "Let my maid help you with your hair." "I suppose you'll do."*

Katherine cleared her throat. "Lilia is your daughter?"

"Yes. She's seven. Tony is six. They're very eager to begin their lessons," he went on, crossing his ankles.

She knew he was only making small talk. No children of her acquaintance would welcome a tutor or anxiously await their lessons. She was sure he said so only in an attempt to put her at ease. But his expression was friendly and earnest, and she replied with a smile. "I'm looking forward to meeting them too, Mr. Colaco."

"Please don't call me that," he said. "It makes me sound old."

"Then what am I to call you, please?" she asked in mild surprise.

"Everyone calls me Alonzo," he said. "You may do the same."

"I couldn't possibly!" Katherine exclaimed, alarmed. "It's too familiar."

"You'll accustom yourself to it," he said with a shrug.

Katherine bit her lip, wondering whether to argue, then decided against it. Her first day was not the day to disagree. She would broach the matter another time.

"And I'll call you Kate," he said.

Her sensitivities received another shock, and her blue eyes flew open. "I am accustomed to being called Miss Porter, or just Porter. The Colworthys called me nurse," she said rigidly.

"That's far too formal," he said unperturbedly. "Porter. As if you were a bellboy. I can't possibly call you that."

"Katherine, then," she conceded reluctantly.

"You definitely look like a Kate. Your dark hair and blue eyes hint at Irish ancestry. And Kate will be easier for my children to pronounce. English isn't their first language, you see. They speak to me in Italian, and they spoke French to their mother."

"Oh! Well, I'm quite comfortable with French."

"That is good, but I'd rather you didn't speak it with them, if you don't mind. They need to learn English. It's one of the things I'd like you to work on with them."

"Their mother, Mrs. Colaco . . . ?"

"Ruth. She died in the spring." His voice was quiet.

"Oh, I'm sorry. I imagine that was very difficult for the children."

His gaze shifted to the window, where buildings passed by in the gathering dusk.

"It has been difficult for all of us," he said.

They rode in silence the rest of the way. Katherine watched the passing fields and forests and imagined what sort of house Mr. Colaco might have. A great stone estate like the Colworthys'? A grand Victorian with a wraparound veranda? Something unusual, she thought, looking at him furtively. She thought him too extraordinary to imagine him living in an ordinary house. A Gothic mansion, maybe, or . . . or a lighthouse on a high promontory. She hid her smile at this thought.

When the train pulled to a hissing stop in Springfield, he leaped into action once more, leaving her on the platform while he went to collect her trunk. Katherine took the opportunity to tug her skirt and bustle neatly into shape, adjust her hat, prod her hair into place, and stretch her arms and legs. She glanced around the station and saw several passengers pulling away in horse-drawn cabs. Parked farther along the dirt road was a gaily painted gypsy wagon with a piebald horse drowsing in the shafts. An old man pushing a small grinder's wheel shuffled past. The muddy street was soon deserted. She wondered if she should try to procure a cab, as it didn't appear Mr. Colaco had a driver waiting for them.

He arrived at that moment with her trunk and set it down carefully on the ground beside her, then pushed his off-balance hat into place. He was tall, a good head above her, and he'd hoisted her heavy trunk as if it were a pillow.

"All right? Off we go, then. Let me introduce you to your new pupils."

To her astonishment, he turned and strode up the street to the gypsy wagon and disappeared behind it.

A moment later, he came back toward her. Walking before him, his hand on the shoulder of each, were two children, a boy and a girl.

They drew to a stop before her and regarded her curiously with identical dark eyes the color and shape of black pearls. They were approximately the same height, with curly black hair and long lashes. Their skin was creamy tan, and their expressions were as frankly uninhibited as their father's.

Alonzo touched each dark little head. "This is Lilia, and this is Tony. My dears, this is Kate. She will be your teacher."

Lilia immediately took Katherine's hand in both of hers. "I'm happy you've come," she said in a sweet, earnest voice, as if she'd rehearsed the phrase. "I hope you will be happy with us."

Katherine swallowed and found her voice. "I'm sure I will be," she said.

The bewitching little face broke into a smile, and the resemblance to her father was immediately apparent.

Tony seemed a little more bashful. He too took her hand in both of his, but he kept his eyes lowered as he said in scarcely more than a whisper, "Me too, teacher." Then he dropped her hand, stepped back to lean against the reassuring legs of his father, and shot her a grin so beguiling that Katherine could hardly think what to say.

She finally said gently, "Thank you, Tony," and looked at Alonzo.

He was looking down at his children with a fond smile curving his mouth. He roughed Tony's hair affectionately and then stooped to pick up her trunk. "Come along, then. Everybody in."

Katherine watched, astounded, as he stowed her trunk in the back of the colorful wagon and lifted his children in after it.

"Did you leave them here all alone to wait for us?" she asked.

"They are very obedient. I told them not to leave the cart, and I knew they wouldn't."

"But what if they had? You can't just leave children alone like that." She bit her lip, wondering if he'd be angry at her for speaking out, but he only smiled.

"If it makes you feel any better, the woman in that store was keeping an eye on them for me. But they're never any trouble." He waved at the store window in farewell to the woman within, then held out a hand to Katherine. "Will you ride in the back with the children or up top with me?"

Katherine was too flabbergasted to speak. Her employer waited, the lines playing about his eyes, his smile impish, and the thought occurred to her that he was enjoying her consternation. He was clearly eccentric, perhaps even mad, and was clearly testing her to see what she was made of. She wouldn't give him the pleasure of amusing himself at her expense. She reined in her astonishment and replied, "I'll sit with the children, I think." She was pleased with how ordinary her voice sounded.

He helped her climb into the back of the cart. It was a snug little compartment, the three walls cluttered with odds and ends hanging from tidy hooks—tin cups, ladles, bowls, ropes of spoons and forks strung together like fish, cheese graters, lanterns, hemp ropes, spools of thread, candles. As her eyes became accustomed to the dimness inside the cart, she saw that the floor was strewn with red and gold pillows. The two children sat with arms wrapped around their knees. A three-legged stool stood in one corner, wedged beside her trunk.

"You sit here." Lilia patted the stool.

Katherine sat cautiously, squirming with her bustle, and blinked as she gazed around her. She'd never been inside a gypsy cart before and had never seen such a variety of things all jumbled together. Perhaps it was a peddler's wagon. It reminded her of the cart an old man used to drive from house to house selling his variety of wares when she was a child. She had loved to peer inside at the treasure trove and had believed everything on earth could be found within. It was a far different thing to ride in one. Where in the world had Mr. Colaco obtained it? Had he borrowed it? And why?

Tony shot her another engaging grin. Then there was a jerk, and the swinging utensils jangled like wind chimes as the cart rolled away.

Her first thought was that this was some absurd joke. Her second thought was that it was humiliating, and she was furious at being treated in such a remarkable manner. Her third thought was of alarm. Was Alonzo Colaco indeed mad? Was he dangerous? Were his little absurdities harmless? She would have to seek out the housekeeper and ask her point blank. For all his charm, she certainly didn't want to remain in a house where the master was unstable.

The square of light that made up the fourth wall began to darken, and soon the back of the cart was completely black. The children, lulled by the swaying of the cart and the rhythmic clopping of the horse, curled up on the pillows and dropped off to sleep.

Katherine, musing to herself that this was the oddest day she had ever had, allowed herself to slump across the trunk and doze to the tune of the chiming forks and spoons.

She awoke when the jolting cart suddenly came to a halt. She rubbed her face vigorously and hoped she didn't look too dreadful. She peered outside but could see only darkness and a few trees glinting in the moonlight. If they'd arrived at the house, why were there no lights? If they hadn't yet arrived, why had they stopped?

She heard footsteps in the grass, and Alonzo appeared in the opening, a dark figure against a darker night.

"We're home," he said softly. "Are they asleep?"

"Yes."

He climbed into the cart and lifted a limp Tony from the cushions. "Poor things. They're worn out with waiting and excitement."

He climbed down, slung the little boy against his shoulder, holding him with one arm, and held out his other hand to Katherine. She collected her skirts, stepped down onto long, cool grass, and looked around. They'd left the road at some point and now appeared to be in a sort of clearing or meadow ringed by tall trees. She could see no house or drive, no light but the moon.

A few paces away was a long, low bulk, a dark, unrecognizable shape. Toward this Alonzo now strode, and as Katherine hurried to follow, she saw that it was a railway car, a long box on wheels. Astonished, she wondered how on earth it had arrived here, in the middle of a meadow, far from any train tracks. Wooden steps led up to the door in its side. Alonzo disappeared inside, and a moment later, a light flared. He reappeared in the doorway.

"I'll just get Lilia, and then I'll show you around," he said.

Mutely, Katherine watched him fetch Lilia from the cart and carry her to the train car. Then he came back to her.

"Please make yourself comfortable. I'll show you where you will sleep," he said and took her arm to help her up the steep steps.

Chapter Four

KATHERINE, STILL TOO STUNNED TO speak, found herself inside. The train car was about eight feet wide and fifteen feet long. It was not a nicely appointed passenger car, with seats and windows, but the type used for hauling goods. The ceiling was high enough for Alonzo to stand upright, and the walls were lined with pine planks to hide the metal and keep it warmer. Two glass-paned windows had been cut into each side and were hung with white curtains. A cozy kitchen area took up one end, with a tin sink, several cupboards and shelves, a woodstove with its chimney sticking through the ceiling, and a square table with three folding chairs. The other end of the car held a sleeping area with a narrow cot along one wall and a second cot head to head with it across the end of the room. On this lay Lilia, her dark curls spread across her pillow. Above her, stuck to the wall like a berth, was a third cot, where Tony lay with a bar railing to keep him from rolling off. On the wall opposite the first empty cot was a bookcase, a vase of wildflowers perched on top of it. The whole room was small but clean and orderly, with cupboards and cubbyholes for everything. It smelled of flowers and soap and freshly cut wood. A lantern burned on the table, casting a comfortable golden glow over everything.

"This is your bed," Alonzo said, indicating the first cot with its patchwork quilt. "There's a closet there for your things and an empty shelf. I'll let you take your things out of your trunk, and then I'll strap it under the car. There's no room for it in here."

Katherine's voice came out in a croak. "I'm sorry, there seems to be some mistake. Do you mean to tell me you *live* in this train car?"

"Why, yes," he replied, his dark eyebrows raised. "Is something wrong?"

"Yes," Katherine said. "Dreadfully wrong. I was under the impression that, well, that there was a house. A real one, I mean. I thought you were—"

"Were what?"

"Well, I mean . . . a gentleman."

"A wealthy gentleman?" he asked. He gave a small smile, but it didn't reach his eyes.

"You didn't tell me you were a gypsy."

His smile bloomed into a full one then, and a chuckle came from deep in his chest. "I'm a craftsman," he corrected her. "A tinsmith and peddler by trade. Not a gypsy."

"A tinker," Katherine responded sharply. "Whatever, I was under a false impression when I agreed to this arrangement."

A flicker of doubt passed over his face. "Are you saying you've reconsidered?" he asked quietly.

Katherine spread her hands to indicate the entire room. "Why did you say nothing of this when you interviewed me?"

He removed his hat and rubbed his forehead thoughtfully. "You agreed to the terms. Ten dollars a month for one year, Sundays off. You didn't ask about the accommodations."

"It never occurred to me there was a need to," Katherine said. "I thought anyone who could afford a tutor for his children must be . . . well off." The words were tasteless, but there was no getting around them. "Can you pay what you promised me, Mr. Colaco?"

"I can," he said stiffly.

Katherine felt a rising sense of alarm. What sort of predicament had she gotten herself into? "I've let my room go, and now I'll have to find another. Oh! And I've spent the last of my savings. I thought . . . How could you have deceived me like this?"

His angular face now registered dismay. Even in her consternation, Katherine mused that his every emotion seemed to flicker across his face like actors dashing across a stage. He would be lousy at keeping a poker face in card games.

"*Deceive* is such a strong word," he said.

"But you misrepresented yourself!"

"I did nothing of the sort." He was beginning to sound irritated, and there was an angry flash in his eye that alarmed her even more. He seemed very tall in the small room.

"You dressed as a gentleman."

"I *am* a gentleman," he said. "I suppose you think a tinsmith can't present himself neatly and conduct himself properly?"

"Ha! I like that," Katherine said hotly. "You've practically abducted me!" As her voice rose, Tony turned over and muttered in his sleep.

Alonzo dropped his own tone to a hoarse half whisper. "Now, see here! You agreed—"

"I agreed to what I thought was an ordinary offer," Katherine snapped. "You said nothing to me about your occupation."

"You didn't ask. I thought—well, I'll be honest. I *hoped* it didn't matter to you." Alonzo shrugged. "Please lower your voice, or you'll wake the children."

Katherine struggled to contain her anger. He really was too impossible. In a calmer voice, she said, "All right. I'll concede that the fault lies with both parties. I didn't ask, and you didn't volunteer the information."

"But you won't stay?"

"It's impossible!"

"Then I'll find someone else."

If there'd been room, she would have stepped back a pace from his smouldering scowl. "Frankly, Mr. Colaco, I doubt you'll find anyone willing to live under these conditions."

She could see the muscles tense in his jaw. "The children must receive some sort of education. I had assumed the local school would take them, but it won't, even though they're of an age. If I'd known . . . Well, anyway, I thought that hiring a tutor would be a good solution."

"Other tinkers' children get along fine without a formal education," Katherine said, perplexed at his intensity.

"'Tinkers' children.' As if they're a separate breed," Alonzo said fiercely. "Do you share the school's prejudices, then, Kate? Are only the children of men who own big, fancy houses deserving of knowledge?" His voice was flat, but the look in his eyes was bitter. "Would you call that fair?"

Katherine stared at him, at a loss for words. Her own education had been provided by her father's hard work and sacrifice. There had been those at her school who hadn't thought she belonged there. Was she now guilty of thinking the same as they? She shook her head. This whole thing was ridiculous. A tutor working for a tinker! The impropriety of it, the *preposterousness!*

Then again, she had nowhere else to go, no money to keep herself until she found something else. She'd have to go to Hugh and Martha, no doubt about it.

She gripped her hands tightly together and forced herself to speak calmly as she said, "Perhaps it isn't fair, but it's the way things are."

"And you're content to let things remain as they are?" His fists were on his hips, his look challenging.

He was a radical, then. A reformist. She had heard of those around her relatives' dinner table, and Hugh had not held a high opinion of them. She closed her eyes briefly. "I won't enter into an argument on social reformation tonight. I'll stay the night because it's too late to go back. But tomorrow I want you to take me back to the train, and I'll require the fare to get me to High Park. I—I have family there."

He looked away, the muscle working in his jaw. "Right. Perhaps it's best you're not staying after all. I seem to have misjudged you. I'll bring your things."

He went out the door with a bang. Katherine pressed her fingertips to her eyelids. The day had been too draining, and she felt unable to cope with anything more. She opened her eyes as Alonzo reentered. He deposited her trunk in the small space between the cots and stood facing her, his features having turned to stone.

"You're probably hungry. I have beef stew and cheese pasties if you'd like."

The thought of cheese pasties existing somewhere in this remodeled train car only added to the absurdity of the situation. Katherine almost smiled but caught herself. She was hungry, but the thought of sharing a meal with this man at the little square table was too much for her. She wanted only to be alone. She shook her head.

"No, thank you, I prefer not to eat," she said.

"I'll just take something, then," he said.

She watched him take a plate from a cupboard, lift a pot from the two-lidded stove, and go out. She waited, but he didn't return, and when she peered from one of the windows, she saw he was kneeling beside the gypsy wagon, building a fire. The orange light danced over his face, bringing his jaw bones into relief, shadowing his eyes. The piebald horse was grazing a little ways away, and clouds were gathering over the moon.

A shiver went through her, and she quickly turned to her trunk and pulled out her nightgown. There was no maid to bring hot water to wash in. There was no one to help her with her buttons and strings. There was no curtain to step behind for privacy. But at least the children were sound asleep, and Alonzo Colaco showed no indication of coming back. She undressed with some difficulty, maneuvering in the tight space with her broad skirts and bustle, struggling to reach behind her to unfasten them. Obviously Mr. Colaco hadn't taken the size of a woman's costume into account when planning the accommodations.

Muttering to herself, she pulled on the nightgown and draped her dress in the empty closet. She went to her assigned cot and cautiously turned down the blankets.

To her relief, the bedding was clean. When she slid between the sheets, she found the cot surprisingly comfortable, firmer than the soft beds she was used to, and the pillow smelled faintly of soap and woodsmoke. The train car was hushed but for the gentle breathing of the children in the darkness. Katherine had intended to lie there fuming over her situation and figuring out what to do next, but without warning she was asleep.

* * *

In the early hours of the morning, she awoke to the sound of thunder. Rain steadily pelted the train-car roof, and as she lay groggily listening, lightning split the sky outside the window. She wondered where Alonzo Colaco was sleeping. Wherever he was, she hoped he was getting good and wet. She giggled wickedly to herself.

Something stirred, and then Lilia's pale face appeared above her, her dark eyes wide.

"Does the storm frighten you?" Katherine whispered.

The little girl nodded and, without hesitation, climbed into the cot beside Katherine and pulled the quilt to her chin.

Taken aback, Katherine lay still, not knowing if she should order the child back to her own bed. This had certainly never happened with Miss Alice. Lilia curled into her, closed her eyes, and slept again within minutes. She formed a warm little bundle against Katherine's side, as comforting as a hot-water bottle. Finally Katherine closed her own eyes, listening to the rain loud on the roof, and fell back asleep.

When she awoke again, the rain had stopped and daylight shone weakly through the windows. Lilia and Tony were gone. Yawning, Katherine sat up and squinted at her watch. It was seven o'clock. Strangely, she wasn't tired after her disturbed sleep, and she climbed out of bed and splashed her face with cold water from the bucket standing beside the tin sink. She struggled to dress herself in the small space and was brushing her hair when there was a light knock at the door.

"Come in," she called, facing the train-car door, unconsciously gripping the brush like a weapon.

Alonzo put his head inside the door. His hair, the color of dark chocolate, was slicked to his head and curled damply over his ears. He wore a plain white shirt, unbuttoned at the throat, with no coat. He looked obnoxiously cheerful in spite of the early hour and their argument the previous evening.

"You're up, then? Good. I feared you'd be a late riser. Breakfast is ready." He withdrew his head and shut the door again.

Katherine pulled her hair into a twist and pinned it; found her shoes, nearly upsetting the bookcase with her bustle; and came out of the train car. A bright fire crackled in a ring of stones beside the tinker's cart, and she saw a blue woolen blanket draped over the limb of a maple tree. Alonzo squatted beside the fire, stirring at something on a griddle rigged up over the flames.

Now that it was daylight, Katherine could see they were in a clearing about thirty feet across, ringed in on all sides by ash, maple, and birch trees. Lilia and Tony were at the edge of the woods gathering branches for the fire. A large gray dog was tied to a stake near the train car, its ears up as she passed.

Katherine sat on a damp fallen log near the fire and held her hands out to the heat.

"Sleep all right, then?" Alonzo asked, not looking up from the griddle.

"Yes, thank you. Lilia climbed in with me early this morning. I think the thunder frightened her."

"Yes, it does sometimes. Sorry about that."

"I didn't mind," Katherine replied. "Did you sleep in the cart? Is it weatherproof?"

"Yes," he said. "And no. There's no door on the back. I was soaked." He gestured with his spatula toward the blanket hanging damply in the tree, but he sounded unconcerned.

"Oh dear."

"Nothing that can't dry," he answered. "I didn't want to use the stove while you were sleeping. I hope scrambled eggs are all right."

"Fine, thank you," Katherine said. She wasn't fond of eggs, but she hadn't eaten the night before and was marvelously hungry. There was also another pressing concern, but she wasn't sure how to phrase the question.

"Do you have—Is there a . . . lavatory?" she asked with as much dignity as she could muster.

Alonzo didn't bat an eye. "Afraid not. You'll have to make do with a bush like the rest of us gypsies."

She clenched her nails into her palms, shocked but not wanting him to see it. "I couldn't possibly. It's—it's *primitive!*"

"Suit yourself," he said, shrugging. He went back to stirring the eggs.

At that moment, Katherine could have hit him. She watched the two children approach, Lilia several paces ahead of her brother, dragging the branches they'd gathered. The early-morning sun turned their hair so dark it had a bluish tinge. Lilia's hair was in ragged curls down her back and looked as if it had never been combed, though her pinafore was clean and white. Tony, in short pants and braces, stood regarding Katherine thoughtfully, as if making up his mind about her. Then he gave her a shy smile and went down on his round knees in the dirt to break the branches into smaller pieces. Alonzo murmured something in Italian, which Katherine didn't catch, and Tony's face lit with pleasure. He fed the twigs to the fire carefully, glancing from time to time at his father for approval.

Lilia settled herself on the log beside Katherine. Her shoes were soaked from the grass, and there was mud on her stockinged knees.

"I sawed a red bird," the girl announced proudly. "Tony frightened it. Will you teach me the names of all the birds?"

Katherine glanced at Alonzo, but he was busy dishing up breakfast. "I'll have to remember their names myself. I've forgotten many," she said noncommittally.

"And will you teach me songs?" Lilia went on, her eyes round in her thin face. "I want to sing. *English* songs."

"We'll see," Katherine said uncomfortably.

Alonzo wordlessly passed her a tin plate containing fluffy scrambled eggs, fried potatoes and onions, and a wedge of thickly buttered bread, along with a fork and a tin mug of cold water. The children received their breakfasts and sat on the log beside her, waiting until their father had served himself too. Then, to Katherine's surprise, they ducked their heads while Alonzo said a short prayer in Italian. Her Latin helped her understand bits of what he said, and she could guess at the rest. As they ate, Katherine mused at what a difference this was, eating outdoors on tin plates, compared to the extravagant meals she'd been served with Miss Alice Colworthy, who, incidentally, hadn't had the table manners this tinker's children seemed to have. They ate politely, they asked nicely for second helpings, and they said thank you. They didn't use their fingers, even with the strips of fat bacon Alonzo served them, and when they'd finished, Lilia collected their plates and put them in a large pot of water, which her father set in the fire to boil.

Katherine had to admit the food was satisfying, even the smoky-tasting eggs. She'd never had them done over a fire before, and it enhanced their flavor. She might even say she'd enjoyed them.

Now necessity overruled decorum. She excused herself and walked into the woods a good distance and, with much muttering, found herself a bush. Alonzo clearly didn't appreciate the problems posed by long skirts and multiple petticoats.

When she returned to the clearing, her own shoes and hem now muddy, Alonzo was drying the dishes while Tony and Lilia ran back and forth to the train car to put them away. When the cleaning was finished, to Katherine's horrified amusement, Alonzo took the crimson shirt he'd worn yesterday, some stockings, and the dish towel and put them all into the pot of boiling water.

"I'll set these to drying, and then I'll take you to the train," he said, standing and brushing his hands on his trousers. He hesitated, and his voice softened as he added, "I'm sorry for the inconvenience I've caused you, Kate. I tend to act before thinking. Please believe I meant no harm. I've just been very frustrated, running into people's prejudices headlong. I hadn't realized how prevalent the attitude was toward . . . Well, anyway, I'm not afraid to admit I have a lot to learn, and I guess this was a daft idea."

"I realize you had good intentions. Thank you." Katherine softened somewhat. "I do hope you find someone to teach your children."

"But that person isn't you?"

She shook her head and glanced to where the children were petting the nose of the grazing horse, seemingly unafraid of the large beast. They were out of earshot. "But I might stay for just a few days," she said, not knowing what she was thinking until she said it aloud. "Just until I'm able to find another position. You cannot hold me to my promise to work for you for one year because it was extracted under false pretences. But to be honest, my only option at this moment is to go to my mother's cousin, and for reasons of my own, I'd prefer not to resort to that. If it's all right, I'll stay here until I find a suitable alternative."

Alonzo stood looking at her a moment, and then he said quietly, "Thank you. Whatever time you will give us, I appreciate."

"I'm sorry you have to sleep in the cart," she added generously.

"I don't mind." He gave a slight bow, his handsome face solemn. "Thank you for staying."

"For a short while," Katherine said.

Chapter Five

WHEN THE BOILED CLOTHING HAD been hung to dry from the tree boughs like ships' pennants, Alonzo announced that it was lesson time. Katherine waited, expecting the children to groan or pout, but they ran to fetch chalk and slates from the train car, then crowded around her expectantly, ready and eager.

"What will you teach us?" Lilia demanded. "Will you teach us the birds' names now?"

"Let's go inside to the table," Katherine suggested.

The children ran in before her, and she found them waiting in their chairs, their faces turned toward her as cheerfully as if they expected candy instead of lessons. Candy. Katherine remembered the gumdrops she'd brought for them, then decided to wait to use them as an incentive should their attention flag.

But their attention seemed inexhaustible. She went over the alphabet with them, which they both knew. Lilia called out the names of the letters, while Tony spoke quietly, one eye on her for approval. They also knew their numbers up to fifty. Katherine set them to reading simple three-letter words. Lilia caught on quickly, but Tony didn't know the sounds the letters made. They worked on this for a while, and then Katherine gave them a rest and taught them to sing "Early One Morning," which delighted Lilia.

"My mother singed to us every night," she informed Katherine. "She was a very good singer, *ma mère*."

"And you will be too," Katherine told her. "You have a very fine voice."

"I will sing you a song," the little girl announced and began to sing. It was a French song, very slow and pretty and in a minor key, about a shepherdess. In her childish soprano, it was exquisite.

When she'd finished, Katherine didn't know what to say. "That was lovely" seemed inadequate.

Before she could think of anything, she heard Alonzo's voice soft behind her. "Your mother is smiling, *cara mia.*"

Lilia beamed, and Tony gave a low chuckle. Katherine turned to see Alonzo standing in the doorway. His eyes were half closed, his smile gentle.

After a moment, he glanced at Katherine and then looked away. "Lunch is ready."

"Already?" Katherine looked at her watch and saw it was after noon. "I had no idea. Your children are excellent students."

"I told you they were eager. Come and eat, loves." Briskly he herded the children out to the fire. Katherine put away the slates and followed.

Alonzo had prepared a simple meal of fried chops, boiled potatoes, salad, and thick bread, and there was a pot of sweet tea. It tasted wonderful, and she told him so.

"I'm surprised what you can create over a fire," she added.

"Thank you. If there is anything in particular you fancy, let me know," he said. "How would you like to spend your afternoon?"

"Perhaps a small recess from our lessons. What are our other options?"

"Walking in the woods. Reading or drawing or napping. Or if you wanted to go into Springfield or Port Credit one afternoon, I could drive you."

Katherine considered. "Today we'll walk in the woods, and I can teach Lilia what bird names I know. But tomorrow I'd like to go into Toronto, please. I need to begin my"—she glanced at the children and ended lamely—"search for other arrangements."

"Take Bo with you," Alonzo said, indicating the dozing dog lying in the wagon's shade. "I don't imagine you'll need him, but it can't hurt."

They set off into the woods, Lilia skipping and holding Katherine's hand and Tony leading the way with Bo on a rope. Alonzo remained in the clearing, carefully hammering the dents out of a tin pot that would join the wares in his cart.

It was cool under the trees, and the air smelled damply of soil and leaves. There was no path, but the earth between the trees was bare except for strewn twigs and a few straggly bushes. As they walked, Katherine told the children the names of the trees—birch, larch, scrub oak, elm, ash, white pine, maple. Her father had been an enthusiastic naturalist, and she thanked him silently now for all he had taught her in her childhood. She showed the children how the silver maple's leaves were glossy on one side and powder gray on the other. She showed them a tulip tree, a great towering thing, and told them how it put out thousands of seeds because only a tiny number of them would ever grow. They saw all kinds of birds, from noisy jays to shy finches, and Lilia carefully repeated their names. Katherine found her memory excellent and was astonished that these children had such a refreshing thirst for knowledge in spite of their material deprivation. Or was it because of? She'd never considered it before.

Then again, she suspected their deprivation wasn't as severe as that of other tinker children. She'd never heard of any other peddler who could afford a tutor—or chops for lunch, for that matter.

She was pondering this when a rabbit exploded out from under a bush a few feet away and took off into the trees. Immediately Bo was after it, barking his head off. But his rope was wrapped around Tony's hand, and the little boy was jerked off his feet and pulled along the ground before Katherine knew what was happening. Lilia screamed and stood frozen to the ground. Katherine dashed to snatch the rope, Bo barking and scrabbling and ignoring her shouts. Somehow she managed to slacken the rope enough to disentangle Tony's hand, and when she released the rope, Bo went bounding off after his prey and disappeared into the trees. Katherine, heedless of the dirt, knelt and gathered Tony into her lap.

The flesh on his hand was seared all the way round from the rope, and blood was beginning to form in drops along the tear. Making cooing, clucking sounds, Katherine bound the hand with her handkerchief as best she could while Lilia hovered in tears. But Tony remained silent throughout, never uttering a sound, though his face was pale and unshed tears glistened in his dark eyes.

"What a brave boy you are!" Katherine exclaimed, smoothing the curly hair from his forehead. Tears rolled unheeded down her own cheeks. "Why don't we go back now and wash this up properly?"

"What about Bo?" Lilia protested. "He'll get losted!"

"Bo can find his own jolly way home," Katherine said firmly. She stood and dusted off her skirt. "Can you walk? Or shall I carry you?"

Tony replied by lifting his arms to be carried, so Katherine picked him up and settled him on her hip. He was much heavier than she'd anticipated, and she found it rough going over the uneven ground, ducking tree branches.

Lilia hurried along beside her, mouth tightly pressed shut, eyes still wet. Katherine scowled away her own tears as she struggled along, upset that her first day had ended in disaster, angry at the disobedient Bo, furious with herself for not foreseeing trouble. And afraid of what Alonzo Colaco would have to say about it. He would probably be glad she wasn't staying after all. First Alice, now this. Was she doomed to go from house to house leaving injured children in her wake?

Tony's arms were around her neck, and he pressed his face into her shoulder. She shifted his weight with shaking arms. My word, but he was heavy! Her breath came in gasps. She would have to stop and rest.

At that moment, Alonzo appeared, jogging toward them through the woods. When he saw her, he quickened his pace, his arms already out to take Tony before he'd even reached them. Katherine handed him over with relief, and Tony threw his arms around Alonzo's neck. Only then did he begin to cry the great gulping sobs of a child.

"What happened?' Alonzo asked, looking more concerned than angry. "I heard Lilia scream."

"Bo ran off after a rabbit, and his rope was wrapped around Tony's hand," Katherine explained miserably. "He's received a nasty abrasion, and there will be some bruising. He was very brave about it."

Alonzo hunkered down on his heels, setting Tony on his lap, and wiped the boy's tears with his thumbs as he murmured softly in Italian. Tony gave a final hiccup and grew still. Alonzo carefully unwrapped the hand and examined the rope burn.

"I imagine that hurts," he said to Tony. "You must have amazing muscles to have hung on to Bo that hard."

Tony instantly beamed. "He pulled me on the ground too," he said proudly.

"My goodness! Such strength. You'll be wrestling bulls next," Alonzo said, wide-eyed. "Let's go wash that off, and then we'll see what tasty treat we can find to reward you with."

"I have gumdrops," Katherine said quickly and winced at how stupid she sounded. Alonzo had not yet met her eye, and she felt sick with guilt.

Tony jumped off Alonzo's knee and marched for home, tears forgotten, but Lilia hung back, lips trembling. "What about Bo?" she asked.

"Bo can take care of himself," Katherine said briskly. She felt no sympathy for the brute.

But Alonzo put his hand on Lilia's shoulder. "I'll go find him as soon as Tony's taken care of," he promised.

Lilia brightened and hurried after her brother. Katherine and Alonzo followed more slowly, in silence.

"I'm so sorry," Katherine said finally, unable to bear the silence any longer.

"For what?" Alonzo answered, sounding surprised. "You weren't the one who ran away. Not yet, anyway." He gazed away through the trees with a faint frown.

She glared at him, suddenly angry. This . . . this *tinker* was trying to make her feel guilty for not going along with his preposterous plans! "At least when I do 'run off,' I won't leave gaping wounds behind," she snapped.

He cocked one dark eyebrow. "Don't be so sure."

Katherine was nonplussed by this. She dropped her pace and let him precede her into the clearing. She wasn't sure what he had meant. Surely the children weren't that attached to her yet, after only one day. Her mind skittered away from pursuing this line of thought. She sat on the train-car steps and watched Alonzo heat water and wash Tony's hand, then bandage it deftly with a wide square of white sheeting. Katherine produced the sweets she'd purchased, and Tony settled down happily with a picture book while Lilia went to gather firewood.

Alonzo was just about to set out to find Bo when the miscreant came bounding back by himself. Skipping out of the trees with his tail in the air and dragging his rope, he bore the rabbit in his mouth and proudly presented it to Alonzo, looking pleased with himself.

"A lot of nerve you have," Katherine remarked to the beast, who grinned back at her and wagged his tail.

"He redeemed himself with his catch," Alonzo said, holding the rabbit up. "I'll add it to the stew."

"You don't expect to *eat* that!" Katherine cried, appalled.

"Why not?"

"Because it's been in his mouth!" she retorted. "He caught it!"

"Is this a problem?" Alonzo asked mildly.

"I cannot possibly eat something that's been in a dog's mouth."

"It will be boiled. It's perfectly safe."

"It might be diseased."

"Not likely. And I'll bet you've eaten duck or pheasant or grouse at some point in your life, haven't you?"

"Well, of course I have."

"Those were all likely retrieved by a dog," he pointed out reasonably.

Of course Katherine had no reply for that.

Alonzo fetched a skinning knife from the cart and began to dress Bo's kill.

Bo trotted off to join Lilia, who greeted him joyfully with both her arms around his neck and a flood of French endearments. Bo turned his sleek head and grinned at Katherine again. *See? They like me*, he seemed to be saying.

"Why does Lilia use French with the dog instead of Italian?" Katherine asked after a moment.

Alonzo glanced up at her. "It was her mother's dog," he replied.

Katherine looked at him squatting beside the fire, knife poised, the half-naked rabbit stretched out on a flat rock. There was fresh blood on the rock, the knife, his hands. She stood and went into the train car. When Alonzo put his head in some time later to announce that dinner was ready, she informed him she wasn't hungry.

"More for us," he responded, shrugging, and went out again, banging the door.

Katherine lay on her side on the cot and curled her arms around her knees. She suddenly felt sad and homesick, though she wasn't sure just where home was. And she was hungry. She thought of the beautiful mutton and grouse and the lemon tarts of which Hugh Fitzgerald was so fond. She doubted he'd ever seen a rabbit with its fur still on.

She fell asleep with the tears drying on her cheeks.

* * *

She hadn't meant to nap, but when she woke, it was late evening, the children were tucked in their bunks, and the lamp on the table was trimmed low. She hadn't heard anyone come in.

Katherine rose stiffly from the cot and went to the window. The stars were out, the moon was a flat white dime over the trees, and she could see a dark figure sitting on the tree trunk beside the fire ring. The low glow of the coals was too dim to reach his face. She watched a while longer, but Alonzo didn't move, so finally Katherine turned away. She was ravenously hungry but didn't feel she should rummage through his little kitchen for food. She climbed into her nightgown, tucked the children's blankets more closely around them, and went back to bed.

She awoke momentarily disoriented to a morning filled with birdsong. The children were nowhere to be seen. She mused that either they were unusually quiet children, or she was a sound sleeper, not hearing them come or go. She dressed, banging her shins and cracking her elbow on the furniture in the process, and went to find herself a bush. It never grew easier, and on a chilly morning, it was especially annoying.

When she returned to camp, Alonzo was crouching beside the fire ring, coaxing dew-dampened kindling to light. He wore a white shirt with a tweed waistcoat and a pair of sackcloth trousers. He squinted up at her through the smoke and nodded. "Good morning."

"Good morning," she said, moving to stand away from the smoke, but it turned and followed her. "Why don't you just use the stove in the train car?"

"I like to conserve oil as much as possible," he answered.

She stood silently, squinting in the smoke. Alonzo glanced at her, then stood and brushed his hands. "I imagine you'll want to freshen up before we go into town. This can tend itself for a moment. Come with me."

He took two towels and a tin box from the train car and struck off into the trees. Wondering, Katherine followed. Some hundred yards into the woods, they came upon a clearing and a wide stream running musically over slippery stones. The banks were thick with grass, and water skaters danced in shallow, sunlit pools. Katherine watched Alonzo hunker down and scoop up water to douse his face and head, spluttering in the cold. He toweled himself dry, making his hair stand on end, then handed her the other towel and the tin.

"Breakfast will be a while, so take your time," he said, and then went back through the trees toward camp.

Katherine eyed the brook with dismay. She had never washed herself in a stream, but on the other hand, she had never felt so in need of a scrub. It was kind of him to think of it. She knelt gingerly beside the stream, apprehensively dipped her hands into the chill water, and brought up a cupful to splash on her face. It was icy but invigorating. She splashed another handful on her face, then unwound her hair and washed it, the water so cold it made her head ache. She found soap in the tin box and scrubbed her face and neck with it. As she straightened to grope for the towel, a cold trickle ran down inside her collar. This only served to remind her how itchy and unwashed the rest of her felt, and she wished she could plunge the rest of her body into the shallow stream.

Well, and why not? She glanced around, but the woods were empty but for the birds. Alonzo wouldn't be back—he'd told her to take her time and was doubtless now preparing breakfast. She was alone. Perhaps just a sponge bath . . .

She quickly stripped to the waist, feeling ridiculously sinful and exposed, and used a corner of the towel to wash. The water was wonderful, making her skin crawl with gooseflesh. The irritableness of the night rinsed away, leaving her refreshed and clean . . . and happy. She turned her face up to the sun and let its weak warmth dry her skin.

A rustling behind her brought her eyes snapping open. Lilia stepped from the trees and joined her, carrying a large pail she now filled from the stream.

Hot with embarrassment, Katherine clawed for her clothes, but Lilia seemed to take no notice of her half-dressed state. She said nothing, and Katherine remained silent also. When she was dressed and her hair toweled dry, she took the heavy pail from Lilia and carried it for her.

When they were nearly to the clearing, Lilia spoke at last.

"You're very pretty."

"Thank you," Katherine mumbled, agonized.

"You look like my mother. There, I mean. Not your face or your hair." Lilia indicated Katherine's chest with childish innocence. "But my mother was not so white."

"Have—You've seen your mother? Bare?" Katherine couldn't help stammering, astonished.

"Of course." Lilia laughed. "She had to feed the baby, you see."

"Oh, of course," Katherine said. "You mean Tony?"

"No, not Tony. The other baby."

Katherine frowned. "What other baby?"

"Michael."

"Oh," Katherine said softly. "Is he in heaven with your mother?"

"Oh no." Lilia laughed. "He's with Mrs. O'Riley."

Chapter Six

THEY STEPPED INTO THE CLEARING and bright sunshine. Lilia ran ahead to join her brother, who was visiting the horse. Katherine carried the water over to Alonzo, who stood feeding sticks into the fire. The wonderful smell of sausages was strong above the smell of burning wood.

"Thank you," he said as she set the pail down. "I see Lilia is letting you do her work."

"I'm happy to help," she said. "I've never had so much free time."

He took the damp towel from her and draped it over a tree branch to dry. As Katherine moved closer to the fire, he reached out and lightly touched a strand of her hair that lay damp on her shoulder. The gesture caught Katherine off guard.

"You should wear your hair down," he said. "It suits you."

"I haven't worn it down since I was seventeen," Katherine said, moving away to sit on the log by the fire.

"You make it sound as if you're eighty years old."

"Nearly."

He chuckled. "Surely not. May I ask how old you are?"

She decided to ignore the breach in manners. After all, what was he to know about social etiquette? "If you must know, I'm twenty-four, nearly twenty-five."

"That's all right. That isn't old." He passed her a tin plate piled with sausage, eggs, fried onions, and toasted bread. "I'm thirty-three, and I don't feel old at all."

"That's because you're fulfilled and happy," Katherine said. "It keeps you young."

There was a pause, and she looked up to see him watching her thoughtfully.

"And you're not?"

"What, fulfilled?"

"Happy."

She smiled uncomfortably. "This is hardly where I thought I'd be at this age."

"Where did you think you would be?"

Katherine stabbed a sausage and inspected its perfect goldenness. "You're a very impressive cook, Mr. Colaco."

"Alonzo, we agreed," he corrected her. "If you're going to evade the question, then I will answer it myself. My guess is that you thought you'd be married to some dashing, successful young man. You'd live in a big home with a cook and a gardener to order around and three or four well-mannered, yellow-haired children. Perhaps a pony out back, and social teas and poetry readings and a pew in church and raising money for widows and orphans. Lace doilies on the backs of the matching Jacquard wing chairs and gold-plated flatware—"

"All right! I have the picture," Katherine interrupted, laughing in spite of herself.

His eyes glittered. "Am I close?"

"Not a bit."

"I don't believe that."

She squirmed. "All right, yes, you're spot on. Of course I want all those things for myself, and I intend to get them someday, though I don't quite know how. But you make it sound like something to be ashamed of. What's wrong with having all that, anyway?"

"Nothing at all, so long as you're happy with who you are. And if you don't take any of it too seriously."

He grinned and turned to call the children to breakfast before she could reply, and she let the subject drop. What would he know, anyway, of social teas and matching wing chairs? As they ate, Katherine watched the children's two dark heads, bent close together, the four little knees in a row, and found herself unexpectedly flooded with a warm, contented feeling. It was quite an impossible situation, sleeping in a train car, bathing in a brook, eating food cooked over a fire. It was entirely absurd and primitive. It was also entirely enjoyable, as if she were at an outing at the beach. *Except for the bush*, she thought to herself. If there were a lavatory, she thought she could be entirely content. For a while, anyway. It was an adventure, an anthropological experience. Martha would have been flabbergasted.

When the dishes were washed and camp tidied, Alonzo hitched up the horse, then disappeared into the wagon and reemerged dressed in his expensive black suit, the suit that had deceived Katherine into thinking he was a wealthy man. This time he wore a white shirt with it and conservative black shoes. With his handkerchief in his pocket and his hair smoothed, he looked like any other well-dressed gentleman.

"I can't go into town looking like a tinker, can I?" he said drily. He clapped his hands. "All right, my loves, into the cart! We're going into the city. Kate has some errands to run."

This time Katherine opted to ride up front with Alonzo instead of in back with the children. He helped her up, then climbed onto the seat beside her.

"All set?" he called.

"All set, Papa!" two voices responded from the back of the wagon.

He chirped to the horse, and they were off, leaving Bo dozing on his rope beside the train car to keep watch.

"Are we going to the train station?" Katherine asked.

"I'll drive us all the way into Toronto today," he told her. "It saves on the fare, and we aren't in any particular hurry."

Katherine felt like a Harvest Queen on a float in a parade. The cart, rattling merrily, was painted in reds, greens, and golds. She was heartily glad that no one she knew could see her perched upon it. In the woods or on country roads was one thing. The idea of riding it in the streets of Toronto was quite another. They looked like something out of a festival.

The autumn day was cool but bright, with a hint of rain clouds on the horizon. The horse trotted, his hooves keeping rhythm with the squeaking of the wheels. Katherine tried to focus on what she planned to do about finding employment, but the gentle rocking lulled her, and she found herself gazing off over the fields and not thinking of anything at all.

"When we reach town, the thing to do would probably be to buy a newspaper," Alonzo said, "to look for advertisements for a position."

"Yes, that's sensible," Katherine agreed. "I can try to arrange appointments for this afternoon."

Alonzo fell silent again, and she glanced at him. He'd removed his hat, and it lay on the seat between them. His long, fine hands held the reins lightly, letting the horse, Bacchus, choose his own speed.

"Why a tinker?" she asked suddenly.

"Pardon?"

"Why did you become a tinker? I don't think you were one in Italy, were you?"

"I was a tinsmith."

"You have excellent English and the manners of a gentleman. I think you could have become any number of things. You could have worked in a shop or been a gentleman's valet. Or you could even have gone on to university and become—I don't know—a teacher."

A grin flashed across his lips, but he said nothing.

"Then why did you choose this life?" she pressed.

He thought a moment, lips pursed. "Reason number one: in Italy, my family were all tinsmiths, my father and his father before him. I enjoyed it and learned quickly. We weren't wealthy, but we had what we needed, and university was never an option. At the time I came to this country, it took nearly all I had."

"What about a secretary, then? Or a man in a shop? Or a butler?"

Alonzo chuckled. "Because of reason number two. I detest being told what to do. I cannot work for another man. I have no patience for rules. I think they were made to be broken."

"Oh, really? I couldn't have guessed." Katherine wasn't sure if she was amused or alarmed. A radical indeed.

"I have no use for the conventions and niceties of society. Never have. The best way to get me to do something is to tell me I shouldn't. I wanted to work for myself."

"Did your wife ever want you to take a steady job?"

He hesitated. "She never complained."

"If she had, would you have found a position? Or is that too personal a question?"

Alonzo's eyes rested solemnly on hers, and his voice was firm as he said, "I would have done anything Ruth wanted. If she'd asked me to fly to China, I would have found a way to do it."

Gazing at him, Katherine felt his intensity, and it shook her to the soul. To be loved by someone that fiercely, to mean that much to someone—she couldn't fathom it. Ruth Colaco must have been happy indeed. Katherine could find it in herself to be envious. It wasn't likely that she'd ever experience such devotion herself. She also knew a stab of pain at the thought of what this unusual man beside her must have felt when Ruth died.

"As I established my family and built up my own business, I noticed that other men all seemed to be so busy working that they had little meaningful contact with their children. I didn't want employment that would keep me away, but I could see myself heading down that same path. I wasn't sure how to avoid it. Then, when it all changed and Ruth died, I decided it was time to go back to a more basic life. A better way to earn my living. As a tinker, I'm with my children all day. They accompany me as I work. I can get to know them. I think it's a good thing with their mother taken so early."

Katherine felt a tight strain in the muscles of her throat, and she swallowed hard. "That's one of the loveliest things I've ever heard a man say. I think Miss Alice Colworthy may have turned out quite a different person if her parents had shown such love for her."

She told him in more detail of her experiences during her brief engagement at the Colworthy residence. He alternately laughed and gasped at the antics of the temperamental little heiress, and when Katherine had finished with the horrendous climax of the adventure in the stable, he slapped his leg and bellowed heartily. And Katherine, for the first time, was able to see the humor in it all and laugh at it herself.

"And what did the lord of the manor say to that?" Alonzo asked, wiping at his eyes with the back of his hand.

Katherine puffed out her chest, pulled in her chin, and said in a good mimic of Mr. Colworthy, "You have fallen down in your responsibilities, Porter. You have lost all control over the nursery. Hadley will drive you to the station."

"Oh my! It's a wonder he didn't make you walk with your trunk on your back," Alonzo said, clucking his tongue.

Katherine reddened. "I suppose getting the sack isn't the thing to tell my current employer, is it?"

"Ah, but I won't be your employer much longer," he said.

"No."

They fell silent but for the creak of the cart and the sound of the horse's hooves and rode that way the rest of the way into Toronto.

* * *

It was as embarrassing as Katherine had feared. Everyone on the streets turned to stare at them as they rattled by. Katherine felt her face grow hot and wished she'd ridden in the back with the children after all. She gritted her teeth and kept her eyes straight ahead, refusing to meet the stares. Alonzo seemed completely unaware of them. He drew the cart up before a news agent's and hopped down to purchase a paper.

"Need anything today, sir?" he asked the news agent as he handed the paper up to Katherine. "Pins, nails, cups, cutlery . . . ? I have a nice tie clip that would suit you."

"Any scissors?" the agent asked.

"Certainly! Several to choose from."

As he conducted his business with the agent, Katherine tried to pretend she was far, far away and had nothing to do with this humiliating situation. She opened the paper and searched through the ads near the back.

The newspaper contained two likely sounding advertisements, one for a lady's companion and one for a private teacher. Katherine swallowed her pride and asked Alonzo if she could borrow enough money to hire a boy to run messages to both prospective employers. She tasked the urchin with waiting at each house to bring back a reply. To her gratification, the boy returned to inform her that both had invited her to attend for interviews that afternoon.

Alonzo, his transaction made, drove her to the first appointment. About a block from the house, she put a hand on his arm.

"Please, if you don't mind, I'll get off here and walk the rest."

He drew Bacchus to a stop and shot her a look from beneath his dark eyebrows. "What, my conveyance isn't highbrow enough for you?"

"Well, it would hardly be suitable to arrive in, would it?" Katherine asked, reddening again.

He grinned and jumped down, then reached up, seized her by the waist, and lifted her bodily down.

"I hope you don't get the job," he said cheerfully.

"You needn't wait for me," she said. "I can walk from here to the other appointment. It isn't far."

"Why don't I meet you on that corner, then, say, about three o'clock?"

"That would be fine, thank you."

She watched him swing up to the seat and drive away. As he went, two little hands waved at her from the back. She waved in return, adjusted her hat, and walked up the street to her interview.

It was the ideal house. A beautiful house. *With a lavatory and a maid to bring your wash water, I expect*, she thought with a smile. She was admitted by the housekeeper and ushered into a cool, hushed hall. From there she was shown into the drawing room, with a thick Oriental carpet and mahogany furniture that oozed opulence. A rich portrait of an admiral hung over the marble fireplace, and a grandfather clock ticked contentedly, like a purring cat. A woman in a blue gown stood beside the mantel in a studied, graceful pose. Her silver hair was piled on her head, sapphires glittering in her ears. She was beautiful—the perfect complement to the house.

"Please come in, dear," she said warmly, her blue eyes swiftly noting Katherine's outmoded dress, hat, and sturdy boots.

"Thank you. It was kind of you to see me on short notice," Katherine said.

"I'm Mrs. Holland. Prunella Holland."

"Katherine Porter."

They sat opposite each other on delicate Queen Anne chairs, hands folded, feet together.

"I was about to take tea. Would you join me?"

"Thank you, that would be lovely."

The woman rang a small bell, and almost instantly a uniformed maid brought in a glittering tray.

"I hesitated to advertise, you know," Mrs. Holland confided cheerfully. "You never know what kind of people you'll have apply. I'll tell you, some of them have actually been frightening."

"I can imagine," Katherine murmured.

"Now, then. I require a companion to spend mornings helping me with what business I may have. I am head of the local Temperance Society chapter and keep quite busy with meetings and correspondence. I have a little trouble with my eyesight and need someone with good handwriting to assist me."

"You will find my handwriting impeccable," Katherine said.

"Afternoons I receive and return calls. You would accompany me."

"I see."

"I trust you support the Temperance Movement?"

"Certainly," Katherine promptly replied. She had never given it much thought. Her father hadn't drunk much, though Hugh had certainly enjoyed his alcohol.

"In the late afternoons, my physician says I must rest, so you would be on your own, but in the evenings you would read to me or go with me should I have any dinner engagements. I dine out regularly."

"Of course."

"For this position, I am prepared to offer thirty-five dollars a month."

"That is generous, madame," Katherine said, sipping her exquisite tea from a Doulton cup. She knew Martha spent that much on a single gown, but for a companion's wages it was very good. Certainly better than what Alonzo Colaco was paying her.

"Now tell me about yourself," Mrs. Holland said brightly.

"Well, I attended a small school in Toronto. Fort York Ladies' Academy."

"Ah, yes. Standard fare, I assume."

"Latin and French."

"Very good. Where were you last employed?"

Katherine skipped neatly over the Colworthys and replied, "I was governess to Miss Theresa Mansell-Waring in Rosedale."

"Ah. And how long were you there?"

"A year and a half, and then the young lady was married, and I was no longer required."

"And prior to that?"

"I was lady's companion to Mrs. Agatha Wilde in Forest Hill."

"Very good. And how long were you with her?"

"Nine months."

Mrs. Holland's eyebrows lifted.

"Sadly, she passed away," Katherine added hastily.

"I see." Mrs. Holland's voice had grown slightly chilly. She sipped her tea. "And before that?"

"Governess to five children for a family in York."

"Five! They must have been glad of the help. You must have been there for some time, I take it?"

"Um . . . well, not *very* long . . ."

The woman eyed her suspiciously. "How long were you there, Miss Porter?"

"Five months. It was a very busy household, and when the opportunity with Mrs. Wilde became available, I thought it prudent—"

"Hmm. And before that?"

"I-I supervised my father's house after my mother died."

"So really, nine months' experience is all you've had as a companion?"

"Well, yes," Katherine said. "But I'm sure you will find me very satisfactory. I am well read and—"

"Yes, yes. I can see your education. No need to flaunt it, my dear."

Katherine bit her lips shut and waited, uncertain what else to say.

"How old are you, Miss Porter?"

"Twenty-four, madame."

"Mmm." She didn't look pleased at this. "You don't have a young man, do you? I cannot allow young men to come calling at all hours."

"Oh no, I don't. I don't have anyone—"

"I am very particular about how things are to be done."

"I understand." Katherine was beginning to feel flustered.

"Did you bring letters from your previous employers?"

"Oh! No. I mean, not with me. I-I can forward them to you." Katherine felt panic churning in her stomach.

"If what they say is satisfactory, I suppose you might do," Mrs. Holland said finally, setting down her tea. "But I have other interviews today. I will let you know. What is your address?"

Katherine sat with her mouth open, feeling suddenly stupid. What on earth was she to say? That she was staying in a tinker's train car in the woods? With the tinker? Unthinkable!

"What is it, girl? You do know where you live?" Mrs. Holland said sharply.

"I don't have a room yet," Katherine said. "I just arrived from Caledon this morning."

"Caledon? I thought you were in Rosedale?"

"Yes, I was." Katherine gulped. She'd forgotten she had omitted the Colworthys.

"Then why were you in Caledon?"

"I was visiting my sister." Katherine said the first thing that came into her head.

The woman's eyes narrowed. "You didn't mention you had family close."

"Er—just my sister Martha and her husband." She knew the lie was plain on her face.

"But why must you rent a room while you look for work? Why not just stay with your sister until you are settled?"

Katherine swallowed and frantically searched for an excuse. "My sister recently had a baby. It would be an imposition for me to stay there."

"It seems to me you would be a help to her." Mrs. Holland frowned. "Don't you think you should be with her?"

"No, I—No." It was going horribly. Katherine could think of nothing but making her escape.

"Well, all right, then. Give me her address, and I will leave a message with her for you," Mrs. Holland said reasonably.

Except Martha was her cousin, not sister, and she lived in Toronto, not Caledon. She should have thought at the beginning to ask Mrs. Holland to leave a message for her there with her cousin . . . but now it was too late to backpedal.

"I could call in . . ." Katherine offered, but her voice trickled away at the woman's expression.

"On second thought, I don't think you would be suitable at all," Mrs. Holland said crisply. "Ellen will see you out."

Katherine found herself on the street. She looked about her, wondering what to do. She began to walk up the road, humiliation and frustration descending on her like a cloud. How could she have been so ill prepared? What had she expected would happen? No one would welcome her into their home based on her word alone. No one, of course, except Alonzo Colaco.

Chapter Seven

As if her thoughts had summoned him, she heard a familiar voice ahead saying, "Quality workmanship, you can see that. I got them from a smithy in Mimico," and then she had rounded the corner, and there stood the tinker's gaily colored cart. Alonzo was discussing a set of tankards with a man who looked to be some sort of house servant. Lilia and Tony, holding the horse's head, saw her and waved.

Katherine felt an immense, unreasonable sense of relief. She waited until Alonzo had completed the sale and the customer had left.

When he turned to her, he said, "Back so soon?"

She tried to smile but wasn't very successful. "It didn't go well."

"Ah. What was the problem?"

She tried to make light of it. Striking a pose, she looked down her nose, her lips pursed primly. "Character from your employer? None? My, my. Address? None? Oh my, my. Not suitable. Not suitable at all."

He laughed. "Oh dear. No, I suppose it doesn't look good. Are you going to the second interview?"

"What's the use? They'll just ask me the same questions. At this point, my prospects are bleak. It would be better if I had a letter of recommendation, but when I asked for one from Mr. Colworthy, he laughed."

"I'll write you one."

"What?" She blinked at him.

"Why not? I *am* your employer, aren't I? I've been very satisfied with your work, and I will say so in writing."

"But I've only been with you two days!" she protested.

"I will word it so as to sound as if I've known you longer. It will be honest, don't worry," he said as she went to argue.

"Well, perhaps it will help," Katherine said doubtfully.

Alonzo sat down right there and carefully wrote out a neat letter on a piece of clean white paper he'd fetched from the back of the wagon. She watched him frown over it, pinching the pencil between his lips, and wondered if writing were a difficult thing for him. But when he finally handed the paper to her, she found his script clear and well formed.

To Whom It May Concern:

Miss Katherine Porter first came to work for me when my youngest child was just turned six. From the first day she has been completely satisfactory, gentle, and confident with the children, well disciplined, and congenial. I have found her intelligence to be of superior quality and am truthfully very sorry to see her go. My children have grown very fond of Miss Porter, and my daughter, now seven, emulates her as much as possible. To my mind, this is the highest compliment she could pay her tutor, and if my daughter applies herself to become as refined and gracious a person as Miss Porter, I will consider myself a most fulfilled parent. I do not hesitate in recommending Miss Porter to you. With best regards and sincere wishes for Miss Porter's continued success,

Mr. Alonzo Colaco, Springfield

Katherine stared at the letter in her hand and didn't know whether to laugh or cry. She shook her head, holding the note out to him.

"You can't write that," she told him.

"Why not?"

"It makes it sound as if I've been with you a year."

"That's what I intended. But it is the truth, however you may choose to interpret it. My youngest just turned six, and my daughter is now seven. And I might add that under the circumstances, you have been quite gracious."

She hesitated, then laughed and put the letter in the envelope he held out to her.

"But what do I say when they ask my address?"

"Tell them you haven't found rooms yet but you can be reached in care of the post office. If the interview goes well, you can arrange a box at the post office in anticipation of their reply."

"That's a good idea. All right, I'll make another attempt."

"I'll drive you," he said.

So once more she rode along the Toronto streets on the bright cart, and once again he let her down a block before the house.

"I'll wait for you here," he told her. "There's a little paper shop I want to visit."

She walked down the road to the house where she was to have her interview, feeling somewhat more prepared. It was a considerably smaller home this time, unostentatious. A balding butler showed her into the drawing room, which was dark and smelt strongly of tobacco. This time her interviewer was a large, heavyset man with a permanently red face. He reminded her unpleasantly of Mr. Colworthy. He wafted her into a chair with slightly too much jocularity, and they were joined by his wife.

Katherine thought the wife was in every way the opposite of her husband. She was thin and limp looking, with frizzy, graying hair. She introduced herself in a near whisper as Amelia Chartrand. She sat in the chair opposite Katherine, shoulders hunched, feet together, and didn't say a word the rest of the interview.

"We are looking for a tutor for our children," Mr. Chartrand said in a loud voice, as if she were hard of hearing. "The girl is sickly; she can't go to an ordinary school, and the boys—well, boys will be boys, eh? Ha, ha! They didn't get along at boarding school."

"I see. You have three children, then?" Katherine asked.

"Four. You needn't bother about the last one though. Nurse sees to him. Not old enough to be your problem."

Katherine glanced at the thin woman sitting beside him and said nothing.

"I presume you know French?" he asked.

"Some French and passable Latin," Katherine said.

"Latin, is it? My, my. There won't be much use for that, I suppose. Just frippery, that is. Like putting pearls on the pig with our brood, but still, I guess it doesn't hurt, does it?" He went on to quiz her about her education and where she had studied and looked more interested with each response she gave. Finally he worked round to the questions she'd been anxiously anticipating.

"Where was your last position, Miss Porter?"

"I've brought a letter of recommendation," Katherine replied and handed Alonzo's letter to him. She watched him scan it, her breath catching in her chest, feeling a terrible fraud, wondering what his reaction would be.

But he merely nodded and handed it back to her without showing it to his wife, who apparently was not to take part in any decisions. "Very good. Very favorable," he said. He went to a drinks trolley that stood near the window and poured himself a splash of amber liquid in a glass. He stood, rocking on his toes, with his free hand behind his back. "Why are you leaving this man's employ?"

"He is planning to move from the area, to Collingwood," Katherine said truthfully. "I prefer to stay in Toronto."

"Very good. I quite understand. About the position—you would be expected to instruct the children in the classics, in music and English—and Latin, why not?—and mathematics, with especial care to their history and geography. Matthew is not doing well in history and geography. You will also instruct them in deportment, and they are to have one hour of exercise in the afternoons. Not Drusilla, of course; she's too weak."

"I see," Katherine said, feeling slightly overwhelmed.

"You would have your own room but would share your day room with the housekeeper. I am prepared to offer you twenty-five dollars a month, paid quarterly. That's seventy-five a quarter." He turned abruptly and rang a bell, and a moment later, the door opened and the children were marched in by a maid. One look at them made Katherine's heart drop into her stomach.

The girl, Drusilla, was the ugliest child she'd ever seen, not so much in her features as in her expression. She had a sour turn to her mouth and an arch to her eyebrows that spoke of temper tantrums to come. She wore a ridiculously ruffled silk dress, and her brown hair was crimped and styled like an adult's. She regarded Katherine coolly, sat down beside her mother, and crossed her legs.

The two boys were dressed in identical jackets and looked to be about six and eleven. The oldest had a distinct black eye and a defiant look about him. The youngest scowled at her, sat down with a plop, and proceeded to jab his sister in the leg with a broken fingernail. She squealed and aimed a kick at his shin. Their father bellowed an order to be still and cuffed the boy on the back of the head.

"These are the children," Mr. Chartrand said flatly. "Drusilla, Matthew, and Peter. Children, this is Miss Porter."

"I don't want a tutor. I want to go to school with Davey," the younger boy whined.

"Of course not. That's a common school for common people," Mr. Chartrand said unpleasantly. "And I've told you I don't want you running about with that Irish brat. Tuck your shirttail in."

Peter ignored him.

Drusilla gave a loud, false-sounding cough. "Can we go now?"

Katherine sat observing the three children, mentally comparing Drusilla's spoiled scowl with Lilia's frank, cheerful expression, Peter's obnoxiousness with Tony's shyness. She thought of the Colaco children's eagerness to learn. Even the Chartrands' clothing, though expensive and stylish, looked uncared for compared to the Colacos', which was stiffly dried on a tree branch. She looked at Mr. Chartrand, large and blustering, who ignored his wife and looked as if he would brook no arguments, and found herself comparing him to mild, humorous Alonzo. She was certain Ruth Colaco had never tiptoed around him like a frail nonentity.

Before she knew what she was doing, Katherine stood, gripping her handbag. "It was very kind of you to see me," she heard herself say. "But this is not the position for me. I'm sure your children would be much happier with someone else. I do hope you find that person soon. Good day."

And she was back out on the street again, her heart hammering, leaving a slack-jawed man behind her. What had she done? she thought in horror. She'd never walked out of an interview before. But it was with a distinct feeling of relief that she headed down to the cart waiting a discreet distance down the street.

Even that was a prime example of Alonzo's courtesy, she told herself. He wasn't ashamed of being a tinker, but he knew to leave the gypsy wagon far enough from the house that no prospective employer would see her getting into it. What was more, he seemed to take no offense over it. She couldn't see Mr. Chartrand being so aware of another's feelings and so utterly unconcerned about his own.

There had to be a good position somewhere. She mustn't be overly anxious. She would wait until she found one where she would be happy.

Alonzo was waiting on the cart seat, the horse dozing in its traces. Katherine peeked into the back, and two grinning faces greeted her.

"Are you finished with your errands?" Lilia asked.

"Yes, for today, thank you."

Alonzo's hand was warm around Katherine's as she climbed onto the seat beside him.

"Well, how did it go?"

"Ghastly," she replied cheerfully, settling her skirts. "I think they wanted me. I didn't want them."

He shook his head, his laugh ringing out over the street. "It must have been awful if you turned them down."

"There were three children—well, four, but the youngest one was proclaimed 'not my problem' on account of his age. The daughter looked sour to the core. Everyone tiptoes around her. The mother may as well not exist. They need a lion tamer, not a teacher."

"You're a hard one to please, Kate. You want it to be easy."

"I have never expected life to be easy," she answered. "Far from it. But I want it at least to be bearable."

"And you'd rather bear with us than with them?" His dark blue eyes slid sideways toward her, half hidden by their thick lashes. A crooked smile played at the corner of his mouth. "I thought you'd jump at the chance for a job where you'd at least have a real roof over your head."

Katherine examined her hands clasped in her lap. "There are some things more important than a roof," she said slowly. "I think the Chartrands didn't have them."

"And we do?"

"At least you love each other. You're happy. That's something the Chartrands will never be."

"Better a crust eaten in peace than a feast taken in bitterness," Alonzo said softly.

"I suppose that's true. I hadn't thought much about it before."

He was silent a moment as he watched the horse's swaying tail.

"My life isn't for everyone," he said finally. "Perhaps it isn't reasonable of me to expect you to live as I do."

"It isn't bad, really," she said. "My bed is comfortable, the food is ample and delicious—though I'm not pleased about the lack of a lavatory."

"But the children? You like them all right?"

"Very much. They're very dear."

"And me?"

She glanced at him, but he remained gazing at the road ahead. "What do I think of you?" She was disconcerted by the question. No employer had ever asked her such a thing before.

"Well?"

She tipped her head to one side. "You're the most unusual man I've ever met, that's certain."

"You're dodging the question."

She laughed. "I guess I like you well enough. I'll admit I wasn't very pleased with you when I first arrived. But you're very sweet with your children, you're considerate, and more than kind."

He looked pleased. "You already know what I think of you because I said it in the letter, and I meant it. You've been a good sport."

"Thank you."

"My children like you too."

"I'd like to think so."

"Then stay," he said, turning toward her. His face was suddenly sober, his voice low and urgent. "I know it's a lot to ask of you. I know it isn't what you want. I know it's unusual. I'm asking anyway. Please stay and teach my children."

She opened her mouth and then closed it again. She didn't know what had happened to her pulse—the thudding of it sounded in her head. *Stay,* he said. But how could she? It wasn't at all what she had expected. *Then change your expectations.* He couldn't ask her to live in a train car and haul water from a river. She couldn't do it. *You've done it for two days already. Ruth managed it somehow, didn't she?* It wasn't decent. She was practically alone with the man, out in the woods, miles from everything. Martha would fall in a dead faint if she knew. *Martha doesn't need to know. No one will know.*

Katherine realized he was waiting for her answer. *Tell him no. Just say it.* But her mouth didn't move.

She was given a momentary reprieve, then, for the clouds that had gathered all day now overflowed in a torrent of water. She gasped, and Alonzo pulled the cart to the side of the road. Jumping down, he tied the horse to a fence, then came back to her and held up his arms. His face streamed with rain, his hair already plastered to his skull. Katherine put her hands on his shoulders, and he lifted her down. Together they ran for the back of the wagon.

Tony was dozing in one corner, but Lilia was wide-eyed with excitement and anxiety.

"Look, Papa!" She pointed to the lightning ripping across the sky.

"It's all right, *cara mia,*" Alonzo said.

The wagon's interior was a snug fit for four. Alonzo sat cross-legged on the floor and pulled Lilia onto his lap, wrapping his arms around her. She squealed and wriggled.

"You're wet, Papa!" she said.

Katherine brushed a strand of hair from her face and held herself as far from the opening as she could without pressing against Alonzo. Her bustle dug into her backside. The rain made musical thunder on the roof.

"You should fix a door across this," she told him. "The rain comes right in."

"There used to be a door. I haven't replaced it yet."

"You'd better before winter if you're going to sleep in here."

His head came up sharply. "Am I going to?" he asked above the rain.

"You don't expect *me* to sleep in here, do you?" she replied, smiling.

His face relaxed into an answering grin. "You'll stay, then?"

And incredulously she heard herself say, "For a while, yes. For a while."

Chapter Eight

THE RAIN SLACKENED AFTER A short time, and Alonzo climbed back onto the seat and chirped to the patiently waiting horse. Katherine remained in the back with Lilia curled up on her lap. The swaying of the cart lulled the child into a doze, and Katherine rested her hand lightly on her small shoulder. She looked from Lilia to Tony, who were slumbering beside each other. With their lashes long on their cheeks and their mouths relaxed in sleep, they looked like matching china bookends.

Their mother must have been beautiful, Katherine thought, though in all fairness, she supposed they could have gotten their looks from Alonzo, with his incredible eyes and thick, dark hair. She wondered suddenly what Ruth had been like. Certainly not like her. She pictured her slim, with long hair, onyx eyes, and a serene smile, like one of the willowy angels she had seen in paintings, hovering over children lost in the woods. She was probably a fun-loving person, happy and laughing, confident and capable. She couldn't picture any other type of woman living such a life with Alonzo Colaco. Had Ruth ever wanted more? Had she ever longed for a house, nice dresses, friends? Had she been ashamed to be seen riding perched on the bright tinker's cart? Or had this life been enough for her?

She smoothed the straggling hair from Lilia's forehead. What had the child meant about the baby Michael being with Mrs. O'Riley? She wanted to ask Alonzo but somehow couldn't bring herself to. It seemed too intrusive. She leaned her head against the jostling side of the cart and fell asleep to the sound of the silverware chiming around her like tiny bells.

She awoke from dreams of brown-haired angels when something softly touched her cheek. She opened her eyes, disoriented, to see Alonzo looking in at her through the opening of the cart, the backs of his fingers resting lightly against her face. For a moment, she thought she was still dreaming. The sky behind him was gray with rainclouds, and she couldn't tell if it was afternoon or evening. He was soaked, as though a barrel of water had been turned over his head.

"We're home," he said. He held out his arms, and Katherine blinked stupidly before realizing he was waiting for her to lift Lilia to him. The child was heavy with sleep and mumbled before looping her arms around her father's neck and dozing again.

Katherine stood stiffly, ducking to avoid knocking her head on the cart roof, and lifted the sleeping Tony, who felt like a fifty-pound sack of meal. Somehow she managed to climb out of the cart, heave him onto her hip, and stagger to the train car.

Alonzo had tucked Lilia into her cot. He came to take Tony and gently placed him in bed, then went to stoke the stove.

"We've missed lunch. I'll throw together a quick tea."

Katherine reached to take the kettle from his hand. "I'll get tea," she corrected him. "You change into something dry before you catch pneumonia."

"Yes, mum," he replied meekly, then shot her a grin and went out to the cart.

Katherine filled the kettle and rummaged in the cupboards for dishes, sugar, a paper bag of store-bought biscuits, and apples. Lilia watched dreamily from the cot, her eyes half closed.

"You remember me of my mother," she said after a while.

"You mean I *remind* you of your mother?"

"Yes," Lilia said. "It's nice."

Katherine didn't know what to say to that, so she said nothing as she fixed a plate of cheese sandwiches, apple slices, and biscuits and brought it over to the cot. Lilia sat up, cocooned in her quilt, and began eating enthusiastically.

Katherine considered waking Tony but decided against it. She laid the small table and was fishing in the cupboards for an onion when Alonzo reentered the train car.

He'd changed into tan sackcloth trousers and a white shirt, sleeves rolled to his elbows, and no jacket. His towel-dried hair curled damply over the tops of his ears and the back of his collar. He surveyed the table, nodded his thanks to her, and sat down. She sat opposite him, but the table was so small their knees touched, and she slid back self-consciously before pouring the tea.

"What happened to the door on the cart?" she asked conversationally, watching him peel the onion in one long brown curl.

He glanced at her from the corner of his eye. "It was damaged," he said mildly. The onion skin dropped to the plate, and he sliced off a thin ring. "Care for any?"

"No, thank you."

He added the onion to his cheese sandwich and took a large bite, followed by an entire cup of tea. Katherine suddenly realized she was watching his jaw muscles work and quickly dropped her gaze to her own meal. Lilia brought her empty plate to the table, and Alonzo put an arm around her.

"Now we have a rainy afternoon to spend," he said. "What shall we do with it?"

"A story!"

Alonzo grinned. "All right, *cara*, I'll tell you a story. But before I do, be a good girl and show Kate your shawl."

Lilia hurried away to a box Katherine had noticed earlier under her cot. The little girl pulled out a mass of white wool yarn and brought it to Katherine.

"You're knitting a shawl? What a clever girl you are. I was twice your age before I learned," she said admiringly, fingering the loose and rather awkwardly made stitches. "You must have worked very hard on this."

"Mrs. O'Riley taught me," Lilia informed her. "Look, I'll show you." She spread the shawl over Katherine's lap and showed her how she could knit. Katherine made admiring sounds, and Alonzo lavishly praised his daughter until she giggled. When her work was bundled away again, she wrapped her arms about her father's waist. "Now the story, Papa. You promised."

Alonzo plopped down on Lilia's cot, folded his legs like an Indian, and pulled her up beside him. "All right, *cara*, which one do you want? 'The Princess and the Dragon'? 'Daniel in the Lion's Den'?"

"Daniel," Lilia ordered, snuggling down with anticipation.

"Mmm. Good choice."

Alonzo began to speak, but Katherine was rather disappointed when the story turned out to be in Italian. Amused at herself, she rose to clear away their meal, listening to the rise and fall of his voice and calling on her Latin and biblical knowledge to decipher the story.

Lilia was rapt with attention. Alonzo played it up, arms waving, face flying from one expression to the next. He glowered and thundered for the lions, who apparently talked in this version. For Daniel, he was innocent and wide-eyed. Tony slept peacefully above his head. When at last Alonzo finished with a flourish, Lilia squealed with laughter. Alonzo sat back with a look of satisfaction. Lilia clapped and begged him in Italian for another.

"Another!" Alonzo glanced at Katherine in feigned dismay. "Have you ever heard of such a greedy child?"

"Please!" Lilia added hastily.

"Which shall it be this time?"

Lilia bounced up and down on the cot. "Make a new one!"

Alonzo frowned in thought. Then his face cleared, and he began. This story seemed a little tamer, with less wild gesticulating, and Lilia listened in absolute stillness, a worshipper before a lotus-positioned idol. Katherine moved quietly about the kitchen, continuing to listen to the cadence of the musical voice and wishing she understood.

When he finished, Lilia cheered. Alonzo came over to Katherine, picked up a tea towel, and began to dry the plates she had just washed.

"You seem to have great talent as a storyteller," Katherine remarked. "What was the second one about?"

"It was about a fairy princess disguised as a servant who moved into a family's home and wrought great changes in all their lives. Flowers bloomed where none had grown before, children sang and played instead of throwing tantrums, the chickens laid double-yolked eggs, and the grumpy old man of the house became a kindly saint."

"I see," Katherine said with a wry smile. "And what became of this amazing fairy princess?"

"Oh, she stayed with them for always and was very happy," he said.

"Why was she in disguise?"

He smiled and carefully folded the dish towel. "Ah, but you see, she didn't know it was a disguise. She herself did not know she was a princess. But the children found out. You can hide nothing from children, even if you hide it from yourself."

* * *

While rainy afternoons with Miss Alice Colworthy had been tedious blood-baths, ultimately ending in tantrums—not always Miss Alice's—rainy days with the Colacos actually proved to be enjoyable. For three days, the drizzle continued, and Katherine spent the hours reading to the children or putting them through their lessons, to which they eagerly responded. She helped Lilia learn a new knitting stitch and taught Tony a rollicking song about a hobo that the gardener had taught her as a child, out of her mother's hearing. Tony shyly performed it for his father, bringing thunderous applause from Alonzo. She wrote dutifully to her cousins, telling them merely that she had found a new position and giving no address. And she and the children spent hours watching Alonzo work.

He spent each day making over old pieces he found in his ramblings. Katherine found it fascinating to watch him working over an old cup or pot, magically transforming it from battered and tarnished metal into smooth, shining silver with his small hammers and melting spoons. His strong, limber hands gently manipulated the little implements as if he were striking a dulcimer's strings rather than a dented old cheese grater.

The children watched him, sponge-eyed, and vied with each other for turns sitting between his knees and holding the tapping mallet with his hand over theirs. One evening he showed Katherine how to work an old tea kettle, his head bent close, his hand warm around hers as she held the small hammer. But his nearness disconcerted her, and the metal grew only more dented with her awkward efforts until finally she laughed and drew back.

"I've ruined it. You'll have to fix it."

"It was a good first try," he consoled her, hiding his grin.

Within minutes he had smoothed the metal out again. He polished the kettle with a bit of cloth and held it up for her inspection.

"You were right," she told him. "You *are* an artist."

"Of sorts," he said, shrugging, but the corners of his eyes betrayed his smile.

Four days a week, Alonzo hitched up Bacchus and drove into Springfield, Port Credit, or sometimes all the way to Toronto to trade and peddle his wares and to run any errands. Before, the children had gone with him and remained quiet and obedient—though undeniably bored—in the cart. Now, however, they could stay home with Katherine in the camp, which they much preferred.

On one such day, Alonzo had gone to the city and the children were out gathering firewood. Katherine was in the train car, awkwardly darning one of Tony's stockings, when Bo began to bark. Lilia burst into the train car, her hair flying, her arms still clutching a bundle of sticks.

"Kate, a constable! Come quick."

Katherine dropped her sewing as a man appeared at the door behind Lilia. Alonzo had stoked the woodstove that morning to save her the trouble of building a fire, which she never had managed to master. As a result, the train car was overly heated. Katherine had taken a holiday from the daily struggle of dressing and had donned only a white cotton blouse and long skirt, omitting petticoats, stays, bustle, shoes, and stockings. She was mortified at being caught in her bare feet, with her hair straggling loose from its bun. She jumped to her feet and thrust her chair away.

"Excuse me?" the officer said, ducking through the doorway. He paused just inside, looking around in surprise. Apparently he hadn't expected to see things so clean and comfortable. He was tall, his hat touching the ceiling. He lifted a gloved hand to touch its brim. "Constable McTavish, mum."

"Good afternoon. What can I do for you, Constable?" Katherine asked, patting a stray hair into place. She knew her hair was in bad need of a wash.

"Well, mum, I need to ask you some questions, please." He looked about twenty-five and uncomfortable in his tight collar.

"Certainly. Won't you sit down?"

"I'd rather you stepped out here, please."

Katherine followed him outside and stood in the sun-heated grass in her bare feet. Lilia hung close behind her, watching. Tony crouched beside Bo, keeping the tethered dog silent.

"The gentleman up the road has made complaints, mum," the constable said apologetically. "He's tried to be reasonable and all, but—well, I have to follow orders, see." He glanced at her feet and looked away.

"What seems to be the problem?" Katherine asked, scraping together her dignity.

"It seems someone has raided his chicken coop and removed three fowl, mum. He's willing to drop all charges if the guilty party pays damages."

Katherine's blood went cold. "You think *we* stole his chickens?"

He glanced at her feet again and shrugged, his face turning a faint pink. "He's always been very reasonable, mum, you can't deny it. He has no objection to gypsies camping on his land, but he draws the line at thievery."

Katherine's ears were flaming. She looked at Lilia, whose mouth had fallen open.

"We are not gypsies," Katherine said indignantly.

The officer backed away a step, holding up his hands. "All right, I'm sorry. I know you prefer to be called travelers. But either way, if you please, I'll need to inspect your camp."

"You may look all you like, but you'll not find any stolen birds here," Katherine replied tartly. "We're not thieves."

The officer tipped his hat again and went past her into the train car. Katherine stood gripping Lilia's hand and listened to him going slowly through the little kitchen, their cupboards and closets, even the trunk beneath the car. Her heart pounded fiercely. Had she done a wise thing in letting him search the camp? She knew the train car was clean, but perhaps somewhere else . . . She hated to even entertain the thought, but Alonzo *did* keep them well fed, and they never lacked for anything. How *did* a tinker keep his family so well provided for? How did he afford to pay a tutor ten dollars a month? How well did she really know him, anyway? Was he capable of theft? She glanced down at the children and was immediately ashamed of herself. Of course she couldn't doubt him. With Alonzo, what you saw was all there was. He was bold and honest—well, except, of course, for misrepresenting himself the first time he'd met her . . . and there was the matter of the character letter . . . She stood chewing on her lip and digging her toes into the earth.

The constable finished his search and stood looking around the camp, his hands on his hips. Then she saw his gaze linger somewhere behind her and his face go blank. Wondering, she turned to look and saw, stretched on a pine-tree bough for all to see, her newly washed undergarments. A pair of long hose fluttered in the breeze like maypole ribbons. She had taken advantage of Alonzo's absence to wash them, and there they were, open to inspection, like white flags on a ship's mast.

She couldn't scramble to hide her underwear; it was too late for that. She stood, embarrassed beyond endurance, wondering what he must think of her. Of course he had mistaken them for a band of gypsies. What else?

The officer cleared his throat and said in a businesslike voice, "Very well, I will leave you for now, but I'm warning you. If any more chickens are stolen, you and your husband will be brought in for questioning."

"He's not my husband," Katherine said automatically.

The constable's eyes narrowed, and he looked her up and down like she was something distasteful in a butcher-shop window.

"You and your man, then," he said, and without another word, he marched to his horse that waited by the road, mounted, and rode away at a brisk trot.

Katherine sat heavily on the steps and put her head in her hands. She had never felt so foolish and caught off balance in her life.

Lilia's small hand fell gently on her shoulder. "Are you all right, Kate?"

Katherine sighed and lifted her head, managing a weak smile. "I'm fine, *cara mia*," she said, and Lilia, reassured by this endearment, ran to join Tony and discuss the event in hushed Italian.

Katherine stood and jerked her underwear off the tree, rolled it into a ball, and bundled it away in her cupboard.

Chapter Nine

IT WAS DUSK WHEN KATHERINE heard the creaking of Alonzo's cart and the sound of Bacchus's hooves on the road. She set down the book she'd been reading and went outside, supper ready on the stove. She had put on her shoes and rolled the waistband of her skirt; she had given up on the bustle altogether as being too impractical under the circumstances.

Alonzo took care of the horse before joining her. She noticed his face was drawn and tired, and his voice was hoarse as he greeted her.

"I have stew ready," she told him. "Come in to the table."

He thanked her and stepped past her into the train car. Lilia came running to give him a hug, but Tony, lost in the new storybook Katherine had given him, looked up with a faraway smile and returned to his reading.

Katherine set the bowl of admittedly watery stew and a plate of bread and butter on the table. Alonzo washed and sat down with an audible sigh.

"Long day?" Katherine observed, sitting opposite him with a cup of tea. Tea she had managed to prepare just fine. Unfortunately, her other culinary skills were limited.

Alonzo took a bite of stew and nodded. If he noticed the carrots were a bit raw or the broth rather weak, he didn't mention it.

"Not up to my usual steam," he said. "I might have a touch of something. What did you do today?"

Lilia was hanging on his elbow. "We picked up acorns, and I learned to add by tens."

"Very good. I shall have to hear you."

"And we did the washing and played Gray Goose," Lilia went on happily. "And then the policeman came, and then we made turnovers. You can have one."

"Policeman?" Alonzo's head came up sharply.

"A constable came round," Katherine said offhandedly. "Someone has been stealing chickens from a farm up the road, and he's questioning everyone in the vicinity."

"He questioned *you*?" Alonzo's voice cracked, and his eyebrows lowered.

"It's not important. He was very polite and apologetic," Katherine said quickly. "He looked around and went away again. He was just doing his duty."

"He said we were gypsies," Lilia added reproachfully. "What's a gypsy, Papa? Is it something bad?"

Alonzo stared as if not seeing her and then blinked once and reached out his arms to hold her lightly. "No, Lilia, it's not anything bad. But we're not gypsies."

Lilia regarded him solemnly. "He said you were Kate's husband too."

Katherine smiled wryly. "I set him straight on that point. But I didn't think before I spoke, and he ended up assuming I was something much worse."

Alonzo's indigo-blue eyes sparkled. "*Is* there anything worse?"

Reddening, Katherine found herself stammering. "That's not what I meant. I-I didn't mean to insult you."

He waved his hand. "I know what you meant." He took a bite of bread and chewed it, watching her contemplatively. "Come out for a walk with me," he said suddenly.

Katherine blinked. "Right now?"

"I'm finished eating."

"All right."

"Me too, Papa?" Lilia piped up, but Alonzo put a hand on her head.

"Not this time, Lilia. You stay and mind Tony."

Tony looked indignant at this.

Katherine picked up her shawl, and they stepped out into the darkening evening. A cool breeze was making the trees dance, and the pewter moon was just rising over their leafy, swaying outline. They slowly walked side by side in silence for a moment along the edge of the clearing.

"I'm afraid I really didn't think things through when I placed that advert in the paper," Alonzo said after a while. "I suspect I've been more foolish than usual."

"What do you mean?"

"I'm not concerned about my reputation or what the world thinks of me," he said, pushing his hands into his pockets. "I've stopped caring for any of that years ago. But I didn't stop to think your reputation might be jeopardized by your living here like this, and that might be important to *you.*"

Katherine thought for a moment before she replied. "It *is* unusual. But I think if no one who knows me thinks ill of me, that's what ultimately matters. And no one really knows, after all . . ."

He shot her a sideways glance. "Would your family approve of your new employment?"

"My cousins don't care much what I do so long as I don't spread scandal back on them. They're more worried about their own reputation than mine. I suppose Martha especially would not be pleased, but not on my account. She'd see all this as an attempt on my part to embarrass her."

"Does she know where you are?"

"No, not precisely." He fell silent a moment, and Katherine bit her lip, instantly remorseful. "I didn't mean—Please don't take that as a reflection on you, Mr. Colaco. Martha doesn't approve of my working *anywhere.* She thinks it improper and demeaning. She thinks I should remain with them and be grateful for all their generosity. I suppose, to be fair, they have been kind to me in their own way. They just never let me forget how indebted I am to them. It . . . rankles a bit."

"I don't imagine you enjoy being beholden to anyone."

She smiled. "No. I might not have minded so much if I'd felt they'd helped me out of love or concern. But to them I was just an excuse to flaunt their wealth and feel proud of themselves. That's why I wish—I *used* to wish—I could become wealthy too, in my own right, just so I could flaunt it in their faces and say, 'See? I'm just as good as you!'" She reddened in the dark. "That sounds dreadfully childish spoken aloud."

He chuckled and looped her hand through his arm. "It's honest, at any rate. Though I don't agree that money has anything to do with a person's value."

"The world may not agree with you."

He chuckled. "I find the world quite often does not agree with me."

"You're a rebel against society, then?" she asked lightly.

"I don't rebel against society. I simply ignore it."

Katherine laughed. "I can see that. But you have to admit it makes life easier if you have a little money. I used to daydream about it quite a lot, growing up, and especially while I lived with Hugh and Martha. I didn't need to be fabulously wealthy, only comfortably so. The best chance for a female of doing that is to marry well."

"And do you think you'll—What is the English word I want?—attain this ambition one day?"

"Not likely." She sighed. "But at least in the meantime I don't have to endure their grudging hospitality. I may not have a lot, but what I do end up with, I will have earned. No one else will be able to take credit for it."

"Ah. And here we have the precise reason I left Italy. You see, we're not so different, you and I. We just have, perhaps, different ideas of what will make us happy."

* * *

Katherine watched Alonzo spend the evening reading to Lilia and Tony as she sewed. The children were curled up on the cot, Alonzo sitting between them with the storybook resting on his drawn-up knee in the lamplight. It was a homey, comforting picture, and with a small pang, she realized she had no part in this family. She was an outsider. In spite of their warm acceptance, she didn't really belong.

She rose abruptly and took a towel, the tin of soap, a toothbrush, and the jar of toothpaste and wordlessly slipped outside. It was fully dark now, and the cool breeze combed the long silver grass and set the trees humming. Bo lifted his head to look at her, then returned to his perpetual snooze.

She crossed the clearing into the woods and, with muttered, genteel curses, found a bush. Come winter, the irritating absence of a lavatory would be unbearable. *If I'm still here then*, she reminded herself.

She padded carefully through the trees along the now-familiar path to the brook. It sounded loud in the stillness. Kneeling, she scrubbed her face in the icy water and brushed her teeth. One day soon she would find a large tin tub she could fill with hot water for a real bath. Alonzo and the children seemed perfectly content with fully bathing—albeit infrequently— in the stream, but though a sponge bath was invigorating at times, she still hesitated to do anything more than that in the cold water. Her skin was beginning to dry and grow coarse, like a farm wife's, and her face was becoming brown and chapped from afternoons spent in the sun and wind.

She stood looking down at the slow-flowing water and wished she could immerse her whole body at one time. It seemed ages since she'd had a good, leisurely soaking. And her hair was positively filthy. It couldn't wait much longer. But the thought of being *completely* bare outdoors still held her back.

"Your problem," she told herself aloud, "is that you're too proud. You have water; you have soap. You have no excuse for being dirty."

The moonlight sparkled on the water like Christmas candles, the space between the lights inky black. She wondered if one would turn black from washing in such black water. She bent down and trailed her fingers in the brook, listening to the hollow sound it made moving over the stones. The water was cold and velvety. If the Colacos could bathe outdoors, surely she could. Just once. Just to hold her over until she could get a big tub.

Decisively Katherine straightened, unfastened her dress, and draped it over a low bush. She forced herself to remove her shoes, stockings, and underclothes, feeling the cold air hit her skin. She remembered seeing the baked potatoes Alonzo had roasted over a fire. When the cold air hit them, their skins split. Grimacing, she pushed the thought away and tiptoed into the stream.

The stones were slippery with some kind of moss. The water came up to her knees. She stood rigidly in the center of the stream, clutching the soap tin, her jaw clamped tightly. It was much colder standing in it than it had been to just pat with a sponge. How on earth did the children manage? She would die of pneumonia. It was ridiculous. It was—*heathen.*

But she had come this far, and she was determined to see it through. Cautiously she lowered herself into the water, squealing as the iciness rose up her body, cursing a little less genteelly. Finally she was sitting on the rocky bottom with the water rushing around and past her shoulder blades. Quickly she soaped up and scrubbed, determined to get clean because she would not be doing this again soon. The white, soapy foam floated away into the night and vanished.

Her vigorous rubbing began to warm her slightly, or else she was growing numb, for the water didn't seem quite as cold as at first. Tentatively she lay back and let the rippling water run over her head. Her hair flowed past her like waving fronds of seaweed. She closed her eyes, letting the irritations and mortifications of the day wash away. She felt her legs trying to float, the tug of the water on her hair, and felt unexpectedly and completely relaxed. The water lapped at her ears and flowed over her forehead onto her face. She imagined herself in a different era, a different world, a wood nymph floating in a primeval forest. An aborigine stretched pale below a winking sky. Perhaps it was heathen. It was also delicious. She thought, just a little, that perhaps this way of living wasn't so bad after all.

She sat up again, fiercely soaped and scrubbed her hair, then leaned back and let the stream carry away the suds. At last refreshed, she breathed deeply, stood, and wrung her hair out like a towel. The cold air slapped her skin, bringing out the gooseflesh, tiny drops of water threading down her legs. It tickled, and she giggled and shivered in pure delight. At last, sober and clean, she tiptoed back to the bank and dried herself off before pulling on her clothes. She pushed her feet into her shoes, collected her things, and headed back toward camp. The evening air turned her wet hair icy cold on her scalp.

Halfway there, a shadow detached itself from the surrounding trees and came toward her down the narrow path.

"You didn't come back. It's dark out. I was getting worried," Alonzo greeted her.

"I took the opportunity for a thorough wash," she said.

"In the river? I thought you refused to immerse yourself entirely."

"Yes, well, I've changed my mind. It really was quite glorious."

He stood looking at her a moment, his face lost in shadow, and Katherine, gazing back at him, found herself clutching her damp towel to her chest. She cleared her throat, but before she could think what to say, Alonzo extended a hand toward her. Katherine took a step back, surprised, but he gave a low chuckle.

"Hold still," he said and slipped his hand behind her neck to pull her long wet hair free of her collar, where she had entrapped it by accident. Then, taking her towel from her, he placed it around her shoulders, spreading her hair over it to keep her dress dry. His hand lingered a moment on her shoulder. "You're trembling," he said, sounding surprised.

"Am I? The water was cold tonight," she said.

"You should wear your hair down more often. It's beautiful."

Katherine swallowed. "It wouldn't be practical—"

"*You* are beautiful, Kate."

She stopped with her mouth hanging open. Beautiful! She had no delusions about being beautiful. Martha had made sure of that. "It's nighttime," she finally replied. "Everything's pretty in the dark."

The corner of his lip turned up a fraction, and his eyes glittered in the moonlight. He moved slightly closer. "You have difficulty accepting compliments, don't you?"

"Only when they're patently false. I prefer honest ones, not glib, empty phrases." Her stomach was feeling jittery, and she felt irritation rising within her. She latched onto it to cover her uneasiness.

"*Glib*? I don't know that word."

"It means throwing out light remarks you don't really mean. *Flippant. Insincere.*"

She saw his face stretch in surprise in the dim light. "You believe I am insincere? I spoke the truth. You are beautiful, Kate."

"I know I'm not. And if you *did* mean it, it's an inappropriate comment for an employer to make to his employee, standing here in the middle of the night, alone in the woods." She wanted to bite her tongue for saying that last bit because it revealed too much of her discomfort, but to her relief Alonzo gave a brief nod and took a step back from her.

"I didn't mean to overstep," he said quietly. "I only meant to compliment you. In Italy, it's an acceptable thing to compliment a woman. Apparently I'm not completely familiar with the rules in Canada."

Katherine couldn't help smiling. "Even if you knew them all, you'd only break them," she said.

His answering grin flashed white in the shadows.

* * *

The next morning Katherine was sitting at the table putting her students through their English exercises when Bo began to bark and she heard voices outside the train car. Going to the door, she saw Alonzo speaking with the constable of the day before. Alonzo had been hammering some boards together, and now he set his hammer down and folded his arms. His face was a picture of innocence and humility.

"Just a routine check, you know," the constable was saying. "Nothing personal, you understand."

"Of course, sir. Anything you like."

"Your name?" He was writing on a tablet of paper.

"Alonzo Giuseppe Colaco," Alonzo said and spelled it for him.

"Your occupation, if you have one?"

"Craftsman."

"Sir?"

"Tinsmith. I make and repair metal items," Alonzo said.

"Ah." The constable jotted this down. "And the members of your family?"

"I have two children, ages seven and six. They're always supervised."

"And your, um, the woman?" The officer glanced at Katherine in the doorway. "What's her name?"

Katherine's chin went up, but Alonzo answered swiftly, cutting her off. "Miss Katherine Porter. She's my children's teacher. And she watches them when I am away."

This caught the constable by surprise. "She's your employee, then?"

"Yes. Anything else?" Alonzo asked mildly.

"I don't suppose you have a permanent address?" the officer asked. "Itinerant?"

"Not at all." The constable had begun to write it, but Alonzo's response made him pause. Alonzo continued. "Thirty-four Collins Street in Collingwood, on Georgian Bay. We'll be returning there in the spring."

"I see. Is there someone with whom we can confirm this information?"

"Mr. John O'Riley, Collingwood," Alonzo said.

Katherine looked up at this name, remembering what Lilia had told her.

The constable put away his notes. "Thank you. I'm sorry to have troubled you. You know how it is with gypsies and vagabonds around."

"Certainly," Alonzo said, shaking the other man's hand.

"There's a Chinese family camping along the river farther down the valley. I'll be questioning them too. No doubt they are the ones responsible for the missing fowl."

A funny expression Katherine couldn't identify crossed Alonzo's face, but he said nothing. The constable rode away, and Katherine returned to her teaching, but her mind was filled with other things, and when Lilia complained of being tired, she stopped her lessons for the day and let the children go.

Katherine occupied herself the rest of the morning sorting through the children's clothes to determine what they needed for the winter and found that they were reasonably equipped but for mittens and heavier underclothes. She was making a list when Alonzo put his head inside the door.

"Busy?" he asked.

She set down her work and rose to join him.

"Constable seemed like a nice chap," he said, sitting down on the front steps and wrapping his arms around his drawn-up knees.

"I suppose you couldn't be of help to him." Katherine sat on the step beside him and assumed the same position.

"You suppose?" He grinned, and when she did not respond, his face sobered, his brow furrowing. "You don't really think I had anything to do with chicken stealing, do you?"

"I couldn't say. I really don't know you," she said with an awkward shrug.

"That's a fine thing to say!"

"But it's true. I would like to think you had nothing to do with it. But I haven't known you long, and I . . . well, I don't know anything about your background or . . . or your life at all."

She waited for him to assure her he hadn't stolen the chickens. She expected him to lean back and invite her to ask any question about him that she liked. But instead he only shrugged and said, "I guess that's true."

"Anyway, it sounds as if he has other suspects in mind."

Alonzo glanced sideways at her. "The Chinese family down the valley?"

"He seemed to think they'll be able to clear up the mystery."

He shook his head slowly, gazing out over the trees with a thoughtful expression. "I doubt very much they are responsible."

"Do you know them?"

"No, I wasn't aware they were there. They must not have been there long."

"Then how do you know whether they're guilty or innocent?" Katherine reasoned.

"I don't. But I would be surprised. You can bet if they did steal the chickens it was only because they were truly starving."

He stood and held out a hand to help her up.

"Come with me a moment, please."

"Why?"

"Please." Alonzo started off into the woods.

"What is it?" she called after him.

"A gift."

Astonished, Katherine followed until he stopped abruptly thirty feet into the trees.

"What do you think?" he asked.

A small square house had been pounded together with a few boards, with a pointed roof and the holes chinked with mud. The door was attached with leather hinges. A metal pipe traveled from the base to a point two feet above the roofline. Katherine stood blinking at it. With a flourish, Alonzo pulled open the door to reveal a wooden rail-back chair with a hole cut in the seat and, below it, a deep hole dug in the earth.

"A lavatory!" Katherine cried.

"Are you pleased?" he asked seriously, his face expressionless but his eyes intensely bright.

"Extremely pleased. What a wonderful surprise! It's very kind of you," Katherine said and was alarmed to feel tears tightening her throat.

He closed the door, and they turned back toward the clearing.

"It's to show you that I'm not a completely insensitive clod," he said. "I meant it as an apology if I upset you last night with my comments."

Suddenly she felt foolish, like a child throwing a tantrum over nothing. "It's all right," she said. "You were right in one thing you said last night; I have difficulty accepting compliments. I still don't believe you meant it because I'm well aware I'm not beautiful, but it was nice of you to say so, and I shouldn't have responded as I did."

Alonzo stared at her in silence for a moment, and then he shook his head slowly, his eyes not leaving hers. Katherine couldn't tell what the expression on his face meant, and it bothered her because he was usually so easily read. She added quickly, "I owe you an apology too for what I said earlier. I don't think you're a chicken thief, not really."

"Thank you. In spite of what all my acquaintances think, I'm not a perfect man"—he flashed her a mischievous grin—"but I assure you I have never stolen a chicken."

Chapter Ten

THE NEXT DAY KATHERINE PUT the children through some exercises to improve their reading. Both could now do simple words like *pot* or *dog*, so she introduced some harder words. Lilia caught on immediately, but Tony struggled to keep up and couldn't quite grasp what she was trying to teach him. After letting him fight with his frustration for a while, Katherine hit on an idea to help with the admittedly illogical spelling variations to be found in English.

"Some of these words rhyme," she explained, pointing to the list. "Even though they are spelled in different ways, they sound the same. Look at this, Tony. *Though* and *throw* rhyme. Do you hear it? *Blue* and *blew* sound the same too."

Tony nodded uncertainly, frowning at the words on the page.

"Don't look too closely at the spelling right now. Here, maybe if we make it into a rhyming game it will help." Katherine took a fresh sheet of paper and wrote the words in two columns, splitting them so each word in the first column had a homonym in the second column. Then she devised a game in which she made up a silly little nonsense song using both words of the pair. *Even though I know it's wrong, I'll throw a rock through your window if you don't like my song.* Or *Billy blew his trumpet so hard his face turned blue and he died in the yard.* The children, listening carefully while studying the lists, drew a line between the words she had used in the song. Before long they were able to make a connection between what they were hearing and what they were seeing on the page. By the time they'd drilled the whole list, all three of them were laughing.

It was nearly dusk when Katherine heard Alonzo's cart pull into the clearing from his trip to Port Credit. She heard voices, and Bo began to bark, so she went to the door to look out. Alonzo was helping a woman down from the back of the cart. Surprised, Katherine watched as a little boy and then an elderly man followed the woman. Calling to Bo to be quiet, Alonzo kept hold of the man's arm, and as the group drew near the light spilling from the doorway, Katherine saw that the man was not elderly, as she had first supposed, but was disabled in some way. He limped badly and walked hunched over, as if his back pained him. He wore a long tunic over cotton pants. His face was unlined from age, though his head was completely bald.

Alonzo guided the man to sit on the steps of the train car, murmuring something in a low voice, and then he beckoned for the woman and child to draw closer. The woman wore an outfit identical to the man's, which Katherine found astonishing, and her sleek, dark hair was pulled into a long braid down her back. As the woman turned to take the child's hand to help him sit on the steps beside the man, the light illuminated her oval face clearly, and Katherine saw that she was Asian.

Suddenly she knew who these people were. Involuntarily she drew in a sharp breath, and over their heads, her eyes met Alonzo's.

"Katherine, this is Jin; his wife, Ah Lam; and—I'm sorry, how did you pronounce your son's name again?"

The woman stared blankly at Alonzo, not comprehending. He reached over and placed a gentle hand on the boy's mop of straight black hair, and her face lightened.

"Huang Fu," she said, nodding.

"Huang Fu. This is Katherine. My children, Lilia and Tony."

Katherine looked down to find that the Colaco children had come up behind her and were pressing their faces around each side of her skirt, peering out. They exchanged nods with the woman.

"Hello," Lilia said to the little boy, but he only hid his face in the man's sleeve.

Alonzo clapped his hands together and rubbed them briskly. "First thing, we shall have supper. Then we will help you set up your tent before nightfall. I think over there under those trees would be a good sheltered spot. It frequently rains just before dawn." He turned and looked up at Katherine, where she hovered unmoving in the doorway. "It's a lovely evening. If I set up a board on two stumps, it will make a fine trestle table, don't you think?"

Katherine became aware that her mouth was hanging open, and now she closed it and turned back to the little kitchen. She had made a pot of potato soup flavored with cubed ham, but the pot now looked dismally small. She rubbed her hand through her hair. Perhaps she could whip up some baking powder biscuits to go with the soup; that wouldn't take long.

Alonzo entered the car behind her and reached for the stack of bowls on the shelf. There were only four. He smiled.

"We'll eat in shifts," he said.

Katherine's head buzzed with a hundred questions, but she pinched her lips shut and set about making the biscuits. She made a double batch, for good measure, and placed them in a cloth-lined basket that Lilia carried out to the trestle table.

When Katherine wiped her hands and joined the rest of the group outside, she found the humble board transformed into something of a party. Alonzo had brought out the chairs from the train car and then rolled a few segments of tree trunk into place to serve as extra seats. Lilia had placed a fistful of flowers in a tin cup in the center of the improvised table. The woman—Ah Lam, Katherine reminded herself—had produced three wooden bowls from her own belongings, so they did not need to eat in shifts.

Alonzo seated Katherine and then served everyone himself, carefully ladling the soup to ensure everyone had an equal portion and passing round the biscuit basket before sitting down himself. He raised his glass to the visitors.

"To new friends," he said.

Jin translated for his wife. Both smiled and nodded in return, but Huang Fu kept his eyes on his bowl, and Katherine decided he must be painfully shy. When he began eating, however, she revised her opinion—it wasn't shyness that kept his eyes on his bowl; he was starving. The little boy shoveled the soup in with his spoon, pausing only to cram a biscuit into his mouth, and she wondered how long it had been since he'd eaten a good meal. He was so petite it was hard to guess his age, but she thought he was about five. His parents ate with equal interest but more restraint.

"Jin and his family are from Beijing," Alonzo told Katherine. "He came here three years ago to work on the railway and has learned some English. His family came to join him last fall. Ah Lam knows only a few words of English."

Jin had been listening carefully, and now he added, "But now I cannot work. Lose job."

"Jin was injured at work," Alonzo said. "When he hurt his back and hip, the railway officials told him he'd have to return to China, but he had no money, especially with his wife and son. They've been living in a tent by the river for the past month and living off of fish and wild greens."

"And chicken?" Katherine murmured, trying not to smile.

Alonzo paused, then grinned. "I didn't ask."

* * *

There was something not quite real—almost magical, Katherine decided—about eating dinner in the middle of a dusk-filled woodland with mosquitoes dancing around the lanterns and stars coming out overhead. The ordinary fare seemed incongruous; she felt she should be dining on moonbeams and fairy dust. And when she stopped to consider that she was sharing this unorthodox meal with French-Italians and a Chinese family, she couldn't help but wonder how she had come to this point. One moment she had been sitting at Hugh's expansive, perfectly correct table, and the next she was slurping soup in the woods with people who would be considered in most social circles as most unsuitable company. She wondered what Jin and his family would do in the long term, for she knew there was little work for the Chinese except the railroad. Perhaps Ah Lam could find work in a laundry, but that was about the only other option available to them. Katherine suddenly felt a bit guilty for whining about her own limited opportunities when she had far more than Ah Lam would ever have.

She glanced at Alonzo, who was leaning forward on his elbows, intent on his stilted conversation with Jin. The lantern light touched his cheekbones and cast his eyes in shadow, making him look rather like a bronze in a museum. He did not see himself as superior to these people, Katherine realized. He wasn't just acting as if they were friends, welcome at his table. He truly considered them such. And apparently he was going to help them move their tent here to the clearing. She wondered why. Surely they could stay where they were by the river, where they could catch fish, and if he wanted to help them, he could take them food from time to time. Why did he need to bring them here?

Katherine felt a flush of shame creep up her cheeks. She realized she was slightly resentful of the family's intrusion, even though she knew it was no fault of their own. Alonzo had gone and fetched them, after all. She had become a bit territorial, perhaps, and had started thinking of this clearing as her own. But it wasn't. It was Alonzo's home, not hers, and he could bring into it whomever he wanted. Even the poorest of the poor, the people society had turned away. People who had limited options and no other home to go to.

People not unlike herself, if she were honest about it.

She felt ashamed all over again for judging these kindly people, for being so aware of their ethnicity, their unacceptability. Alonzo could overlook all that—in fact, she doubted he was even aware of anything to overlook. Could she do the same?

After supper, Katherine began to clear away the dishes, and Ah Lam jumped to her feet to help. Together they carried everything into the train car, washed it, and put it away. Words weren't necessary between them; women's domestic chores were the same universally. In the lamplight of the car, Katherine could see Ah Lam better. Her oval face was the color of milky tea, her eyes a chocolate brown, and her hands rubbed red and raw from much washing outdoors in cold water. Ah Lam seemed surprised by the snug arrangements in the train car and examined everything with many exclamations and nods of approval. She ran an admiring hand over the clever built-in cupboards and the pretty quilt on Lilia's bed.

"Is good," she said, patting the hanging bunk where Tony slept. "Very pretty."

"Thank you. Alonzo built all of this himself. Lilia sleeps there, and Tony's bed is that one on the wall," Katherine told her. "That is my bed, there."

She doubted Ah Lam understood what she was saying, but the woman nodded.

"All very good," she said. Then she came to touch Katherine gently on the sleeve of her dress and looked up into her face with shining eyes. "You very good," she said. "Thank you."

Katherine felt a tightening in her throat and smiled brightly to fend off tears. She wasn't good at all. She had just sat through an evening half resenting this woman's presence. No matter how nice Ah Lam seemed, Katherine did not want her here.

Well, this small, quiet woman was apparently going to be her neighbor and new friend, so she must cope with it.

No, she must do more than cope. She must accept and welcome this family the way Alonzo did. Katherine gently put her arm around the other woman's shoulders and turned her toward the door. "Let's go help the men set up your tent," she said.

The tent turned out to be a square cloth cobbled skilfully together from pieces of canvas and cotton sacking, draped over a center ridge pole, and staked at each corner. Both ends were open to the night air. Ah Lam placed several blankets on the ground, tucked their meager belongings around the edges, and stepped back to view it with satisfaction. Katherine looked at it more doubtfully, then went into the train car and brought out an extra quilt from her bed, which she pushed into Ah Lam's arms.

"It's cold at night," she said. "Those open ends won't stop the wind."

Ah Lam may not have understood all she said, but she understood the gesture and took the quilt with thanks. She spread it out over the other blankets, and Huang Fu crawled into the center of the nest and chattered happily in Chinese, apparently pleased with the addition.

As Katherine turned back toward the train car, she found Alonzo standing behind her.

"That was a kind gesture," he said.

Katherine shook her head and continued walking, and he fell in step beside her. "It isn't enough. They can't possibly stay in that tent all winter."

"I don't think they plan to. Jin told me they're trying to find work for Ah Lam. Once they do, they'll find a rooming house in the city."

"A rooming house won't be very comfortable either, I expect," Katherine said. "But it will be better than this arrangement. Provided they can even find someone who will let a room to a Chinese family."

"There are a fair number of Chinese in Toronto," Alonzo said. "They'll get by."

At the door of the train car, they said good night, and Alonzo continued on to the cart with the lantern, climbing inside. Katherine looked up at the stars for a moment, thinking over the full evening once more, and then went inside to bed.

* * *

The next morning Katherine stepped outside to make her way to the lavatory and found Ah Lam squatting beside a campfire near their tent, stirring something in a frying pan. Jin sat on one of the tree stumps in the early sunlight, sipping from a mug, his legs stretched before him. Katherine gave them a wave and continued on into the woods.

When she returned, Lilia and Tony were at the open end of the tent, coaxing Huang Fu to come out and join them.

"Leave him alone," Katherine instructed. "He's shy."

"We want him to play with us," Lilia said.

"When he's ready to play with you, he will. Besides, it isn't playtime right now; it's get-ready-for-breakfast time, and after that, it will be school-lessons time."

For the first time since she'd come, Katherine heard her small charges groan at the suggestion of lessons.

"But after that, may we play?" Lilia begged.

"Yes, and maybe by then Huang Fu will be ready to join you."

But Huang Fu did not play. Katherine kept an eye out all day and noticed that the little boy stayed close beside his father. Sometimes he just sat talking with him, and sometimes he jumped up to run small errands, fetching his father a mug of water, spreading a blanket over Jin's knees against the chill air, going to find sticks and twigs for the campfire. He seemed perfectly content to attend to his father, so Katherine discouraged Lilia and Tony from badgering him to play. Time enough for that later, she thought.

That afternoon when she stepped outside to throw some scraps to Bo, Ah Lam approached her.

"Please to come," she said haltingly. "Talk Jin."

Katherine followed her to the tent, where Jin sat with Huang Fu beside him. Ah Lam knelt on the grass beside him and looked expectant.

"Please to sit down," Jin said to Katherine. "I cannot stand."

Katherine looked around, but the nearest tree stump was some distance away, and she doubted she could lift it anyway. So she gathered her skirts and sat on the grass as Ah Lam had done. She reflected that Ah Lam's trousers and tunic were much more convenient and wished she could get away with wearing them.

"My wife see last night," Jin said, looking a bit uncomfortable. "We friends now. I ask . . . question."

"Yes, all right."

"Yes. You call him Mr. Co—" He stumbled over the name.

"Colaco."

"Yes. And Ah Lam say he sleep in cart last night."

"Ah. Yes."

"Not your husband?"

Katherine smiled. "No. He's my employer. I teach and take care of his children."

"Ah!" Jin translated this for Ah Lam, and her eyes widened. Excitedly she chattered back, gesturing toward Katherine.

"My wife ask you teach children English."

"Yes, that's one of the things we're working on. They grew up speaking Italian and French."

Ah Lam spoke again, and Jin looked astonished and then slightly angry. He shook his head firmly.

"What did she say?" Katherine asked.

"No. Ah Lam too much ask. Not good."

"What did she ask?"

"She not understand. Too much ask."

Ah Lam continued to press, however, and at last Jin reluctantly translated.

"My wife ask you teach Huang Fu English. I know is too much. Is foolish."

"It's not foolish at all," Katherine said. "I imagine it would help him a lot to be able to speak English. Life in Canada is hard enough for you. Knowing the language would give your son a great advantage."

Jin gazed at Katherine a long moment, then said slowly, "You do this for Huang Fu?"

"Of course. Tony and Lilia would love to have him join them. Would Huang Fu be agreeable to it? He is young enough that learning a new language should be no problem for him, but he seems rather shy. Would he let me teach him?"

Jin spoke a moment to Ah Lam, and the woman's face lit up. She nodded eagerly and clasped her hands together. "Thank you. Very thank you!" she told Katherine.

"Hmm. Well, we'll give him this afternoon to get to know us better and start lessons tomorrow," Katherine said. "I've never taught someone who speaks no English at all, but I think it will be an interesting challenge." And she was surprised to find she was looking forward to it.

The trestle table appeared again for supper that night, and Katherine made sure she cooked more than enough food for everyone. Ah Lam contributed a salad of wild greens, which Katherine was nervous about trying, but it turned out to be delicious. The wind had picked up from the north though, and they all sat huddled in their coats and blankets for dinner.

"This arrangement isn't going to work much longer," Katherine told Alonzo. "Fall is upon us."

"Tomorrow Ah Lam go to Toronto. See if work," Jin announced. "But sad for me, Ah Lam work and not me."

"I'll give her a ride to Toronto in the cart," Alonzo said.

Jin and Ah Lam exchanged a few words, and then Ah Lam looked away, her lips pinched together.

"Is there a problem?" Alonzo asked.

"No, no problem. You are very kind. Kind offer to take Ah Lam."

"She doesn't seem pleased about it. She doesn't want to find work?"

"Oh, yes, very much."

Katherine, watching Ah Lam's expression, suddenly felt she knew what the issue was, and the thought made her grin in spite of herself. She had more in common with this woman than she'd realized.

"Perhaps Ah Lam feels the same way I do about riding down the public thoroughfares of Toronto on a gypsy wagon."

Jin's eyes slid toward her, alarmed, and then away, and Katherine knew she had guessed correctly. "No mean to insult," he muttered. "Ah Lam be happy accept very kind offer."

Alonzo chuckled. "Everyone has their pride. There's no offense taken, Jin. I'm fully aware my cart is outrageous." He glanced at Katherine, and she saw the mischief dancing in his eyes. "It suits me though, and I'm afraid it's the only conveyance I have to offer."

Jin said something rather sharp-sounding to Ah Lam, who lowered her face toward her bowl. Jin coughed. "Ah Lam is happy accept ride to Toronto."

Alonzo thought a moment, then said, "Jin, may I ask a personal question, as a friend?"

"Yes?"

Katherine laughed. "That is just what he asked me this afternoon, almost to the word!"

Alonzo looked startled. "He did? What did he ask?"

"Ah Lam was wondering if we . . . well, what the arrangements were between us. They'd thought we were husband and wife, but when she saw you go to the cart last night, she wondered. That and the fact that I call you Mr. Colaco. I explained I teach Tony and Lilia. We arranged for me to teach Huang Fu English as well. Oh!" The thought suddenly occurred to her, and she felt her cheeks grow warm. "That is, if you have no objection to him sitting in on their lessons. I should have asked you first. You're the one paying for the instruction."

"Of course it's all right," Alonzo said. "I don't mind Huang Fu sharing lesson time with the children."

Jin smiled broadly. "Thank you. Most kind. Will help Huang Fu very much. Now, what question to me?"

"I wanted to ask, have you seen a physician about your back and hip? Perhaps something can be done to help you."

The man shook his bald head vigorously. "No money for doctor. I use herbs and soak the . . ." He trailed off, not knowing the word, and pointed to his hip.

"The joints?" Alonzo asked.

"Yes. I soak joints with herbs. Helps a little."

"Tomorrow why don't you come with me and Ah Lam in the wagon, and I'll take you to see a physician as well. He might be able to do something for you."

"But—"

"I will pay his fee," Alonzo added. "It's not a problem."

Jin looked surprised and turned to his wife, saying something in Chinese. Ah Lam put her face in her hands.

"Very kind," Jin said. "Why you do this?"

"It's not a big thing," Alonzo said carelessly. "We are friends now."

Katherine lowered her voice. "Would a Toronto physician see a Chinese man?"

"I should think so. And if not, there will be someone in the Chinese community who practices their traditional medicine."

"I will watch Huang Fu tomorrow while you go," Katherine offered. "He can have his first lesson with the children."

"It's all decided, then," Alonzo said.

Chapter Eleven

THEY SET OFF RIGHT AFTER breakfast, and Katherine faced a full day of watching three children, but somehow this did not intimidate her as it would have before, especially not with these particular children. Once Huang Fu warmed to her, he proved to be cheerful and eager to learn, and she suspected his intelligence was keen. He picked up new words quickly and didn't seem hesitant to try them out with the other children. She kept the lesson simple, focusing on useful nouns and phrases, and he absorbed the new information readily. By noon he could name most of his body parts, count to ten, introduce himself, and identify several objects in the train car by name. He found the alphabet beyond him though, so she didn't press him to begin reading instruction. His voice was quiet, and she found his accent charming. Tony and Lilia stayed on task much better than usual, fascinated by this new child in their midst.

She released them to play outdoors while she cleaned and thought about what to make for lunch. She had just started slicing cheese for sandwiches when Huang Fu knocked at the train-car door. When she opened it, he held out a large fish he held by the gills.

"My goodness! Did you just catch that just now?" she asked, amazed.

He didn't reply but pressed the fish into her hands and then pointed to the stove. Clearly he was providing lunch that day.

"Thank you, Huang Fu," Katherine told him. He grinned and ran off to join the other children, who were playing with Bo. Katherine gingerly took the fish into the kitchen to clean it. If that little boy was thoughtful enough to provide lunch, she wasn't going to disappoint him. She mused that not all that long ago, she wouldn't have known what to do with a fish, much less gut and clean one. Now, though she disliked the task, at least she was capable.

The sense of having learned something, of being more self-reliant, made her happy.

When the cart returned that evening, Katherine went to meet it and could tell immediately that the day had not been successful. Ah Lam looked drawn with exhaustion, Jin frowned sadly, and even Alonzo had lost his usual spark.

"No luck finding work?" she asked.

"No one will hire her," Alonzo said quietly, jumping down to unharness Bacchus. Jin moved slowly off toward his tent, Ah Lam helping him. Alonzo watched them go, then told her, "Even the laundry said they had no vacancies."

"That's a shame," Katherine said. "And what about the doctor? Did someone agree to see Jin?"'

"Yes, that wasn't a problem, fortunately. But he didn't feel he could do anything to help but prescribe rest. He thinks Jin has compressed vertebrae in his back, and the joint in his hip is deteriorating from all the hard labor. He won't be able to do heavy work again."

"That's awful," Katherine said. "What are they going to do?"

"I considered teaching him basic tinsmithing, but he could never afford his own tools or cart and horse, and he couldn't afford to rent a shop, at least not at this point."

"Is there another trade he could learn that wouldn't require him to have a set of expensive tools?" Katherine asked.

"Not that I can teach him."

Katherine thought a moment, and her eyes went to the tent Jin and Ah Lam had disappeared into. "He can sew," she said.

"What's that?"

"Jin can sew. He put together their tent quite cleverly with what scraps he had, and the seams are very well done. Perhaps he could apprentice as a tailor."

"I doubt any Toronto shop is going to hire a Chinese man," Alonzo said practically. "But maybe someone within the Chinese community would take him on. It's a good idea. I'll put it to him and see what he thinks."

* * *

The following Monday Ah Lam brought Huang Fu for his lessons and knocked tentatively on the train-car door, but instead of dropping him off and going back to her camp, she touched Katherine gently on the wrist and held up something for her to see. It was a sheaf of paper of various colors cut into rectangles.

"Yes, Ah Lam? Is this something you want to give me?" Katherine asked, confused. "I have plenty of notebooks and slates for the children to write on."

"For children," Ah Lam said, fanning the papers in her hand and gesturing toward the table where Tony and Lilia already sat waiting. "See please."

Katherine stepped back and opened the door wider, and Ah Lam entered and approached the table. She smiled at everyone in turn, and then she selected a piece of orange paper and laid it on the table in front of Lilia. Curious, Katherine watched to see what the woman wanted.

Ah Lam set down the other papers, then deftly folded the piece of orange paper, rubbing the creases to sharpen them. Before Katherine could quite follow what she was doing, Ah Lam held up a paper swan.

Lilia gave a squeal of delight. "Look! Look what Huang Fu's mother made!"

"That is amazing," Katherine said, coming closer. "Can you do that again?"

Ah Lam selected a piece of blue paper and, in no time at all, folded it neatly into a budding rose. She presented this to Katherine.

"I didn't follow how you do that. Can you show me?" Katherine lifted Tony from his chair, sat down in his place, and situated him on her knee. "Children, today Ah Lam will be your teacher. Mine too."

The afternoon passed swiftly, so engrossed were they in their new entertainment, and by the time Alonzo came in at dusk, the train car was filled with clever birds, other animals, and flowers perched on every surface and hanging from every possible space.

"Papa, look at what we made today!" Tony shouted, coming to grasp Alonzo's hand and pulling him farther into the room. "I made this one. It's supposed to be a dog, but it didn't work very well. But look at the one Kate made. Isn't it good?"

Bemused, Alonzo gazed around at the transformation of his car, and he shook his head in wonder. "Where did they all come from?"

Katherine laughed. "Ah Lam showed us how to do it. She says, if I understand her correctly, that people in Japan do this, but she learned how as a small child. Is that right, Ah Lam?"

Ah Lam nodded, smiling sweetly. "Mother teach. I very small."

"These are quite wonderful," Alonzo told her. "And I think you have solved at least part of your problem, at any rate."

"No understand," Ah Lam said. "Slow please?"

"Wait a moment." Alonzo went out of the train car and, a few minutes later, returned supporting Jin up the steps. He gestured toward the paper figures decorating the car and turned to Jin. "Please tell Ah Lam I think she could earn money with this talent. She can make little paper figures to sell to people on the street in Toronto or maybe even sell paper flowers in shops. I have never seen anyone do this before, and probably no one in Toronto has either."

Jin's eyes widened as he looked at Ah Lam's handiwork. "You think people pay money for these things?"

"Yes, I think maybe they would."

"Is just playing."

"No, it's a real skill. These are beautiful and unusual. If you agree, I'll take some of them in my cart next time I go to Toronto and show them to my customers as I make my rounds. Then we'll know if people are willing to pay for them."

"Yes," Jin said, nodding. "Yes, thank you. Very good."

When Alonzo returned from the city the next evening, he was beaming. Jumping down from the cart, he went to Ah Lam, who sat stirring the ashes of the cook fire, and helped her to stand. He pulled a packet from his pocket and handed it to her. Puzzled, Ah Lam opened it to see several silver coins winking up at her. Her exclamation brought Jin hobbling hurriedly to her side.

"I sold all of the paper figures I took with me today," Alonzo told them. "People especially liked the paper roses and irises. I brought you more paper. If you make more, I can sell those too."

Ah Lam stared in wonder from his face to the money in her hand while Jin translated, and then she turned a great big smile toward her husband.

He laughed and clapped his hands to his bald head. "I never believe, but I see it is true," he said and laughed again.

* * *

The next evening Lilia said she felt funny and refused any supper. When Katherine touched her forehead, the little girl felt hot, and when Katherine suggested she go to bed early, she went without argument. In the night, Katherine awoke to hear Lilia crying softly.

"What is it, little one?" Katherine whispered, reaching over to feel Lilia's cheek. It burned her fingers.

"My head hurts and my—this hurts." She guided Katherine's hand to her throat in the dark. "*La gorge.*"

Katherine rose and pulled on a shawl and slippers. She opened the door of the train car and felt the cold wind on her face. She strode quickly across the grass, stood on the step of the gypsy cart, and called softly inside.

"What is it, Kate?" Alonzo was instantly awake, sitting up, a dark shadow in the cart's interior.

"Lilia is quite ill. She's very hot."

He climbed out of the cart and went with her into the train car. Katherine lit a lamp and saw with a shock that, in spite of the chill, Alonzo slept in only a pair of sacking trousers, leaving his feet and upper body bare. The lamplight cast his olive skin in a warm glow, highlighting the sculpted contours of his torso. She realized with some confusion that she was staring at the smooth, curved plane of his back as he bent over the cot. She pulled her mind firmly back to the matter at hand.

Alonzo knelt beside Lilia and murmured something, and Lilia nodded and touched her throat again. Above her, Tony mumbled in his sleep and turned over.

"Bring me a cold, wet cloth, please," Alonzo said, lifting Lilia and removing her nightgown. Katherine hurried to fetch a cloth and a bowl of water. She stood watching as Alonzo gently bathed the small body with the cool water. His hands moved with surety, economy, wasting no motion. He went to the cupboard, mixed a solution in a cup, and brought it to Lilia to drink. She did so, grimacing at the taste.

"A touch of fever," he said, wrapping his daughter in the blanket. He stood, lifting her against his chest. "I'll take her out to the cart with me to keep an eye on her."

"You can stay here," Katherine offered instantly.

"It's cooler in the cart."

"Shouldn't she be kept warm?"

"Not when she's like this. The cool air will help. Thank you for waking me." He disappeared into the darkness with Lilia, closing the door behind him.

It was some time before Katherine could settle herself to sleep again. She kept picturing Lilia's distressingly feverish face and Alonzo's efficient hands gently smoothing her hair.

Lilia's fever was down by morning, and by evening she was back to her old self. They watched Tony closely, but he showed no sign of contracting the illness himself. But two days later, Katherine woke with a searing sore throat and a squeezing headache.

"Kate's turn to be sick," Alonzo said, watching her slump over her tea at breakfast. He reached over and put a cool palm against her forehead. "You're burning up. Go back to bed."

"I'm all right. It's your day to go into the city. The children—"

"I'll go tomorrow," he said. "Another good thing about being a tinker: my time is my own. I can make up whatever schedule I please. Go to bed and rest. It will only linger longer if you don't. I'll tell Ah Lam lessons are canceled today."

Katherine suddenly felt disinclined to argue. When breakfast was finished and Alonzo had retired with the children to work in the cart, she changed into a house robe and climbed into bed. She thought she'd just rest awhile, but she fell asleep before even completing the thought.

* * *

At some point, Katherine remembered waking with Alonzo's hand on her forehead and then choking down a vile liquid from a cup he pressed to her lips. The room tilted sideways and went dark, and she slept again. Sometime later—she didn't know how long—she was aware of something wet and cold being placed over her eyes and then icy sensations from under her arms. She smelled vinegar, tangy and sharp. Somewhere in her muzzy brain it registered that she had been stripped to her camisole, and she thought she ought to do something about it, but somehow she couldn't seem to worry much. When the cold moved behind her ears, she tried to move away from it, shouting in irritation, but heavy hands held her shoulders to the bed. She snatched at the wet cloth over her eyes and flung it from her, and a disembodied voice said firmly, "That will be quite enough of that."

At one point, she thought her mother was there beside the bed, her face gently smiling, her touch tender, and Katherine felt tears slide down her temples into her hair. She was tormented by feverish dreams, confusing images without plot or pattern. And always, through everything, the hands were there—turning her, placing the cloth on her forehead, smoothing her hair, gently touching, always touching. At times it was soothing, and at times it made her irritable. Sometimes it felt like a man's hands and sometimes like her mother's. But mostly their touch made her cry. She couldn't seem to keep the tears from rolling toward her ears. Again and again the hands would wipe them away, lift her head to replace her pillow with a fresh one, cool against her cheek.

When finally she came fully awake, the windows were dark and a lamp burned low on the table. She swallowed tentatively, and her sore throat was nearly gone. Her robe was damp and clammy. Stiffly she turned her head. Tony's cot was empty. Alonzo lay on Lilia's cot, his head a foot from hers. He was stretched out on his stomach as if he'd fallen exhausted into bed. His lax face was turned toward her, his lashes long on his cheeks, the planes of his face softened in sleep. His arm was hanging over the edge of the bed, his hand lying on the floor.

Katherine lay limply, feeling as if she'd just run a long way, and continued to gaze at him. It was new seeing him at this close distance. He had rolled the sleeve of his shirt up to his elbow, and she could see the black hair of his lean arm against the olive skin, the powerful muscles now slack in his shoulders beneath the fabric, the rise and fall of his breath. As she watched, she heard a slight change in his breathing and knew he was awake, though he didn't move.

Then his eyes half opened, gazing straight into hers, pinning her. For a moment, she couldn't look away. Then he blinked once, breaking the spell, and smiled. He lifted his fallen hand and reached to softly touch her cheek. "You're back," he said.

She merely nodded, too tired to say anything.

"You gave us a scare. Feeling better?"

"Tired."

"No wonder."

"I'm sorry I was a bother. Was I too difficult?" Her tongue felt thick and foreign in her mouth.

He sat up, rubbing his face. "Not a bit. And Ah Lam was a great help."

"Ah Lam?"

"She took turns with me, caring for you. Never seems to get tired, that woman. She has a real gift for kindness."

Katherine wiped her eyes with her wrist. "That explains it. Sometimes I felt my mother was here. Her hands were so gentle and soothing."

"That would be Ah Lam. Are you hungry?"

"Thirsty. But I need to . . . go outside." She was mortified at having to say it.

He nodded. "I'll help you." He pulled on his jacket and boots and placed a shawl around her shoulders. Before she knew what he was about, he scooped her up in his arms and was leaving the train car. The night air was icy through her damp clothing.

"I can walk," she cried, clinging to his neck and then, embarrassed, loosening her grip.

He nearly dropped her and staggered to regain his balance. "Your legs are cooked noodles," he said. "Trust me."

He carried her through the dark to the lavatory, set her down, and went out again, closing the door. Katherine's head was light, and she was grateful she needn't find a bush anymore. When she teetered uncertainly out, he picked her up again, one arm under her knees, the other around her back. This time she didn't protest. She looped her arms around his neck and let him carry her back to her cot.

"Where are the children?" she asked as he tucked the blanket around her feet.

"I moved them to the cart for now. I didn't want them to disturb you."

"How long was I ill?"

He was moving about, making tea in the golden lamp light. "This is Sunday night. You've been delirious with fever for two days."

"I have?" She was astonished. "I didn't realize."

"I gave you laudanum yesterday and birch-bark water. It has medicinal qualities."

"How do you know?"

He winked. "Old gypsy secret. Ah Lam made some kind of concoction with herbs, too, that seemed to settle the fever."

She shifted into a sitting position and accepted the cup he held out to her. "I'm sorry I was so much trouble."

He grinned and sat on the edge of her cot. "Never that. Though you do have an amazing right jab."

"Pardon?" She stared.

He rubbed his jaw, eyes glittering. "You didn't take kindly to the birch water."

"I struck you?" She was horrified.

"Like a professional pugilist. If you can't find a position as a nanny, you could go into the ring."

"I'm so sorry!"

He took the empty cup from her and set it down. "Do you want to change your nightgown?"

She shrank back. "No, I'll wait until morning."

"It's damp."

"I'm all right."

He nodded. "Do you want me to fetch Ah Lam to help you?"

"No, let her sleep. I don't want to disturb her more than I apparently have."

"Rest, then. You'll be stronger in the morning."

She lay back, and he tucked the quilt around her shoulders in a motherly fashion.

"Thank you," she said, looking up at him. "I don't know what I would have done if you hadn't been here."

"It's my fault you are here," he reminded her. "If you'd been in the city, you'd have had a real doctor and better care."

"There isn't better care," she said with certainty.

He rose and looked down at her, then bent and kissed her forehead briefly as if she were Lilia. He turned away to lower the lamp wick, kicked off his boots, and climbed into the other cot. He turned his back and immediately fell asleep.

But Katherine lay awake a long time, clutching the quilt to her chest, her forehead burning where his lips had touched it, before sleep finally came.

Chapter Twelve

SHE RECOVERED QUICKLY NOW THAT the fever had broken. By Wednesday morning, her jitteriness was gone and she was able to conduct lessons at the table. Lilia chattered to her happily, telling her all she'd done while Katherine had been ill, and Huang Fu was cheerful and quiet as always. But Tony's reaction surprised her. The first time he saw Katherine, he ran to her and threw his arms around her waist, pressing his face against her stomach. When she knelt to comfort him, she discovered his lashes were wet with unshed tears.

"Why, what's the matter, Tony?" she asked.

"I thought you were going away," he whispered, lips trembling.

"No, I'm not going away. I was only ill for a while," she said gently.

"I just thought . . ." He struggled to explain. "Mama was ill, and she went away."

Katherine put her arms about him, and he rested his head on her shoulder. "I'm all better now," Katherine told him. "I'm not going to die."

She glanced up and saw Alonzo watching her solemnly, his eyes darkened with some emotion she couldn't read. Briskly she involved Tony in a game, and his fears were soon forgotten, but they remained with Katherine for a long time. It was natural that Tony would have the fears he had, but she was shaken by how strongly he had become attached to her, and—she had to admit—she to him. And she *was* going to go away someday, after all. She felt she was digging herself into a rather large and bleak hole the longer she stayed. And yet she didn't want to leave. Not yet.

Over the next few weeks, life assumed a sort of rhythm. Tony and Lilia returned to the train car, and Alonzo moved back to the cart. He went several times a week to Toronto. Sometimes the children, and even Huang Fu, went with him, always to return with sticks of candy or some new item of clothing. There would often be a gift for Katherine as well, a net bag of oranges or tablets of crisp writing paper. And once they came back with two pounds of clotted-cream fudge.

"To celebrate All Hallow's Eve," Alonzo told her.

She had forgotten it.

Every time he went to the city, he took with him a collection of paper figures Ah Lam had made, and at night he returned with an envelope of coins for her, having sold every one of them. The flowers were especially popular, and Alonzo made a deal with the keeper of a flower shop to stock her paper creations and sell them alongside his real flowers. It didn't generate enough money to support the family, but it certainly helped, and Katherine could see Ah Lam's confidence and happiness grow each time Alonzo handed her the envelope.

Jin and Ah Lam occasionally went into Toronto with him too, continuing the search for a position for Jin. Jin liked the idea of becoming a tailor and felt it was work he could do without straining his back and hip, but finding a position as an apprentice was not a simple thing. Most of the Chinese tailors and seamstresses he spoke to could not afford another employee, and none of the fine shops on Yonge or Queen Street would consider taking him on. Jin patiently continued to apply, and in the evenings, he hunched beside the campfire with needle and thread and some spare fabric, practicing his skills. To everyone's amusement, he was far better at sewing a seam than either Katherine or Ah Lam.

It seemed to Katherine, as she went throughout the day, teaching and playing with the children, peeling potatoes and hauling water from the stream, that time had ceased to exist. She looked less and less frequently at her watch. She had to ask Alonzo what the date was. One day flowed into another. The only indication of the passage of time was the changing colors of the trees and the increased chapping of her lips and hands. She hardly noticed as November slipped past.

It grew too cold to eat *al fresco* on the trestle table in the wind, so Alonzo purchased canvas, and Jin sewed a large tent from it, which they strung up with rope between two trees. They erected the table within it, and with lanterns and hurricane lamps blazing and the wind prevented from entering, it was a cozy place to dine. Bo took to sleeping inside it, and on frosty nights, the horse made himself comfortable there too. With the remnants of the canvas, Jin fashioned flap doors for the ends of his family's tent to protect them from the wind as well.

It was December before Katherine knew it. In a kind of peaceful fascination, she found herself watching winter descend upon the isolated clearing. She no longer felt Jin's family were intruders; they disturbed the place no more than did the wind in the pine trees or the rabbits that lurked at the forest's edge. They had become simply a part of the place, and she enjoyed Ah Lam's quiet companionship and generous help. Huang Fu fit in with the other children as if he had always been part of the sibling group. His English was progressing nicely, provoking Tony and Lilia into greater efforts with their own language skills, and Ah Lam had started learning more phrases too. She no longer had to rely on Jin to translate for her all the time. Jin and Alonzo spent long hours talking quietly in the cart while Alonzo worked.

Katherine remembered her initial resentment of their presence with embarrassment. She couldn't have asked for nicer neighbors. She just wished she could provide better lodging for them. December was beginning to turn the ground to iron, and the frost was thick on the canvas tents each morning. She tried to coax Ah Lam and Jin into taking turns sleeping in the train car, but they would not hear of it. Jin assured her they were all right in their tent.

Katherine thought about how many times she had wished to live in a big, fine house, but now she wished it for a different reason. A larger, finer house was not a symbol of status to her now so much as something that could be shared to help others, and she wished for one so she could bring her friends indoors. Her daydreams began to take on a slightly different hue, focused more on others' comfort than on her own. She was aware of this switch and thought wryly that in all likelihood she was maturing . . . albeit a little late.

Whereas at the beginning Katherine could never have imagined herself able to tolerate such living conditions, now she could hardly imagine herself living anywhere else. She told herself her new-found contentment was an effect of the cooling weather, the snug cosiness of the train car, the open affection of the children, and their gratifying progression under her tutelage. She enjoyed her companionship with Ah Lam and her family. She was beginning to enjoy her forays into hands-on housekeeping and found she was succeeding more than failing. And, of course, she enjoyed talking with Alonzo at the end of each day, watching him work, hearing him laugh. After awhile, she stopped trying to explain it to herself and just enjoyed it, moving about in her unhurried little world like a butterfly after its struggle to escape the cocoon, fanning its wings softly in the sunlight.

In early December, familial guilt flared, and she wrote to Martha, dutifully informing her she would stop in during the holidays to visit. She was rather anxious as she prepared for it, sorry for the disruption to her idyll, but to let the Christmas holidays go by without contact was petty and would be unforgivable. While she didn't want closeness with the Fitzgeralds, she also didn't want out-and-out warfare with them.

Alonzo drove her to the train station and left her with good wishes. Katherine took the train to High Park and then a hansom cab to Martha and Hugh's stately home, with its manicured grounds and high iron fence. Hugh was sure to remind people that in spite of his thriving textile mill, he was "old money," that he had acquired his home through inheritance and not through his business achievements, which he saw as "cheating."

Katherine had always been awed by the ostentatiousness of the house, the imposing stone entry, the glittering chandelier poised above the door like icy daggers ready to drop on her head. Now, as she stood regarding the hushed and archival drawing room, polished and glowing, where the butler had deposited her, she momentarily had the panicky feeling that she'd stepped directly back in time and was once more the awkward, poor relation in last year's styles and scuffed boots. She glanced at the polished mirror on her left to reassure herself that at least she no longer looked the part. She'd worn her best green dress and health bustle, done her hair with particular care, and pumiced her hands to softness. Nothing could be done about her chapped complexion, but she thought that on the whole she looked passable. If only she could quell the sickening feeling in her stomach that assaulted her each time she stepped into this house of miserable memories.

Martha came sailing into the drawing room looking like whipped cream, her dress feathery white lawn, her blonde hair pulled up with pearl combs, her white skin lotioned and fragrant.

"Katherine, darling! I'm so glad you've turned up!" Martha kissed her cheek and stepped back, her smile bright even while her blue eyes were sharply assessing. She was eight years Katherine's senior but looked about nineteen and was short and slender in spite of the two children she'd borne. Staring at her, Katherine felt ridiculously tall, and her stout shoes seemed indecent on the pale-green and rose carpet.

"I wanted to write and tell you of course to come, but you didn't give me your return address, silly girl," Martha was saying now.

"Didn't I?" Katherine asked casually, sitting on the silk-cushioned sofa. "How forgetful of me. How are you, cousin Martha?"

"Perfect as ever. You must see the boys. They are much taller since you last saw them." There was a note of reproach in her voice. "I'm sorry Hugh is away today. You just missed him. He returned from Edinburgh last week, and he's in New York this week. Such a bore." While she spoke, Martha poured the tea a uniformed maid had brought them. Katherine held her paper-thin china cup and let her cousin go on about her family, her voice like carefully composed music.

"But what about you?" Martha asked finally. "What are you up to now? You look brown as a nut. Have you been playing a farm laborer?"

"I started a new position in September. A Mr. Colaco. He's a widower with two children," Katherine said, a touch defiantly.

"Poor Katherine. Is it too awful?" Martha purred.

"Actually, I'm quite enjoying it. There's a girl and a boy, and they're very well behaved and bright." She deftly skipped over Huang Fu. Somehow she didn't think Martha would quite understand that arrangement. "I've been concentrating on their English. Their father is Italian, you see, and their mother was French, so their English has suffered somewhat. I mean, Mr. Colaco has excellent English, with hardly any accent, but he speaks to the children primarily in Italian. The little girl has a very good singing voice, and the boy, Tony, is quite sweet."

As she'd hoped, Martha was soon bored of the topic and instead moved on to a discussion of her own Curran and Eddie, a subject she never tired of. Personally, Katherine had never liked her young cousins, ages eleven and eight, who seemed altogether too aware of their own importance. But now she acted deeply interested and asked about their school and their equestrian lessons, her new employment safely forgotten.

They moved into the library after tea and sat by the fireplace. Katherine dutifully admired the tapestry Martha was working on and the Christmas gifts she and Hugh had squirreled away for the boys.

"Hugh's brother Reginald and Elizabeth are coming for Christmas this year," Martha informed her. "Lord Wiarton invited them, of course, but they preferred to come here."

"Of course," Katherine murmured.

"We're having a dinner party Christmas Eve. Obviously you're family and should be there too. We're having the Gayles and the Chisholms over—just a small party. You are coming, aren't you?"

There was no mention of wanting her there. It all came down to duty again. Martha was obligated by blood to invite her, and Katherine was as obligated to accept. She hesitated over her answer though. "Thank you for the invitation, but I'll have to ask my employer. I don't know what his arrangements will be. He may want me to watch the children." She fumbled for an excuse.

"Surely not Christmas Eve?"

"My time isn't my own, Martha. I'm employed now."

"You needn't remind me," Martha said irritably. "Then bring the brats with you, and they can play with the boys upstairs. Hugh will be most disappointed if we're not all together."

"I'll see," Katherine said noncommittally. "Mr. Colaco will want the children home Christmas morning, I'm sure."

They passed a formal afternoon of pleasantries and didn't mention the dinner again. At last Katherine announced that it was time for her to go.

Martha gave a sigh. "One day you really must come for longer than a few hours," she said. "I'm losing touch with you, Katherine. You never have time for us."

Katherine accepted her coat from the sour-faced butler and thrust her arms into it. "I'm sorry, Martha, but you know how it is."

"I don't know why you insist on working. You *know* we would be happy to—But we won't go over that again." She sighed again and waved a limp hand at Katherine. "Do ask, though, about Christmas Eve. Surely he can spare you for the holiday."

"I will ask."

They went to the door, and Martha surprised Katherine by laying her hand on her sleeve. "Is everything all right with you?" she asked earnestly, looking up into Katherine's face with her eyebrows knitted. "You seem different somehow. As if your mind is somewhere else."

"Oh? Sorry."

Martha's eyes narrowed, and she took her hand away. "I don't like to see you worked so hard. It isn't right."

Katherine thought of her leisurely hours spent reading stories to Lilia, playing rhyming games with Tony and Gray Goose with Huang Fu. She thought of Ah Lam's help with the cooking and washing up. "I'm not overworked, Martha."

"Still, I wish you would come back here, even for a while. You would be more than welcome, you know that." The sincerity in her voice was puzzling, even alarming.

Katherine softened slightly. "Thank you for your concern, but I'm all right, really."

"Do you need anything at all? Hugh can arrange a loan . . ."

"Not at all. We've been through this before. I'm not accepting charity."

"We're your only family," Martha reminded her stiffly. "It isn't charity. It's very ungrateful of you to say so."

Katherine closed her eyes briefly and forced her muscles to relax. "I know you mean well, Martha. You and Hugh have been excellent to me, and if I ever do need help, I'll come to you. But right now I'm enjoying being on my own."

"You're too proud," Martha said but smiled. "You're too independent."

"You've never liked that, have you?" Katherine tried to laugh.

She watched Martha's smile fade slightly on her ivory face. "I just like to be needed sometimes," she said softly.

The comment was startling. Katherine regarded her, unsure what to say, and then, for the first time in her life, she impulsively leaned forward and kissed her cousin's cheek. "Take care of yourself, Martha. I'll let you know about Christmas Eve."

In the cab, she watched the scenery pass by and thought about the visit, feeling oddly troubled. For four years, Katherine had taken Martha's criticism to be superiority and imagined that she had gloated over her younger cousin's failures and admissions of need. But now she wasn't so sure. Perhaps Martha's disapproval had come from insecurity lying beneath the waxed veneer. She supposed it would be understandable, considering Hugh's extensive traveling and cool nature. He loved his wife in his way, but he certainly didn't need her except to run his home. And to be honest, Mrs. Hislop, the housekeeper, did most of that. Even Martha's sons were self-sufficient and undemonstrative. But the thought of Martha needing *her* was hard to assimilate.

"Does she want me to come back so she can rub salt in my wounds?" Katherine murmured to the window. "Or because she needs to be reassured of her own usefulness?"

When she arrived at the Springfield Station, she took another cab and directed the driver along the road into the countryside. Alonzo had offered to meet her, but she'd declined, not knowing when she'd be back. It was dusk, and a cold wind was coming out of the north when they reached the turnoff to the clearing and she called to the driver to stop.

"This can't be right, mum," he said as she climbed out. "The village is another mile up ahead."

"This is fine, thank you," Katherine assured him. "It's right over there through the trees."

"I don't like leaving you in the middle of nowhere and at night, mum."

"It's all right," she said, paying him. He was a thin man with red eyes and chilblains on his hands. She left him standing in the road and walked along the rough track under the trees. Fifteen yards in, she entered the clearing. Behind her, she heard the driver stumbling after her.

"Please just let me walk you home," he said, catching up with her. "I'd feel better about it."

"It's very kind of you," she said patiently. "But I am home. This is it."

He blinked at the gaily painted cart, the train car, the tents, the horse cropping the brown, brittle grass. A light glowed in the car window. Bo barked once from the steps. "This is where you live?" the man asked doubtfully and looked down at the money in his hand.

"Yes, thank you."

He turned back up the track toward the road, shaking his head. "I never would have guessed you was a traveler's woman. I thought you was—er—good night, mum."

Katherine watched him go, feeling her ears grow hot and debating whether to call him back and ask him exactly what he thought she was. But what was the point? His opinion didn't matter. She would never see him again. She walked across the clearing to the train car and smelled the dead ashes of the cook fire, whipped up by the strengthening wind. The trees ringing the clearing tossed about, sounding like surf. She opened the door and stepped into the warm room, letting Bo in behind her.

Alonzo was sitting on Lilia's cot, watching her knit. Tony was lying in his cot above them, half asleep. A pot simmered on the stove, smelling wonderfully of onions.

"You're back all right, then?" Alonzo said. "Did you have a good visit?"

"Very good. We actually separated at the end without drawing blood." She hung her coat in the cupboard.

"You sound surprised."

"I am, rather."

"There's stew left if you're hungry."

"Thanks. I'm starving." She pictured Martha cringing at the phrase and smiled to herself as she dished up a fragrant bowl and sat at the table. Alonzo's stew looked and smelled infinitely better than her own. "I've been invited to dinner Christmas Eve. I told her I'd have to speak to you first."

"Of course you should go," he said promptly.

"If you had plans, she said I might bring Tony and Lilia with me and they could play with her boys. They're eleven and eight, so somewhat older, but they have a lot of their old toys still in the nursery."

He shrugged his shoulders. "That's kind of her. But would you be spending the night?"

"Probably. We would be out very late. I told her I didn't think you would like that idea."

"I'll have to think about it," he said, glancing at Lilia, who was listening curiously. "It would be good for my children to play with other children, but perhaps on a different night."

"You wouldn't want my cousin's children for their playmates anyway," she said frankly.

"Ah," he said, smiling, and nudged Lilia with his elbow. "Enough for one night, *cara*. I'll read you one story and then bed."

Katherine sat sipping the hot stew and listening to the rise and fall of his voice as he read to his children from *A Child's History of England*. Bo curled against her feet under the table. The wind rushed around the train car like some live thing. The lamp flickered and then steadied.

At nine, the clock on the cupboard chimed, and Alonzo closed the book and kissed each child on the forehead. "Sleep now. We'll finish tomorrow."

Lilia protested briefly, then subsided under the blankets. Alonzo tucked Tony in, then went to the door with a parting nod at Katherine. She set her cup down and went to her cot.

"Take one of these quilts," she said, pulling one free. "I don't need two, and you can tell by the ring around the moon that it's going to be a cold night."

Alonzo took it from her. "A very thoughtful gesture," he said.

"Not at all. I'm feeling guilty, staying in this cozy train car while you're out in the cart."

He grinned suddenly, eyes sparkling. "You could sleep in the cart, then, if you like."

"I'm not feeling *that* guilty," she replied promptly. "But take the blanket."

He went out laughing.

Chapter Thirteen

THAT WEEK JIN FOUND A position with a Chinese tailor in Toronto.

"Is good work, and we have two rooms above shop," he announced, clambering down from the cart with difficulty as soon as it rolled to a stop. Ah Lam hurried to help him, and he excitedly told her his news in what Katherine now knew was Cantonese. Ah Lam clapped her hands together and laughed.

"The tailor who owns the shop will let him have the apartment above it rent free until his apprenticeship is over," Alonzo told Katherine as he began to unhitch Bacchus. "He won't receive wages until he's fully qualified, but he won't have to worry about a place to live this winter."

"That's lovely news, but how will they survive with no wages?" Katherine said.

Alonzo shrugged one shoulder. "Oh, Ah Lam can still sell her paper figures, and I can spot them a little money to tide them over. It's not a worry."

"How can you—" Katherine caught herself, realizing how rude it would be to ask her employer the state of his finances. She was suddenly aware of just how casual her relationship with Alonzo had become. She turned and took Ah Lam's hands in her own.

"I am happy for you," she said. "But I'm sad for myself. I will miss you."

Jin began to translate, but Ah Lam didn't need him to. She gripped Katherine's hands in return and smiled, her eyes suddenly damp. "Good friends," she said, looking from Katherine to Alonzo. "Very much thank you."

"You very good friends too," Katherine said, laughing. "And I will miss having Huang Fu for a pupil. He's such a good boy. I hope he will have the opportunity to go to school one day."

"You come visit us," Jin told Alonzo. "Yes?"

"We will keep in touch, old friend."

Within the week, they were gone, Alonzo driving them into the city with all their belongings packed in the back of the cart. The clearing seemed hushed and empty after they drove away, and Katherine found it difficult to keep Tony and Lilia focused on their lessons. They were irritable and disinterested, and finally she called a halt to learning and let them help her bake Christmas cookies instead. This cheered them somewhat, and they were tolerable again by the time Alonzo returned.

"I met their new employer and landlord," he told Katherine, carrying in the groceries he had purchased while in town. "He's from Beijing as well, though he's been here twenty years, and he seems nice enough. Their rooms over the shop are small and have no running water, but there's a pump downstairs, and the place is heated. It's an improvement over their tent, at any rate. They seem pleased. There are several other Chinese working there, so they'll have a community."

"I'm glad they won't have to spend the winter in that tent. It will feel strange not having them here after these past weeks," Katherine admitted. "I got used to their company."

Alonzo studied her a moment. "Perhaps it's difficult for you not having another woman around."

"I didn't feel so when I first came here," Katherine replied. "And no doubt I'll adjust back again. But for a while, yes, it was nice."

Alonzo looked at the package of tea he held as if wondering where it had come from and then placed it on the shelf. With his back to her, he said in a low voice, "I've never thanked you properly for welcoming them and at short notice. When I first brought them home, I didn't stop to consider what you might think of it, and for that I apologize."

"It's your home," Katherine said, surprised. "You can bring whomever you want into it."

He turned and spread his hands. "But I should have thought of your feelings about it first. I know in the world you come from, the Chinese are not generally treated as equals. They're acceptable as laborers but not as neighbors."

"I can't deny that," Katherine said quietly. "But that doesn't mean it's right. I suppose growing up I thought the same way because I didn't stop to consider it. It was just the way things were. But now that I've gotten to know Jin and Ah Lam, I don't think the same anymore."

"I'm glad."

"So am I."

He put away the last of the purchases and wiped his hands on the towel. "I like to think that one day society will come to its senses and get rid of some of the illogical and unfair rules and assumptions that exist now."

"If I can change my view of something, I suppose society can too. It just has to happen one person at a time."

Alonzo cast a glance at her over his shoulder and laughed. "Stick with me long enough, Kate, and I'll turn your whole way of thinking topsy-turvy."

She suspected he had already begun to do just that.

* * *

The weather grew bitterly cold after that. When Katherine awoke the next morning, the grass was crunchy with frost, and a thick lid of ice had formed on the pail outside. Alonzo seemed unaffected, appearing bright and red cheeked for breakfast. He told the children to sponge bathe in heated water from the stove, however, for the brook was now too cold and would soon ice over completely.

"I don't want any more fevers in this house," he told them firmly. "Bathing outdoors in the summer is rustic. In the winter, it's plain foolishness."

That Saturday it snowed, a light dusting that lingered after the sun rose. The winds turned fierce, whipping the powdery snow into little piles against all objects, bending the trees until they protested and Katherine feared they would snap. Alonzo rigged an improved windbreak for the horse, stretching the canvas over a strong wood frame and anchoring it firmly beneath the trees. He also made certain the food supplies were well stocked in case it became difficult to get to town. Bo abandoned the outdoors and took to sleeping by the stove. Katherine kept the children indoors much of the time too. The cold could be kept out with mufflers and thick coats, but the wind seemed to find its way through all barriers.

One night, eight days before Christmas, the wind grew to a ferocious roar. Katherine lay in bed, the blankets pulled to her chin, and listened to the sound of it ripping through the trees. It rocked the train car on its wheels and whined at the windows. Lilia and Tony slept restlessly in their cots, mumbling, and Bo raised his head in the dark, alert. And then there was a different sound, terrifying, a sort of scream and crash. Katherine was on her feet and at the door even before the heavy *whump* had finished. In the light of the moon, she could see only the flattened grass. The icy wind hit her full force. Careful to close Bo in the train car behind her, she clutched the front of her nightgown in a futile attempt to keep out the cold and ran in bare feet through the frozen grass to the cart.

What used to be the cart.

An oak tree had uprooted in the gale and fallen directly across the gaily painted tinker's cart, the tree's tangled branches totally obscuring their victim. It was impossibly heavy, the length of it stretching back to the clump of its root ball, which lay obscenely bare under the moon like Medusa's profile.

"Alonzo! Oh, no, no!" Panic gripping her chest, Katherine pulled at the trunk. She couldn't budge it. Its girth was so thick she could barely get her two arms around it.

Her breath started coming in gulps, her heart knocking against her ribs. She climbed with her nightgown hiked to her knees to rip at the branches. The smaller ones bent back but would not snap in her hands, and there were layers and layers of them. It was too dark to see properly. Her hands stung with scrapes. Her body shivered uncontrollably. She heard herself shouting, crying as if from far away, as if another person were making the sounds. "Alonzo! Can you hear me?" *God, please let him be alive. Please don't let the children wake up.* "Answer me, Alonzo!" Her hands clawed at the leaves.

The horse. She would get Bacchus and hitch him to the trunk somehow, pull its crushing weight off the cart. She jumped down, turned to run, and froze. Above the rush of the wind, she heard a sound that stopped her.

"Kate!"

His voice. He was alive. She whirled around, confused. The sound wasn't coming from the smashed cart. Across the clearing, silver in the moonlight, she saw a figure running. She hiked up her gown and flew, bare-legged, to meet him. His arms went out, and she ran into them. She clung to him, crying, and felt his hand cradling the back of her head, pressing her face to his shoulder.

His lips moved against her temple. "It's all right. I'm here. What is it, *bella*? What's upset you?"

"I thought you were dead," she sobbed. "I couldn't find you!"

He made a slightly astonished noise and then chuckled. "Why would you think I was dead? Only gone to your precious lavatory, that's all. Hush now."

Relief made her gasp. She could hear the hysteria in her voice but couldn't seem to control it. She muffled her face in his chest. "I thought—the tree. I heard a scream. I thought it was you."

He held her away from him, his face an odd collage of angles and planes in the shifting moonlight, his eyes shadowed in their deep sockets. "What scream? What tree?" His voice was bemused and gentle, as if he were talking to Lilia awakened from a bad dream.

"Come and see. It fell on the cart, and I thought you were crushed under it." She began to tremble again. "You could have been."

His smile faded. He looked beyond her to the dark shape of the smashed cart, to the distorted shadow of the tree, to the tortured roots exposed in the silvery moonlight. He released her shoulders and walked slowly toward it. He stood staring at the wreckage, silent.

Katherine came to stand beside him, uncaringly wiping her nose with the sleeve of her nightgown. Her feet were frozen numb. Her hair whipped around her face.

"Providence," Alonzo said flatly.

"Your poor cart. All your wares," Katherine mourned.

"The scream you heard was probably the wood ripping. It can sound like that."

Katherine shuddered. "Yes. I-I didn't think. I thought it was you, but I heard it before I heard the tree fall. If you hadn't gotten up . . ."

His arms went around her once more. "But I did. Don't think about it. It's all right."

Katherine's own arms went around his middle, and she huddled in his warmth, trying to make her body stop trembling. "I was praying the children wouldn't come out and see. I didn't know what to do. I was going to get Bacchus, but I don't know how to hitch him up."

"Come on, you're frozen through."

He led her away from the cart, one arm tightly about her shoulders, and into the train car. There, Katherine sat at the table, her arms about herself, while he lit the lamp, filled the kettle, and stoked the stove. The children slept, washed in the golden glow of lamplight.

"You're going to catch pneumonia," Alonzo said quietly, bringing the blanket from her cot to wrap around her. He bent to eye level, looking at her sharply, one eyebrow raised. "Now, are you feeling calm? No more tears?"

She shook her head, feeling foolish now. "I'm sorry."

"Sorry for what? Being afraid?"

"For acting hysterical." She managed a totally unconvincing laugh. "For running around like a helpless fool. I should be fussing over you, not the other way round. You just lost everything."

He shook his head and sat opposite her. "I've lost nothing," he said. "I'm lucky to be alive."

"But your livelihood depends on that cart, and all your things . . ."

"Those are replaceable. All that I value I have right here." He motioned toward the children. "Drink your tea now."

She shook her head. "I can't believe you can be that matter-of-fact about it."

"What else can I be? Ranting and raving won't change matters. I know." He sat looking down into his cup, and a faint smile played about his lips. "That's how the door to the cart was damaged, you know. I was ranting and raving and put my foot through it. I felt so foolish about it afterward. Such a stupid thing. All it did was destroy the wood." He grinned suddenly. "Not that that matters now. The whole thing is in splinters." She gave a violent shudder, and he reached across the table and put his hand over hers. "Go back to bed now and get warm."

"What about you?"

"I can put a tent up tomorrow. If it was good enough for Jin, it's good enough for me. But I'll have to squeeze in here for tonight, I guess." He glanced at her from under his lashes. "Would that shock you dreadfully?"

"No." She laughed. "I'll take Lilia in my cot with me, and you can have hers, Mr. Colaco."

"Alonzo."

"What?"

"I distinctly heard you call me Alonzo when you were shouting just a minute ago."

"I suppose I might have."

"Then can't you call me that now?" he asked.

"Certainly not," she said, rising and putting her cup on the counter. "The circumstances are totally different."

He shook his head and went to lift Lilia into Katherine's cot. Katherine carefully squeezed in beside her, and Alonzo turned out the lamp. The train car returned to complete darkness. She heard him remove his shoes and climb into Lilia's cot.

He sighed up at the ceiling. "I'll have to see if I can salvage some of my clothes from the cart tomorrow. I may have to buy another cart if this one is beyond repair."

"Can you afford it? I mean—I'm sorry. I don't mean to be rude. But that's awfully expensive."

"I'll manage," he said simply.

"If you need to withhold my wages for a while, I'll certainly understand."

"Nonsense. I have some money put away, Kate. Don't fret."

She hesitated, listening to the wind, then asked softly in the dark, "What was it you were raving about? When you put your foot through the door?"

He was silent a moment, and she thought he wouldn't answer. Then he said quietly, "After Ruth died, for a while, I held God responsible. One evening, I . . . well, I was expressing to Him my view of it."

"I see."

"Good night, Kate, what's left of it."

"Good night, sir."

"Alonzo."

"Alonzo," she said, smiling into the darkness.

He sighed. She could hear him breathing in the quiet.

"Thank you," he said then.

"What for?"

"It's nice to know someone considers my injury or death worth getting hysterical over," he said.

Katherine chuckled and snuggled closer to the sleeping Lilia.

Chapter Fourteen

When Katherine awoke in the morning, the wind had died down somewhat and the windows were so frosted over that nothing could be seen through them. The stove ticked quietly as the metal cooled from last night's fire, and there was a peaceful rustle as the ashes fell. Lilia lay deep in sleep, her mouth open, one arm flung above her head. Alonzo was just waking, stretching. He turned his head, saw Katherine watching him, and smiled at her across the gap.

"This is a nice way to wake up," he said quietly so as not to disturb the children. "It's so warm compared to the cart! I've never felt so good."

Katherine sat up and slid carefully away from the sleeping little girl. Her feet hurt when they touched the floor. Examining them, she saw scratches from the previous night's events. She should have had the presence of mind to put on her shoes, she thought woefully. She hobbled to check the stove and refill the kettle, then limped back to the closet to find her bathrobe.

Alonzo had been watching her. "I've got just the thing," he said now. He got out of bed and took a white jar from a cupboard. "Sit down a minute."

Katherine sat on the nearest chair, and he knelt in front of her. Taking the lid off the jar, he scooped out a thick brownish cream that smelled nastily of fish grease and began to rub it into her feet. Katherine sat stiffly. The sensation of someone massaging her feet was a new one, and she wasn't sure how to react. It seemed dreadfully improper, and yet it felt so good she couldn't protest. She closed her eyes and let him work the cream into the broken skin and felt herself grow boneless and peaceful. She was sorry when at last he stood and wiped his hands on a towel.

"I'll do it again tonight. By tomorrow you won't feel a thing," he said.

"Thank you. I won't ask what is in it."

"You don't want to know," he said, putting the jar away. "I guess I'll go inspect the damage now."

"I'll have breakfast ready when you get back."

After he'd gone, Katherine dressed quickly and fixed a large breakfast of sausage, eggs, toast, and fried potatoes. She found herself humming a little as she moved about the kitchen and thought back to the first few days she'd spent with the Colacos. She'd been unfamiliar with all but the simplest cooking; her father's cook had done it all throughout her childhood and Martha's cook after that. She remembered her first attempts at breakfast—burnt bacon, bits of shell in the watery eggs—and smiled. She had definitely improved, she thought as she placed the steaming dishes on the small table. What was more, she'd discovered she enjoyed cooking.

The children woke, and she dressed them and started them eating. Then she put on her coat and went outside.

Alonzo had dragged the fallen tree away from the cart with the horse's help and had begun to pile the wreckage into two mounds, salvageable and unsalvageable. The latter was bigger than the former. She stood and watched him a moment, her hands deep in her pockets. He worked quickly to stay warm. His quilt and some clothing lay on the salvageable pile, and she moved to gather them up.

"Breakfast is ready," she called as she walked back toward the train car.

He nodded, and she went inside. She spread the clothes on the cot and sorted out which ones needed washing or mending. There was a twig caught in his scarlet shirt. She felt her hands begin to tremble again and firmly brought them under control. It had been a narrow miss, but all was well, she reminded herself.

When Alonzo came into the train car with a blast of cold air, she was briskly clearing the children's dishes away and had wash water heating.

"Are you going to Toronto today, Papa?" Lilia greeted him, bouncing up to hug him.

"Not today." He glanced at Katherine with a grin. "Not for a while. Today we're going to work at home. I have plenty for you to help with."

"I'll help too?" Tony asked hopefully.

"Of course. You too." He sent Katherine another glance. "And today I'm going to teach Kate how to hitch up Bacchus."

Katherine stopped and looked at him.

He shrugged. "You should know how. It's a useful thing."

"Let your father have his breakfast now," Katherine told the children. "Tony, run and put on your shoes, and Lilia will take you out to the lav."

"I can go myself," Tony said disdainfully and went to find his shoes.

"How bad is it?" Katherine asked after they'd gone.

"It did a good job on it," he said ruefully, gazing into his cup. "I can still use the wheels and some of the boards, but the frame and axles are history."

"What about all of your things inside?"

"Oh, I can fix a few dents and dings. That's all right. Most of it I can mend or replace. At least I hadn't gone to the expense of replacing the door yet."

She stared at him, uncertain whether to laugh or cry. She was sure Edgar Colworthy wouldn't have taken such loss so casually. "You're an astonishing person," she said finally. "I don't know how you can face the loss of your livelihood with such little concern."

"It's hardly that," he said, looking uncomfortable. "I still have my skill; I still have my tools, thank heavens. And I have enough money put away to keep us for a while. I'd say I came out of this in pretty good shape. Good luck, wouldn't you say?"

She agreed doubtfully. "I'm glad you weren't smashed."

He nodded solemnly. "So am I. And I'm glad you're all right."

"Me?"

He fiddled with his fork against his plate. "When I came out of the woods last night and heard you screaming, I thought—I don't know what I thought. All sorts of things. Maybe the stove had blown up or a tramp had broken in and attacked you."

"Oh my." She chuckled.

"Well, you did sound pretty frantic."

"You can hardly blame me. I thought I had two orphans on my hands."

He was about to speak when the door burst open and Lilia tumbled in, wide-eyed.

"Papa! The cart!"

"I know, *cara mia*," he said cheerfully. "Today we're going to see if we can build a new one. Would you like that?"

"Can I choose the color to paint it?" Lilia cried, delighted.

"*May I*," Katherine corrected automatically.

"Any color you want," Alonzo said.

"I want it blue," the little girl said promptly. "Not dark. Light. Like Kate's dress."

Alonzo turned and scanned Katherine's dress appraisingly from head to toe, and Katherine felt herself begin to flush pink under his lingering scrutiny.

"Yes," he said, nodding in satisfaction. "That's a perfect color to choose."

"Blue like heaven," Lilia said solemnly.

"Where will you sleep now, Papa?" Tony asked.

"A tent will do just fine, just like for Huang Fu's family," Alonzo said confidently. "I've always enjoyed camping. And it's only until I can fix the cart again."

Alonzo spent the morning digging through the wreckage. He saved out the few scraps that were still useful and chopped the rest for kindling, stacking it under a tarp behind the train car. Then he saddled the horse and rode into Springfield. At his urging, he carried a letter to post from Katherine to Martha, informing her that she would be pleased to come for dinner Christmas Eve and would stay the night, returning Christmas Day.

Alonzo returned, driving a battered hay wagon. He told Katherine cheerfully as he unhitched the horse, "It was just my luck to hear they were having an auction today. I can build sides and a roof on it. A little paint and it will be better than new. And it's much bigger in back than the cart was. You see? I'll have more room to spread out."

Katherine eyed it doubtfully, but Lilia cried happily, "Blue, remember, Papa."

"Blue it is. With white and gold curly letters on the side." Alonzo laughed. "But it will take some work to fix it up. I'll be in the tent awhile, I think."

"But winter is here. Won't a tent be too terribly cold?" Katherine asked.

"It will be fine for now, and I'll work fast. You'd be amazed by how much I can do when I have an incentive."

"Well, take all the spare blankets, then. I feel terrible that I'm inside, warm and dry, and you're out in a tent."

"Can't be helped," Alonzo said. "I can't move into the train car permanently, now can I? I mean I *could*, but the good citizens of our village would be shocked, and so, I fear, would our Miss Porter."

Katherine rolled her eyes at him. "I'll help you with the tarp," she said primly.

* * *

The day before Christmas, Katherine confined the Colacos to the outdoors and carefully wrapped the small presents she had bought for them on a trip to Toronto: a set of coloring pencils for Tony, a cloth doll for Lilia—she had noticed with astonishment that the children had no playthings to speak of—and, after much deliberation, a pair of leather gloves for Alonzo. She left the small packages on the table. She packed an overnight bag, topping it with the small purchases she'd made for her family, and changed into her green velvet dress. She hadn't worn a full bustle and train since her visit to Martha and hadn't missed the fight it took to get them on. She took special care with her hair and polished her shoes to a gleam. When at last she was ready, she hardly recognized herself in her finery.

The Colacos were waiting for her in the wagon. Alonzo had offered to take her to the train, and the children were coming along for the ride. There wasn't yet a roof or walls on the wagon, but the children huddled together in the back, warmly swathed in blankets, their smiling faces peeping out, giving them the appearance of sausage rolls. Bo, shut up in the car, barked as they rattled away toward town.

The weather had warmed slightly, but there had been a lot of snow. Soft icing lined the tree branches and melted to mud under the horse's hooves. The gray sky looked heavy with snow clouds in the distance. They passed a horse and carriage on the road that were so covered in mud Katherine couldn't tell the true color of the horse.

When they reached the station, the platform seemed unusually crowded, even for Christmas Eve. She and Alonzo shouldered their way awkwardly to the ticket kiosk.

The white-haired man behind the grate shook his head sadly. "I'm sorry, that line is closed. It probably won't be open until tomorrow afternoon."

"What do you mean?" Katherine exclaimed. "It can't be closed."

"What's the problem?" Alonzo asked.

"Train hit a herd of cows, wandered onto the tracks. Happened just twenty minutes ago. Train rounded a corner, and there they were. No time to stop. Awful mess. Terrible thing to happen Christmas Eve. I'm sorry. I can get you to Mimico. Would that do?"

"No, it wouldn't. Thank you all the same," Katherine said.

"How far down the line are the tracks closed, please?" Alonzo asked.

"You'd have to drive to Teasdale Station the other side of Mimico and go on from there. All other junctions are closed off between."

As they moved away, Katherine frowned. "Teasdale is so far, and I would have to switch trains down the line. It will be midnight by the time I arrive. I'll just have to miss it, I guess. It can't be helped."

"Nonsense. I'll just drive you to High Park directly," Alonzo said as they returned to the wagon.

She stared at him. "I can't possibly make you drive all that way. It's a good two hours at least, in the best of conditions."

He shrugged in his offhanded way. "I'm not doing anything else at the moment."

"It's Christmas Eve," she protested.

"Yes, it is, and you should be with your family."

"And you should be with yours."

"I *am* with mine," he said, winking at the bundles in the back of the wagon. "One of the advantages of a mobile family."

"I can't let you. Why are you being so nice to me?"

He grinned and, seizing her unexpectedly about the waist, hoisted her bodily onto the wagon seat, then jumped up beside her. "You argue too much," he said amiably. "You need to remember your place. I'm your employer, remember?"

With an odd start, she realized she had indeed forgotten. "I know that," she said irritably, twitching her skirts into place. "But I can't make you drive so far out of your way."

"I assure you, no one *ever* makes me do anything."

"It's not that important to me."

He cocked one eyebrow. "Spending Christmas with your family isn't important to you?"

"That's not what I meant," she said. "It's just not vital. I don't want to inconvenience you."

"Do you want to go?"

"Of course. I'm expected."

"Then stop arguing and tell me how to get there."

She slumped, laughing. "All right. You win. But you're going way beyond duty."

"Never duty," he said, clicking to Bacchus. "Never that."

* * *

They arrived at the Fitzgerald home well after sundown, the children asleep in their blankets under a light dusting of snow. The beautiful house was lit at every window, and torches marched down each side of the drive. Broad red ribbons were wrapped around the trunks of the two trees flanking the end of the drive. Alonzo halted the wagon at the front steps and sat staring at the house.

"It's very lovely," he said at length and glanced at her.

"I've always thought so," Katherine agreed.

"A bit overwhelming, maybe."

"Hugh, my cousin's husband, is very proud of it."

Alonzo climbed down and was lifting Katherine to the ground when the front door opened. Martha stood in the doorway, the light pouring out around her red-velveted shoulders. She shivered exaggeratedly and waved her hand. Behind her, the butler stood looking aggrieved.

"Hurry, come in, come in. I was beginning to think you'd forgotten us," Martha called out. "What on earth is that contraption? Where's your cab?"

Katherine went up the steps to meet her while Alonzo followed with her overnight bag. The women embraced briefly, formally.

"I'm sorry I'm so late. The train hit a herd of cows and—"

"My gracious!"

"Not while I was in it. But the line was closed, and I had no way of getting here sooner."

"You poor dear. I understand completely." Martha drew her into the warm entry hall. "You do look a fright. Your nose is the color of a strawberry. Come upstairs, and my maid can straighten your hair. Just set the bag down, man," she added irritably to Alonzo. "Tippetts will take it upstairs."

Katherine watched him quietly set the bag just inside the door. She cleared her throat and turned to Martha. "Mr. Colaco was kind enough to drive me all the way here," she said flatly.

There was a pause while Martha tried to remember where she'd heard the name before. Then she glanced at Alonzo, a puzzled frown on her pretty face.

"This is Mr. Alonzo Colaco, my employer. This is Mrs. Martha Fitzgerald, my mother's cousin."

Alonzo smiled, removed his hat, and briefly took Martha's hand.

Martha turned a delicate shade of pink. "I'm sorry," she said. "I thought you were some farmer who gave her a lift. I do apologize. You . . . you just have an extraordinary conveyance."

"It's quite understandable," Alonzo said kindly without offering any sort of explanation for the hay wagon.

Katherine hid a smile.

"Still, I suppose that's more practical on the roads than a carriage in this weather," Martha said, supplying an explanation for him and regaining her poise. "Won't you come in, Mr. Colaco? You must be frozen. It was so kind of you to drive my cousin. Such an inconvenience to you. Katherine has a way of needing to be rescued every so often."

Katherine flinched. So the little jabs weren't to be suspended, even for the holiday.

"Thank you, I will step in for just a moment. My children are in the wagon, and so I shan't stay."

Once more Martha was thrown off guard. "In the wagon? But why are they—? They must be freezing. You must bring them inside."

After some flurry, the children were carried in and the horse led off by Hugh's carriage boy. Alonzo set Tony and Lilia on the floor of the hall and unwrapped the blankets like an artist unveiling two statues. They stood blinking, half awake, smiling at the faces around them like lost, dark-eyed cherubs.

Martha clasped her hands together. "The sweet little angels. They're simply charming. They're not twins, are they? Are you hungry, my dears? Betsy, please take them to the kitchen and have Annie do up something nice. And, Tippets, take our guests' wraps. What are you thinking?"

The butler stepped forward to take their coats. The children looked at Alonzo, hesitant, and he nodded to them. They followed the maid out of the room.

"You're very kind," Alonzo said to Martha.

"They seem well behaved," Martha replied. "I have two sons myself. Perhaps your children would care to play in the old nursery awhile and you could join us for dinner. We would be most pleased."

Surprised, Katherine looked at Alonzo. In his good dark suit, white shirt, and ordinary boots, he looked like any normal, respectable gentleman. If her cousin had known his true occupation, however, she was sure Martha would never have made the invitation. Though she was unfailingly polite, she had adopted more than a little of Hugh's snobbery.

Alonzo looked alarmed. Quickly he said, "Oh, no, thank you, I won't interrupt your holiday gathering."

"Nonsense. It's Christmas Eve. What better season to meet one's neighbors? It's practically our fault you had to come all this way. You can't turn around and go back out in that cold."

Alonzo looked at Katherine, who raised her eyebrows helplessly. He nodded slowly. "All right, thank you. I will. But I can't stay long. I thought I would take my children to midnight mass, and it's half an hour's drive from here."

Katherine froze.

"You're a Catholic?" Martha asked faintly, her smile a little tight around the edges.

"I'm Italian," Alonzo said, grinning broadly. "Is that all right?"

Flushing deeply again, Martha said quickly, "Yes, of course. I merely— My husband . . . um. In spite of his name, my husband is a staunch Orangeman. I realize you're not *Irish* Catholic, but still, I think it may be wise to avoid the topic in conversation, yes?" She said it brightly, as if suggesting a delightful game, but her eyes were chilly blue stones that conveyed her seriousness.

"Whatever you suggest," Alonzo said graciously.

Martha turned those eyes briefly on Katherine, then snapped her fingers and called sharply, "Tippets!"

The butler reappeared.

"Mr. Colaco will be joining us for dinner."

The butler smoothly nodded and went to inform the staff.

"We've already begun dining, I'm afraid, since you were so awfully late," Martha said. "Would you care to freshen up before joining us?" She looked pointedly at Katherine's hair.

Katherine smiled sweetly and declined. They followed Martha into the dining room. As they entered, Alonzo shot Katherine a look full of mischief, eyes glittering merrily, and she wondered with nervous little quivers in her stomach what was going to happen next. She had no idea how he would behave in polite company. Though he could assume the manners and appearance of a gentleman, Alonzo also had a devilish streak in him. He plainly admitted he didn't approve of convention and custom. Hugh was the epitome of them. It was with a sense of dread that she followed Martha.

Chapter Fifteen

"Ah, Katherine. I was beginning to worry," Hugh boomed. He stood to greet them, his handshake as hearty as his voice. Hugh was a man who could not be in a room and go unnoticed. She thought he'd put on weight since the last time she'd seen him.

"Everyone, you remember my cousin Katherine, and this is her . . . friend," Martha amended neatly. "Mr. Alonzo Colaco. He's Italian."

Of course, Katherine thought. Heaven forbid any of their distinguished guests find out Katherine was working to support herself. It would reflect so poorly on Hugh.

Around the glittering, laden table sat six other people. Katherine recognized James and Emily Gayle, the older and graying, judge-faced friends of her grandparents. They lived in opulent retirement in Rosedale. Across from them sat a slightly younger couple, Robert and Judith Chisholm. Robert had read at Oxford with Hugh, and Katherine didn't know them as well.

Next to them were Hugh's brother Reginald and his wife, Elizabeth.

As Reginald rose and came to kiss her cheek, Katherine felt the old, familiar rush of confused emotion that assailed her whenever she saw this cousin-by-marriage, a mix of awe, admiration, and irritation. She always felt reduced to the wit and importance of a ten-year-old in his presence. She watched him coming, his once-hard-and-lean frame now starting to fill out, hair dark, his manner dripping with studied charm. His very bearing flaunted the station he enjoyed through his wife, who was the daughter of an MP. While Hugh was unconsciously condescending, his brother Reginald worked actively at it.

Katherine returned his greeting and received Elizabeth's cool kiss. Martha indicated a chair before the extra place setting a maid was hurriedly but silently placing, and for a moment, Katherine stood in hesitation, fearing that Alonzo wouldn't know what to do. But to her relief, he caught his cue and smoothly stepped forward to seat her as genteelly as if he moved in such formal settings daily.

Introductions were made all around, and the interrupted meal resumed. Katherine sat in her nice green gown, still chilled from the long journey, and looked around the table.

To her amusement, she noted that every female eye in the room, from the hostess's to her serving maid's, was on Alonzo. Elizabeth, sophisticated, her blonde hair piled high to draw attention away from her horsey face, her velvet dress the latest fashion and cut low on her milky bosom, had broken off her conversation with Mrs. Gayle to greet them. Now she sat blinking, her conversation forgotten. Mrs. Gayle herself, who had emeralds the size of walnuts in her ears, didn't seem aware that the conversation had been broken off. Her cornflower eyes had fastened themselves on Alonzo's face and had not moved.

Alonzo, to his credit, didn't seem to notice the attention. He spoke to his host in a pleasant murmur, smiled unabashedly at everyone, and—to Katherine's relief—picked up the proper fork.

The hum of conversation resumed. The candles sparkled, the food was rich and plenteous, the wine offered repeatedly. Katherine couldn't seem to relax and enjoy the meal though. She found herself wondering increasingly why she had come here. She couldn't follow the conversation and felt no interest in the women's gossip. She was no longer used to the rich food and could only nibble at it. She may have moved in this circle for four years, but she certainly had never belonged to it. Always she had been the outsider. After the years of absence, she found she still didn't belong to it, and she feared she never would no matter how much she may have wanted to. *This is the one whose father went bankrupt*, the others would be thinking to themselves. *This is the homely one who never married. How unfortunate. So good of Hugh and Martha to take her in.* It was just another bit of gossip to them.

"And what sort of business are you in?" Hugh's voice interrupted her spiraling thoughts.

She looked up in alarm and saw Alonzo sitting calmly beside her, his wine glass in his hand. She knew he didn't belong here either, any more than she did, but he still managed to look relaxed. She held her breath, wondering if he were going to announce he was a tinker. Perhaps he might have, but her agonized look stopped him.

Smoothly he replied, "I'm in minerals. Primarily tin."

"Ah. Mining? Manufacture?" Hugh asked.

"Buying and selling," Alonzo replied, smiling.

"Really? How fascinating," Martha said, sounding slightly breathless. "Hugh is in textiles himself." She gave Katherine a sort of approving look, as if she were somehow to be congratulated for Mr. Colaco's occupation.

Like Martha, Hugh was fondest of talking about himself, and for a while, everyone forgot Alonzo and Katherine as Hugh carried on a monologue about his various business interests.

But as dessert was being served and just as Katherine was beginning to think perhaps all would end smoothly after all, Judith Chisholm leaned forward in a sparkle of diamonds. "I certainly would have remembered your face if I'd seen you about, Mr. Colaco. Where do you live?" she asked, toying with a stray dark curl on her shoulder. If her husband were not at the table, Katherine might almost have thought she was flirting.

Alonzo, who had remained silent most of the meal, now replied, "I winter in Springfield. In the summer, I go home to Collingwood."

"That's where you're from?"

"Well, it is now. Of course, originally I'm from Milano."

"Of course. That delightful accent," Judith gushed enthusiastically. "Have you been in this country long?"

"About twelve years."

"I'm surprised you speak English so well," Mrs. Gayle piped up.

"He has two darling children. They're upstairs now," Martha added.

"Really? And your wife, Mr. Colaco?" Elizabeth asked, watching Judith narrowly.

"Unfortunately, she died last spring," he said briefly, as if apologizing for mentioning anything sad at the festive gathering.

"Oh, I'm so sorry," Mrs. Gayle said sincerely. "Was she ill?"

"Yes." He nodded once and didn't elaborate.

"I'm sure it must have been very difficult for you, especially with the children," Judith murmured.

"Yes."

"But I imagine you've managed to get on with your lives."

There were speculative glances at Katherine because Alonzo had, after all, been introduced as a friend, and, of course, they didn't know her real relationship to him.

Hugh cleared his throat. "I haven't seen you about before either, sir. Were you by chance at MP Hoffley's banquet last summer? No? Percy Chomondsley's? Timothy Eaton's?"

"I'm afraid I travel a great deal with my work," Alonzo said pleasantly. "I don't attend many functions."

"I see."

Elizabeth leaned forward now. "How did you meet our cousin, sir? I'm afraid I haven't kept in as much contact with her recently as I should."

Katherine looked at Alonzo.

He gazed back at her with a faint smile. "We met at the Duke of Paisley Teahouse on Yonge Street in Toronto," he said softly. "I came in, and there she was at a table by herself. Of course I couldn't leave her sitting there all alone, could I?"

The men at the table chuckled. Martha glanced at Katherine with eyes that danced with amusement, but she said nothing.

As the table fell quiet again, Elizabeth turned her appraising blue eyes on Katherine and addressed her with a nasty little smile. "It's been ages since we've seen you, Katherine. What *have* you been doing all this time?"

Farther down the table, Reginald looked up sharply. Martha and Hugh exchanged glances.

Katherine stared at Elizabeth, who blinked innocently back. She knew perfectly well where Katherine had been. She'd asked the question only to see Katherine squirm, to hear her lie to the Gayles and Chisholms about how she'd spent the past months because, of course, Katherine couldn't possibly tell their guests the truth. It would disgrace the whole family, especially their host, to announce in front of guests that one of them had been reduced to such circumstances that she had had to hire herself out.

Katherine glanced around the table, uncertain what to say. Martha was chewing her lip. Hugh looked annoyed. Reginald was scowling at her hard, willing her to lie. Elizabeth continued to smile blandly, enjoying her awkwardness. And suddenly Katherine was angry, not just with Elizabeth for putting her in such a position but with the rest of the family as well for expecting her to lie to save their dignity. All the old resentment for their pomposity, their self-interest, their insincerity rose up and choked her. They didn't care a thing for her, only for their own reputations. She looked from one face to another, seeing the same expression on each. Alonzo stared at his plate.

"Katherine?" Judith Chisholm murmured in puzzlement.

Katherine put down her serviette and heard herself say briskly, "I've been working as a children's tutor and a lady's companion, as you well know, Elizabeth. Have you grown forgetful?"

It was worth it just to see the surprised expression on Elizabeth's face. *Let's see how you deal with that*, Katherine thought smugly. *You didn't expect that, did you? You assumed I'd play your game.*

Martha looked stricken.

James Gayle cleared his throat. "A lady's companion? Why ever would you want to be such a thing?"

"It's a whim of hers," Martha began overbrightly, but Katherine smiled and interrupted her.

"It's not a matter of wanting, Mr. Gayle. It's a matter of necessity."

Hugh coughed.

James Gayle turned to him with a pained expression. "What is this, Hugh? Surely you didn't turn the girl out in her unfortunate circumstances?"

"Of course not," Hugh bellowed, turning dark red.

"What is it, then? Are you in some sort of financial difficulty? I consider myself your friend, Hugh. You must feel you may come to me with no hesitation if you—"

"No, no. There's no difficulty," Hugh sputtered. "Katherine is just being overly dramatic."

"I'm sure Hugh is very sound financially," Katherine said cheerfully, "if we are to judge from how frequently he mentions the fact."

"Katherine!" Martha hissed.

Katherine ignored her. "When my father died without leaving a penny, the Fitzgeralds fulfilled every familial duty, I assure you. But I couldn't keep accepting charity indefinitely. Could you, Mrs. Gayle, in my place?"

"I suppose not," Mrs. Gayle murmured vaguely.

Katherine took a sip of wine and wondered if it was going to her head. She felt refreshingly happy. "Under the circumstances, I thought it best not to grow too reliant on their generosity," she said.

"That's a good independent attitude," Robert Chisholm said stoutly. His wife gave him a withering look, and he subsided back into his wine glass.

"You will have to excuse my cousin," Martha said swiftly to her guests. "Goodness knows we tried to teach her the social graces while she was with us. Sadly, she came to us too late in life for our instruction to have had much effect."

"Now, now," Reginald said uncomfortably and fiddled with his fork against his plate.

"I don't mean to sound ungrateful," Katherine said. "Hugh and Martha were there for me in my hour of need. I'm sure they're aware of how indebted I am to them. But I mustn't let that hour of need become a lifetime."

"Yes," Mr. Gayle said. "Er, I mean no. Quite right. I always admired independence in a woman, isn't that right, Emily?"

"Yes, dear," Mrs. Gayle said, frowning.

"But a tutor?" Mrs. Chisholm piped up. "Surely there must be something easier you could have chosen. I know I gave *my* tutor a dreadful time!"

The others twittered politely, and the tension around the table began to ease, giving Katherine hope that the topic would be changed.

But Hugh remained scowling. "Foolish notion in the first place," he muttered. "No need for her to go to work at all. I would have supported her, you know. I'm not one to shirk a responsibility, even if she's not from my side of the family."

"Of course not," Elizabeth murmured soothingly.

"Her father was just as mule-headed. I would have set her up proper, found a decent match for her. Seen her settled instead of living with strangers. Least I could do."

Elizabeth glanced at Katherine, and there was devilry in her look. "If you had planned on marrying *her* off, Hugh, that hour of need indeed may have stretched to a lifetime."

There was sudden silence at the table. Alonzo's eyes were fixed on Elizabeth's. Even Martha's face showed she knew Elizabeth had gone too far in front of company.

Reginald squirmed in his collar and tried to make a witty remark. "My word, a regular cat fight."

No one laughed. Elizabeth smiled blandly and reached for her glass.

And then Hugh's bovine face crinkled, and he gave a chuckle. "A lifetime." He chortled. "Maybe so. I get it. Very quick, Elizabeth. You mean it may indeed have been a lifetime before any man would marry her."

As he continued to laugh, the nervous flutters in Katherine's stomach shrank together and consolidated into a hard, determined ball. If they wanted a storm, a storm they would have. She set down her fork a little unsteadily. "We'd better be going, Alonzo, if we're to be on time for midnight mass."

"Mass!" Hugh's laugh ended in a violent cough. Martha put a hand on his arm, and he shook her off.

Alonzo rose smoothly, his face betraying nothing, and came to pull out Katherine's chair. "Thank you for a lovely dinner," he said to Martha. "It was very kind of you to include me."

"You are a *Catholic*, sir?" Hugh bellowed.

"He is Italian, after all, isn't he?" Reginald said. "What did you expect, Hugh? A Mohammedan?"

"Katherine, you bring a Papist into this house? To my table? Knowing full well what I think of them?" Hugh bellowed. "Martha, were you aware of this?"

"Well, yes, dear, but it's only dinner—"

"You allow her to have such friends?"

"He's not her friend," Martha blurted. As all eyes turned toward her, she realized she had come too far to turn back, and she saw an opportunity to get some of her own back. Flashing a glare at Katherine, she said, "He's her employer. She teaches his children. Our Katherine has no friends, at least certainly no male ones. No romantic interests."

Elizabeth snickered. "I should have known. I was awfully surprised when he came in. Far too good-looking to be interested in *her*."

Katherine was following Alonzo from the room, but now she stopped and turned back. Her face was impassive, her tone dead quiet and controlled as she said, "Are you so sure?"

"Pardon?" Elizabeth was taken aback.

The years of criticism and taunting came welling out of Katherine's memory to blind her. In her sudden fury, she spoke without caring or thinking. "Alonzo is far more to me than an employer. Since I've been living with him, he has been kinder to me than any of you have ever been. And . . . and he cares for me as much as I care for him!"

There was a moment of absolute stillness. Reginald was on his feet. Martha's mouth fell open. Judith Chisholm turned a speculative eye on Alonzo. Katherine suddenly realized how her words had sounded and how they could be misconstrued. She felt the bottom fall out of her stomach and thought she might be sick, but with effort, she kept her chin up defiantly. It was too late to claw the words back or qualify them.

"Well, well, our little Katherine is full of surprises," Elizabeth said, but her laugh was strained. "Do you expect us to believe this little fantasy? Anyone else, perhaps, but not you, Katherine."

"You, sir," Hugh barked, lurching to his feet. "Is this true? What are your intentions toward my ward?"

Katherine looked fearfully at Alonzo. His face had turned to chiseled stone. He leveled his gaze at Hugh. "She's of age. I don't see that it's any business of yours, sir," he said. And he took Katherine's arm and pulled her from the room.

Chapter Sixteen

THEY DROVE IN THUNDEROUS SILENCE. The children, still disoriented from being pulled from their play so abruptly, sensed the tension and were silent in the back of the wagon. It was too dark for Katherine to read Alonzo's expression. She wanted to crawl under a rock and die. What had possessed her? She gulped the cold night air until it hurt her lungs, and she vowed never to drink so much wine again. What must Alonzo think of her? She had never been so mortified. He would fire her, of course. What else could he do? She deserved it. But where would she go? She'd effectively burned the Fitzgeralds' bridge. She huddled in her misery.

"Well," Alonzo said at last. "Do you feel better?"

She looked up at the lightness in his voice.

"Have you accomplished what you meant to do?" he asked.

"I—Oh, I'm sorry! I didn't think before I spoke," Katherine cried in a rush. "It didn't come out right. I just looked at Elizabeth sitting there all smiling like a snake, and Hugh was laughing, and I just lost my mind. Elizabeth and Martha have always aggravated me, but it's never caused me to be so . . . so stupid."

"I was trying so hard to behave myself too." He chuckled.

She was dazed. "You're not angry with me?"

"Whatever for?"

"Because of what I said."

"You said I was kind to you. I thank you for thinking so."

"I practically said we live together," Katherine wailed.

"In a way, we do."

"I-I said we cared for each other!"

He shrugged. "And we do. Don't we? I consider you a friend. I would like to think you regard me as the same."

"But they'll draw the wrong conclusion entirely from the way I said it."

"Well, as for that, they are free to draw whatever conclusion they like. It wasn't meant as a lie."

"Then you aren't angry?"

"Why would I be? The question is why did you say it?"

She shook her head. "I don't know. It was all the arrogance, I suppose. The feeling that no one really cared what I did so long as I didn't humiliate *them*. Expecting me to hide what I do in order not to embarrass the family. Expecting me to be grateful for the assistance they've given so grudgingly. Treating me like family in front of other people but not in private."

"The comments about you having no romantic prospects?" he asked gently.

She nodded and felt the tears come to her eyes. Angrily she swiped them away. "It's true though. I shouldn't be upset when it's true. I've known for a long time that marriage wasn't likely to be in my future."

"What makes you think so?" he asked, looking astonished.

She looked away into the darkness, and after awhile he gave a quick nod. "If you don't want to discuss it, I will respect that. But please believe me when I say—let me think of the correct English words—I don't see any barrier to the possibility of marriage in your life."

"No, you wouldn't, would you? You don't see rules or barriers. You don't see the way society really is."

"And you don't see how *you* really are, Kate. Your cousin has put all kinds of doubts and criticisms in your mind. I can see that. But, Kate, they're unfounded."

Katherine swiped at her eyes again. "There you are, being kind again."

"It's the truth." He paused. "And you spoke the truth tonight too, Kate. I do care for you."

"Thank you. And I care for you. Sir," she added, beginning to smile.

"So have you sufficiently embarrassed your family now?" He was clearly amused.

Katherine gazed up at the stars, frozen still in the cold sky. "Yes, I think so," she said.

"No regrets, then," Alonzo said firmly.

"But I am sorry about how Hugh reacted to your being Catholic. I don't know why he gets like that. I think his father or someone was killed in Ireland . . ."

"Don't worry about it. You're sorry for too many things."

"Am I? I'm sorry."

He chuckled low in his throat and put his arm comfortably about her shoulders. "Stop talking, Kate. Look at the sky."

So she sat looking up at the stars and listening to the horse's hooves on the frozen road.

* * *

They attended midnight mass after all, at St. Michael's Cathedral. It was a new experience for her, and she wasn't sure what to do. There was a lot of standing and kneeling, which was difficult as each was holding a sleeping child. A new organ had been recently installed, manufactured by Warren and Son, and the music it poured from its multiple throats was heart shaking. She had never heard such a sound in all her life. She thought the cathedral itself spectacular, like a gigantic jewel box. Archbishop Lynch officiated, and the flow of his words, the smell of incense thick in the air, the hush of hundreds of bodies around her, the exultation of the hymns—Katherine soaked all of it in, her heart pounding with awe and delight. Beside her, Alonzo's voice on the responses was a fervent baritone. When it was over, Katherine could hardly believe how fast it had gone. They made their way out through the crowd, the smell of candles and incense following them.

Alonzo made a bed in the back of the wagon for the children, tucked the blankets over them, and helped Katherine onto the seat. They clopped slowly through the nearly deserted streets and away from the city. It had grown bitterly cold, frost already forming, and the sky was black and shining like candlelight reflecting from an inverted onyx bowl. Katherine felt immensely content.

"I'm glad you enjoyed it," Alonzo said, seeing her expression as they passed under a street lamp.

"The music was overwhelming," she said. "And the choir was heavenly."

"I used to sing in a choir," he murmured, shaking his head. "Imagine it. I wasn't a bad soprano when I was nine. But one day I was asked not to come back after I put a frog in the font."

"I'm not surprised." Katherine chuckled. "Thank you for bringing me. I never knew what beauty I was missing."

"We'll make it an annual event," he replied.

Katherine sobered. This time next year, where would she be? Would she still be with the Colacos? Would she have found a different position? The questions made her uncomfortable.

They arrived home at four o'clock in the morning. They carried the children into the train car, and Katherine made tea while Alonzo took care of Bacchus. When he came inside, they sat at the table in the lamp's glow.

"I'm sorry you didn't get to spend the holiday properly with your family in their beautiful house," Alonzo said thoughtfully. "But merry Christmas anyway."

"To you too," she said. "But you know, gold-plated flatware or no, I'd rather be here than there anyway."

He smiled. "Thank you."

"Do you have any family? Brothers or sisters?"

"Three brothers, all in Italy. My parents died years ago."

"Are you the oldest?"

"Youngest."

"Why did you come to Canada? You must have been brave to come on your own."

He shrugged. "A new place. New sights, new opportunities. Room to stretch my wings. Like you, I wanted to prove myself. And I would say Canada has been good to me."

She glanced around the snug train car. It wasn't her idea of elegant, but it did have a certain cozy charm. What had he once said? Better a crust eaten in peace than a feast taken in bitterness. "I would say so too," she said.

"What's this?" He had noticed the three small parcels on the table that she'd left there that afternoon—just as she'd unceremoniously left, in her retreat, her family's gifts on the Fitzgeralds' hall table for them to find.

"Just a small something," she said. "To wish you a merry Christmas."

"May I open mine now? It's nearly morning."

She laughed. "You're like a little boy. Yes, you may."

He removed the wrapping and examined the gloves in silence a moment, then slipped them on his hands. "They're perfect. It's very nice leather. I shall certainly put them to good use." He removed them and reached over to lightly touch her arm. "It was very thoughtful of you. Thank you."

"You're welcome." She felt ridiculously pleased.

He jumped up from the table, went to the trunk under Lilia's cot, and rustled around a moment, coming back with a small, red-wrapped package.

"You may open yours now too," he said.

"Oh, that wasn't necessary, Alonzo," she said, standing to take it from him. She unwrapped the package and stood staring at a pair of soft white leather gloves just her size.

"Great minds think alike," Alonzo murmured.

Katherine put a hand to her throat, trying not to wake the children, but the silliness of it was too much for her. Tears in her eyes, she looked up at Alonzo, about to laugh at the coincidence, and then the sound caught in her throat as his mouth came down on hers.

Her first impulse was to pull away, but his hand held the back of her head. She stood stiffly, her thoughts completely blank in her astonishment and confusion. His face was still cold from the outdoors, and a trace of incense was caught in his clothes. She didn't know what to do. So she stood.

When he released her, she found she couldn't look him in the face. She turned away and fumbled with the gloves still clutched in her hand. She bent to retrieve the wrapping paper from the floor. She cleared the cups from the table. When Alonzo still hadn't moved or spoken, she finally ventured a look at him. He stood looking down at the table, his face expressionless, his eyes half closed. His hands were on his hips. Suddenly she didn't want him to speak, to say anything, whether to justify or apologize.

In a sort of panic, Katherine picked up her coat and went out of the train car. Sitting in the lavatory, shivering in the cold, she put her head in her hands and tried to form coherent thoughts. She couldn't understand why he had done it. It had to be the coincidence of their gifts, the stupid things she'd said tonight. It hadn't meant anything. He had looked angry, staring down at the table. The kiss had shattered the easy camaraderie of the evening. Had he expected something more of her? Did he still? Was he waiting in the train car for her at this moment with . . . more in mind? His words that evening came back to her. "I do care for you . . ."

Her stomach lurched, and she wished she were more sophisticated, like Elizabeth. Elizabeth would know what to do. She wouldn't be awkward and tongue-tied. She would have laughed the kiss off, made some offhanded remark about missing mistletoe. She certainly wouldn't have fled to the freezing lavatory.

"I can't very well sit here all night," she said aloud. Angry now, disappointed that the evening had gone awry, and fearful of what she would find waiting for her, she marched herself back to the train car.

Alonzo sat outside on the steps, his collar turned up and his hands jammed into his coat pockets. A lamp burned at his feet on the lowest step. Katherine slowed and drew to a stop a few feet away.

"I've stoked the stove. It should last until morning."

"It *is* morning," she replied.

He looked up at her then, and the lamplight cast his features into relief. "I'm sorry," he said abruptly.

"No need," she said, trying to sound casual. "It's all right."

"Not for the kiss. I meant it," he said softly. "I'm just sorry if it upset you. I didn't intend it to."

Katherine shook her head. "No. Just . . . startled me, is all."

"Give me your hand."

She hesitated, then reached out, and his fingers wrapped warmly around hers. They held hands over the space between them.

"You know I would never press my advantage. I would never harm you, Kate."

"Of course. I know that."

"Good night, Kate."

"Good night, Alonzo."

He released her hand, took the lamp, and strode to the tent he had pitched where the train car would block the wind. She watched him enter it, and the lamplight glowed through the white canvas. She could see his shadow, large against the side of the tent as he moved around. She turned and went into the train car, undressed quickly, and slid into bed.

Exhausted as she was, she didn't fall asleep until the sunrise was pearling through the window.

* * *

She awoke to the wonderful smell of sausages frying and full daylight streaming in. Lilia stirred and burrowed farther into her blankets, and Tony gave a grumpy murmur and turned over in his bunk.

Alonzo waved a spatula at the stove. "Merry Christmas!" he called. He wore his scarlet shirt, and he looked as fresh as if he'd slept a full night.

At his greeting, Lilia's eyes popped open, and she scrambled out of bed to wake her brother. "Tony! *É Natale!*"

The children tumbled across the floor to where bulging stockings hung beside the door. Sitting up, Katherine wondered when Alonzo had hung them.

"*Buon Natale*, Papa," Lilia called. "But why are there three stockings?"

"Because you aren't the only person in the house," Alonzo replied cheerfully. "Greedy child. The third one is for Kate."

Katherine pulled the quilt up to her chin and pinned it with her arms. "Me?" she laughed. "I haven't hung a stocking since I was seven."

"It's for you," Tony said, bringing it to her. "See what's inside."

So she put her hand in and pulled out the gifts, tumbling them onto the bedspread. There was an orange, a selection of hard candies, lavender sachets, a satin pin cushion, and, in the toe of the stocking, a small green box containing a silver stickpin. Its top was shaped like a rose with a drop of red glass embedded in its center.

She looked up to see Alonzo watching her carefully.

"You shouldn't have. I mean, thank you. But you didn't need to."

"Everyone must have a stocking Christmas morning. Look, St. Nick even left me a new razor and strap."

"That was very nice of him, Papa. But why doesn't he ever use a razor himself?" Lilia asked.

"A good question. Next time I see him I shall ask him."

"Do you think Huang Fu has a Christmas stocking too, Papa?"

Katherine looked up. The children had not mentioned their friend often, and she'd thought they were beginning to forget him. Now she could see she was wrong.

"Perhaps," Alonzo said gently. "When the weather is good we'll go to Toronto to see him, and you can ask him yourself. Would you like that?"

"Yes, please!"

Lilia had unwrapped her doll, placed beside her stocking, and now came running to show it to Katherine. They spent a luxurious morning drawing with Tony's new pencils, reading the new English storybooks St. Nicholas had brought, and eating sausages, fried potatoes, and sticky buns. Katherine taught the children a Christmas song about a donkey, which they performed for Alonzo, who had waited outside in the cold while they rehearsed. Katherine made paper puppets for them to reenact the Nativity play. Lilia was especially fascinated by the story but insisted on placing the paper infant Jesus in the inn and not the stable contrived from a box and decorated with bits of actual hay.

"Not with the animals," she protested when Tony tried to correct her. "It isn't clean. Do you think Papa would let them put Michael in a dirty pile of hay? Of course not. Joseph got him into the inn. You watch."

At the mention of Michael, Katherine glanced at Alonzo, but he was sharpening Tony's pencils with a penknife and did not look up.

That afternoon, while the children were out playing in the snow with Bo, Katherine decided to broach the subject. "Lilia keeps mentioning Michael. Who is he?"

Alonzo was clearing away bits of paper from the table. He swept them into a pile in his hand and dumped them in the stove before answering shortly, "He's her brother."

"Where is he?" she asked, wondering if she were treading on forbidden ground. But his face remained impassive as he replied, "In Collingwood. I left him with John and Lucy O'Riley in Collingwood until we go back."

Katherine slipped the scissors they had used into her sewing basket. A fragment of wicker had worked loose, and she fiddled with it. "Why isn't he here with you?"

"It's difficult enough to travel with two children. A baby would be impossible."

She glanced at him. "I imagine you must miss him very much."

Alonzo's hands grew still, and he stood looking down at them. Quietly he said, "Ruth died a week after giving birth to him. Septicemia."

"Oh." Katherine felt her face go hot. "I didn't know. I suppose it's natural to . . . to resent him somewhat."

He turned to face her, his eyebrows knitted in puzzlement. "I miss him deeply. He was the last thing Ruth gave to me, the last bit of her to remain. To leave him behind was to lose her all over again."

Katherine started to put a hand on his arm, then stopped herself, suddenly reluctant to touch him. "Why don't you go back? Now, I mean, and not wait until spring?"

He looked away and shook his head. "Not yet," he said. "Spring is soon enough. I'll be ready in the spring."

Chapter Seventeen

THE NEXT FEW DAYS IT snowed heavily, but the train car was bright and warm, and there was plenty of food. Alonzo finished building the back of the wagon just in time and fitted it with a straw-filled mattress and piles of quilts. He asserted it was warmer now that he was up off the ground, the snow providing a layer of insulation on the top of the new cart, and that the next time he had the chance to go to town he would get a small woodstove for the back.

"I'll be downright toasty, no matter the weather," he declared.

"You didn't paint it blue," Lilia pointed out.

"I will in the spring, I promise," he assured her. "If I tried now, the paint would freeze."

The children had their lessons in the morning, but each afternoon Katherine bundled them up warmly and took them outside for fresh air and exercise. They were particularly fond of Fox and Geese, and Katherine stamped out a trail for them in the snow behind the train car. They were playing this the day before the new year, and Katherine was the fox, running after Tony and laughing. The children were spattered with mud, and Katherine's hair was straggling from her bonnet, her skirt soaked, when she looked up and saw Alonzo coming toward them across the snow. His face looked grim.

Breathless, Katherine pulled herself up and turned to face him. "You're back from town early. Is something wrong?"

He stopped a few feet from her, frowning, and she felt her stomach tighten with sudden worry. Was it the frightfully dirty state she had allowed his children to get into that had upset him? Was something wrong with the horse?

Before she could ask any questions, he suddenly bent down, scooped up an armful of snow, and, with a shout, showered her head with it. Squealing, she ducked away, but to her astonishment, he joined in the game. He was an aggressive fox, dashing around the track and sweeping up his scrambling children, throwing them over his shoulder with a roar and making off with them. The children were delighted, screaming as he caught them, triumphant when they caught him. He never managed to catch Katherine, however, though twice she was forced to pick up her skirts and sprint to avoid him.

At last, when they were soaked through and the track was reduced to slush, Katherine observed the children's red cheeks and announced it was time for them to go inside. They protested, too excited to give up their game, but Katherine held up a hand.

"Run and change into dry clothes," she directed, "and I'll make hot chocolate."

Tony and Lilia scampered for the train car, their woolen knit caps bobbing in unison, but Katherine and Alonzo followed more sedately.

Alonzo was breathing hard, and his eyes shone. "I'm getting too old for this," he remarked as they tramped slowly through the snow toward home.

"You run like a young man of twenty," Katherine said charitably. In spite of her damp condition, she was hot from exertion. She loosened her bonnet and took it off, shaking her head to free her hair, which had abandoned its bun. The cool air brushed through it deliciously, spreading it into a dark shawl on her shoulders. The snow was dove-gray in the growing dusk. It lay like icing along the tree branches and was piled in deep, smooth drifts where the wind had sculpted it. She felt incredibly happy.

As they approached the train car, Katherine stopped before a particularly inviting drift, eyeing it, and then, without further thought, she turned around and fell backward into it. Giggling, she moved her arms and legs to make a snow angel. "I haven't done this in years," she said cheerfully, eyes closed against the white-pink sky. When Alonzo didn't reply, she looked up and found him watching her with an amused smile.

"What?" she asked as primly as she could from her ridiculous position.

In reply, Alonzo turned around and fell with a *whump* beside her. Lying peacefully in the snow, he made his own angel.

"Far too long," he murmured pleasantly. He climbed carefully to his feet, then reached for Katherine's hand to help her stand. They stood looking down at the angels with satisfaction.

"Those turned out well," Katherine said.

"They look good side by side," he agreed.

Something in his voice made her look up at him. Alonzo still held her gloved hand. He gave it a small tug and turned her to face him.

"You have been an angel to me and my children," he said quietly. "You gave us a chance when no one else would have."

"I could say the same to you," Katherine said, embarrassed.

"I am grateful every day to have you here." He looked down at his glove holding hers, and a smile quirked his lips.

Katherine felt a warm rush in her cheeks and wondered if the sight of the gloves reminded him, as it did her, of his kiss on Christmas Eve. When his eyes met hers, she was sure of it. She opened her mouth to speak, not even knowing what she was going to say but wanting to break the sudden silence.

He spoke first. "I caught you off guard before. This time I'm giving you fair warning. A . . . what do you say? . . . a shot across the bow. I want to kiss you again." And he did so, tenderly, almost cautiously, as if expecting her to fly away.

But somewhat to her surprise, Katherine didn't fly away. Instead, she found herself responding, drawing closer to him. His skin was cold, but his mouth was warm, an intriguing combination, and she quickly became oblivious to all else. How long they stood together, she didn't know, but when he finally pulled away, she felt a strange loss. Dazed, she looked up at him. He returned her gaze with a kind of wonder.

"I had no idea . . ." he murmured.

Instantly Katherine was appalled at herself. Too much had been revealed in that kiss, leaving her feeling shaky and exposed. This was her *employer*. This was her friend. And she was suddenly frightened of anything happening to that friendship. It had come to mean much more to her than she had realized. She found her voice at last. "That . . . that shouldn't have happened."

"It's all right, Kate."

"No, it isn't," she said briskly.

His face was troubled. "But I really think—"

"It wasn't appropriate. I work for you, Alonzo."

He remained standing in the snow, staring at her bleakly.

"Are you afraid of me, Kate?" His voice was quiet.

Her lips began to tremble, and she bit them together, knowing it gave her a ferocity she didn't intend. "No," she said flatly. "I'm afraid of myself." She went into the train car and closed the door.

* * *

Alonzo didn't come inside for another hour, and Katherine wondered what he had been doing all that time. When at last he came inside, he was white with cold, and his damp clothes were coated with a thin film of ice. He entered the train car in time for supper, which he ate in silence, keeping his eyes averted. The children sensed something was wrong and were silent. Katherine found the quiet stifling after the noisy joy of the afternoon, and the children's solemnity was unnerving.

After dinner, she bundled the children in their coats and sent them with a pail to the river to get water for washing the dishes. There was water in the barrel behind the train car, but she wanted a moment to speak with Alonzo alone.

"Kate, about—"

"Please," she said firmly, cutting him off as soon as the children were out of earshot. "Let me speak first. I need to be very clear. There is to be no repetition of what happened. I speak to myself as much as to you."

Alonzo reached out and caught her hand. "I didn't plan for it to go quite the way it did, Kate, I promise you. It was just the day, and you beside me, and I was happy. I meant it to just be—Well, it got away from me."

She pulled her hand free. "I wasn't exactly beating you off, was I?" she muttered.

He reflected a moment, then smiled. "No, you weren't, as I recall."

"We're both to blame. But we both need to watch ourselves in the future. We're much too alone out here, and the children really don't count as proper chaperones."

"Yes, Kate," he said, but she suspected he wasn't as meek as he sounded.

* * *

Katherine awoke with the windows dark and a steady wind howling around the corner of the train car. Lilia was sprawled in her bed, her arms flung above her head in sleep, and Katherine could hear Tony's heavy breathing. She wondered what had awakened her and was turning over to go back to sleep when she saw a dim light out the window. Katherine rose and looked outside.

A hurricane lamp burned across the clearing, and in its faint light, she could see Alonzo bent against the wind. A tent stake had come loose from Bacchus's windbreak, and one side of the canvas was flapping wildly while

Alonzo struggled to capture it. Each time he seemed to master it and reached for his hammer, the wind would catch at the canvas and rip it from his grasp. Bo bounced around him unhelpfully and barked once sharply. The horse tossed its head and pranced nervously with each flap of the canvas, refusing to come near it. As Katherine watched, great drops of sleet hit the window pane with a noise like thrown gravel.

She pulled on her robe, stuffed her feet into her shoes without stockings, and let herself outside, barely catching the door before the wind could fling it wide. The wind took her breath away, instantly chilling her to the core. She trudged head down across the drifted snow and caught up the hammer where Alonzo had flung it. As he forced the tent side down again, he reached for the stake and caught sight of Katherine behind him.

"You hold it. I'll pound," she called above the roar of the wind in the trees.

He used his weight to hold the tent flap down, and Katherine thrust the stake into the metal eyelet and hammered it into the hard ground. When she had secured it most of the way, Alonzo took the hammer from her and finished pounding the stake in. Katherine wiped the sleet from her face and called to the dog, who seemed to find all this nocturnal human activity exciting. Alonzo went to catch Bacchus and soothe him with a caress and, after a while, managed to coax the horse back into his shelter. The horse shook his mane and stamped uneasily but remained inside.

"To the house, Bo!" Alonzo ordered sternly, and the dog obeyed. Alonzo grasped Katherine's elbow and escorted her back to the train car. But when he paused on the steps, she gripped his hand and pulled him inside after her. Together they pushed the door closed against the wind and bolted it so it wouldn't spring open again, the task made all the more difficult by Bo wriggling and entwining himself damply around their knees.

They both leaned against the door, breathing hard and wiping melting sleet from their hair and shoulders. Katherine lit a lamp and set it on the table. Bo stood wagging his tail furiously with a big grin on his face, then shook to spray droplets of water all over the train car. Alonzo began to laugh.

"Hush, you'll wake the children!" Katherine scolded, but she was smiling too.

"I forgot my hurricane lantern outside," Alonzo said.

"It will be all right where it is," she told him. She pushed her unbound hair out of her face and turned to the kettle on the stove. "Let me get you something warm to drink. You're soaked and must be frozen."

"Not soaked, only damp," Alonzo said cheerfully, but he sat at the table and watched as she fetched mugs and made tea. The sleet peppered the window, and he glanced at it warily. "Thank you for letting me in," he said in a low voice.

"It's nearly morning anyway."

"A lovely way to ring in the new year," Alonzo said, and Katherine stopped to blink at him.

"So it is! I'd lost count of the days. Happy 1881." Katherine sat at the table opposite him and cupped her cold hands around her mug. She knew that a few short hours ago her cousin's parlor had been crowded with guests, all poised with champagne glasses raised toward the Seth Thomas clock, waiting for its chime. She felt oddly distant, as far removed from the festive scene as if she were in Egypt. She could picture Martha in her party gown, Hugh smiling self-importantly, and she was glad she had been spared the ordeal.

She looked up from her reverie to see Alonzo smiling at her. He lifted his mug and clinked it gently against hers.

"To the new year and what it may bring," she said.

"To the old year and what it has brought," he added.

Katherine sipped her tea and tried to look out the window at the clouds scudding across the moon, but she saw only her own face reflected in the window, the golden glow of the lamp behind her. It made her look as if she had a halo, she thought, and then that reminded her of angels and Alonzo's comment . . . and the kiss. Had that been only a few hours ago? The blood rose in her cheeks. It felt as if it had happened only moments ago.

Alonzo was silent, savoring his tea. He sat close enough that she could feel his warmth radiating against her arm. If she moved a mere inch, she would touch him. She curled her fingers more tightly around her mug. Bo, disgruntled that the adventure was over, settled on the floor beneath the table with a sigh. Alonzo glanced down at him, and Katherine found herself looking at her employer's lashes, long and dark against his bronze cheeks.

"It's no good, is it?" she said quietly.

Alonzo turned his head to look at her.

"Under the circumstances, I don't think our present living arrangements are going to work."

"What do you mean?" he asked.

"If I stay . . ."

He tensed. "If?"

"If I stay," she repeated, "it will just happen again, won't it?"

He was quiet a moment and then said, "I can't in all honesty say that it won't. I confess I would like it to."

"That's the problem," Katherine said, refusing to admit that she wanted it to happen again too. "I think I need to go. I've been here too long." Her voice sounded hollow to her ears.

"Kate, listen." He set down his mug and reached across the small table to take her shoulders in his hands. "I realize what happened may not have been proper according to social rules, but I've never been one to worry about rules."

"Fancy that," she replied, trying to smile.

"Even I realize an employer shouldn't kiss his employee under normal circumstances. But you know as well as I do that it was *right*. I haven't felt so right since Ruth died."

"Please don't say that," Katherine pleaded, trying to rise, but he held her firmly.

"I know you felt it just as I did, Kate. The moment I touched you I knew. We're right for each other. The children could see it ages ago."

She shook her head. "I won't deny I feel a certain attraction to you. But . . ." She stopped in confusion.

He tipped his head, his eyes piercing hers. "But what?"

"It can't happen."

"Why not?"

"It just can't."

"I want you with me always, Kate."

When she didn't answer, he straightened. "Why do you hesitate? You said it to your family yourself; I mean more to you than just an employer."

"But I don't know if what I feel is enough."

"You mean you don't know if it's love?"

She spread her hands. "I don't really have experience with these things, Alonzo. I don't know how to answer you. I know I . . . I do care for you a great deal."

"Again with the caring!" His voice rose with frustration.

"But try to understand; I've seen so little of life. I had plans for my life, dreams . . . And they may not happen, I doubt they will, but . . .

but I'm not sure I'm ready to let go of them completely yet. I may not be as resigned as I thought . . ."

He sat back as if she had struck him. "Resigned!"

"Oh, that isn't what I mean, and you know it! Now I've offended you," she said.

He drew a deep breath and studied her a moment, thoughtfully. "Is it because I'm a tinker? Do you think less of me because I don't surround myself with all the fancy things you think are important?"

"No, no," she said automatically, but her voice sounded hollow to her ears once again. She struggled to express herself. "I just—It isn't what I had planned for my life. Try to understand. Our worlds are so far apart."

"Not so very far apart," Alonzo said, frowning. "Perhaps at one time that was true, but you've come down in the world since your youth, haven't you? Oh, and now *I've* offended *you.*"

Katherine fumbled for a handkerchief, couldn't find one, and wiped her nose on her sleeve, trying to force back the threatening tears.

"Look," Alonzo said more quietly, covering her hands with his on the table. "All right, there are gaps between us that society thinks are important. I acknowledge that. But we've been doing all right so far bridging them, haven't we? I may not live with all the trappings other men do, but my life reflects what's important to me. And now you need to decide what's important to you. What do you really want, Kate? A life with me, as I am . . . or the chance to have a life of . . . of gold-plated flatware and doilies on the tables and shiny, beautiful clothes . . ."

"You're making fun of my dreams."

"I'm not."

"You make it all sound shallow."

"I don't mean to. If those things are important to you, that's how it is. I'm only asking you to look into your heart and be honest about what really *is* important to you."

Katherine felt the tears begin to course down her cheeks. "I don't know. I used to think I knew."

There was a pause.

"Then," he said softly, "you must figure that out."

"But I can't think clearly when I'm so close to you," Katherine exclaimed. "I think I have myself all sorted out, and then you come along, and I'm all in turmoil again. I need to go away for a little while to think."

He raised his hand and traced her cheek with one finger. "I'm afraid if you go, you won't come back."

She couldn't reply, for she knew it was a possibility.

He studied her a moment and then nodded. "I can see you're right. Whatever decision you make must be made with a clear head. You must be sure of your heart. Sure about me. Perhaps I should take you to stay with your family for a while."

"No," she said. "I couldn't possibly think rationally there. I wouldn't be welcome now anyway. I'll find another position somewhere . . . for a while." She rose and reached for their mugs, but he stood and stopped her with a hand on her arm.

"I love you, Kate, more than life. I want to be your husband. Let your decision be based on that knowledge." He clicked his tongue to call Bo, and they went out the door, closing it with a bang against the wind.

Shaken, Katherine bolted the door against the storm, doused the lamp, removed her damp robe and shoes, and slipped back into bed. But she lay awake a long time, gazing toward the window and the icy night beyond. He wanted to marry her. He loved her. She felt empty at the thought of leaving him and the children. So what was stopping her from accepting his offer?

Say it, Katherine, she hissed at herself. *It's not about gold-plated flatware. It's about deciding if you want to be a tinker's wife. Live a tinker's life. Have constables mistake you for a gypsy and have to haul water from the river to wash your frying pan. It's about deciding what's more important to you—your pride, your comfort, what people think . . . or Alonzo.*

She turned over in bed and punched her pillow into softer submission. No matter the turmoil in her heart, of one thing she was certain: if she saw marriage to him as a humiliation, an embarrassment, if she couldn't unreservedly say *he* was her dream, it wasn't fair to him.

He deserves better than that, she thought. *He deserves a wife who will love him as he is, unconditionally.*

She didn't know if she was that person.

For so many years, she'd thought to find happiness in material things, in status and social position. She'd longed to fit in the realm in which her cousins moved. Her only goal—vague as it was—had been to reach that realm somehow, prove she was as good as anyone, and flaunt her success in Hugh's and Martha's faces. Put so baldly now, it sounded awfully petty.

Alonzo had begun to show her how happy life could be without all those things. But could she give up a lifetime of dreams, those desires, forever, and close that door once and for all?

In exchange for what? she asked herself. A cramped train car. The disdain of cab drivers. A life of stoking a fire and washing her own clothes. Being ashamed to have Alonzo drive her down the street.

Tony. Lilia.

Don't forget Michael.

Alonzo.

Did she look down on him for the life he lived? She was afraid of the answer, for it held her character. And her future.

Chapter Eighteen

THEY DIDN'T SPEAK ABOUT THEIR conversation again but were studiously polite and careful around each other. Katherine hated the tension that had arisen between them, but she didn't know what else she could do about it.

Alonzo drove her to Toronto the following Monday, and she applied to an employment agency as a lady's companion. She told the elderly woman who took her application the complete truth about her past employment, even about Miss Alice's fall from the hayloft and her current, unusual position. For her reason for leaving, however, she said only that the position was obviously not what had been advertised and she'd given Mr. Colaco all the time she cared to. The woman took this information with clucks and exclamations.

"My poor girl, how shockingly terrible for you. We'll find you something nice, shall we? In fact, I think I have the perfect position for you. They're in rather a hurry to find someone and will be willing to overlook . . . er . . . any oddities in your employment history. If I recommend you, they will hire you."

"What position is it?" Katherine asked with trepidation.

"Lady's companion to Mrs. Millicent Pendover in Chatham Square. I'm sure it's just the position for you. Mrs. Pendover is an aged lady, and her body has caused her much trouble of late. She's confined to a wheelchair and must have assistance dressing, eating, and writing—that sort of thing. But her mind is sharp as a knife, and she specifically requested 'an educated girl who could carry on intelligent conversation.' Those are just the words she used. The Pendovers are a longtime Toronto family of good background. Mrs. Pendover is an entertaining woman, and I suspect your adventures will provoke more mirth than alarm. Shall I arrange an interview?"

"Yes, please, this afternoon if possible," Katherine said before she could hesitate. "Thank you, it sounds just the thing."

As it happened, the lady was available that afternoon. Katherine asked Alonzo to take her to the appointment without letting herself hesitate or debate, and he drove her without speaking.

"I don't know how long I'll be," she said as she climbed from the cart.

"It doesn't matter. We'll wait."

"May we go see Huang Fu?" Lilia said. "While we're waiting for Kate?"

"Not today, *cara mia*," Alonzo said. "He's a bit far from here. But if you're very good, I'll take you for hot chocolate while we're waiting."

* * *

Mrs. Pendover lived in a massive but beautiful house at the squared-off end of a wide, treed street in the center of Toronto, not far from Yonge Street. A very proper housekeeper ushered Katherine into the parlor, which was gaily decorated in a rather flamboyant floral pattern. An armful of evergreen boughs sprouted from a china vase on the mantel, and there was a distant scent of hothouse roses. The windows overlooked the garden, where the sun glittered on fresh snow, and there was an ornate red bird feeder nailed to a tree. Katherine felt immediately cheered. Surely anyone who set out such lovely bird feeders would be a kind sort of person.

Millicent Pendover proved to be not only kind but lively. Though she was restricted in body, her mind was keen and alert, and her speech was punctuated with delighted laughter. She looked about ninety and sat in a high-backed wheelchair with a pink shawl over her sticklike legs. Her brilliant white hair was pulled into a bun, and her blue eyes were crinkled with smile lines. Katherine warmed to her instantly and answered all the woman's questions honestly, hiding nothing but the recent transpirings between herself and Alonzo. She even told her about being mistaken for a gypsy and having to bathe in the brook.

"You can see it simply isn't an acceptable arrangement," she concluded.

Mrs. Pendover tilted her head and lifted a gnarled finger. "You say it wasn't an acceptable position, and yet you stayed there all autumn."

"Yes. I told Mr. Colaco I would stay until I found something else."

"I suspect you haven't looked very hard."

Katherine hesitated, then smiled. "Perhaps not."

"Hmm. Well, I do not approve of the situation at all, but all the more reason to extract you from it. You show good sense, child. Very well. If you're amenable, I'll hire you on."

"Thank you, Mrs. Pendover. I'm very amenable to it."

"Call me Millie," the old woman said with a display of still-healthy teeth.

"And you may call me Kate," Katherine replied.

"How soon can you start?"

"Immediately, if you like," she replied. "I brought my things in case . . ."

"How very efficient. Bring them in, my dear."

Alonzo and the children had returned from getting their hot chocolate and were waiting at the curb across from the house. The children did not take the news well that Katherine wouldn't be returning home with them.

"Why are you going away?" Lilia wailed. "You can't go."

"I must," Katherine said, trying to sound firm and confident. "The woman in this house is very elderly and frail. She needs my help. I'm going to live here and help her."

"But *we* need you. We had you first!" Tony pouted.

"Don't you like us, Kate?" Tears welled up in the little girl's eyes.

Katherine swallowed against the tightness in her throat. "Of course I do," she murmured, smoothing Lilia's hair. "I'll always love you, and Tony too. But you have your father to look after you. This woman has no one. You've always known I can't stay with you forever."

"Why not?" Tony pouted.

Katherine drew them close and kissed each one on the forehead, but she didn't trust herself to speak further. She had no answer for them anyway. She stood beside her trunk where Alonzo had placed it on the road. Alonzo waited, arms folded, leaning against the wagon's side. His lips were set in a pout so like Tony's that she nearly laughed, but the sound caught in her throat and died immediately.

"Well," she said awkwardly.

"Yes," he said, nodding.

The children, however, were not going to let her go so easily. They scrambled from the back of the wagon and launched themselves at her. Lilia sobbed openly, and Tony wrapped his arms around her legs and refused vehemently in three languages to let go.

"I'll visit you," Katherine promised, her voice straining to get past the tightness in her throat. "I'm not going away entirely. Of course you'll still see me again sometime. Just not every day."

"Who will be my teacher now?" Lilia protested.

"I will be." Alonzo had watched the scene in stiff silence, but now he stepped forward and picked his daughter up as if she were an infant. "I'll teach you. And soon, in the spring, we'll go back to Collingwood, and you can tell Mrs. O'Riley of all your adventures. You'll like that."

"I want to stay here with Kate," Lilia cried, her chin jutting out in defiance.

Alonzo stopped trying to console and convince. The noise was beginning to attract attention on the street. He deposited Lilia back in the wagon, pried Tony loose, and dropped him beside his sister. The children knelt, clinging to the tailgate and scowling.

Katherine didn't know what to do. She was near tears herself, but she knew if she gave way to them it would only set the children to howling again. She drew a deep breath and held out her hand to Alonzo.

"I'll visit later, when I'm settled," she told him. "I'll let you know one way or the other."

He ignored her hand. He stood looking down at her, the muscles in his jaw working, his eyes searching hers. Then he bent and kissed her. His touch was brief and gentle, but it seared her lips. "I know already," he said quietly. He climbed up behind the horse, and they were gone, moving swiftly and with a great deal of noise down the road.

If Mrs. Pendover noticed Katherine's red-rimmed eyes, she didn't comment on them.

* * *

Katherine threw herself into her new position, believing—hoping—that the way to subdue the turmoil in her mind was to smother it with work.

She found Millie Pendover undemanding but still requiring a lot of care. Between clothing, bathing, and feeding her, reading to her, and taking down letters by dictation, there wasn't a lot of time for brooding. At first she found it awkward to handle someone else's body and help with such intimate activities, but Millie had both patience and a sense of humor. She wasn't at all inhibited about instructing her in what needed to be done, and Katherine learned quickly. As the first week drew to a close, she grew more comfortable with her new, rather tiring routine. But it *was* too bad she had to resume the regular wearing of a bustle.

She was somewhat amused and more than a little dismayed to find that she had also lost the knack of living in a proper house. The big dining room seemed impossibly far from the kitchen; she was used to being able to reach the tea kettle on the stove without having to rise from the table. She would turn a corner in the hallway and come across a servant unexpectedly and be so startled she'd jump; she'd forgotten how to live with workers who moved in quiet efficiency in the background. Her bed seemed extravagantly wide and overburdened with quilts. She surprised herself by missing the smoky aroma of the campfire and sometimes fancied she could smell it. She even had to reacclimate herself to using a proper lavatory.

But she tried her best not to think of the children or Alonzo at all. Separation from them was even more painful than she'd anticipated, and she tried to keep it buried under the busyness of day-to-day life.

Millie kept an open door. There were endless streams of guests for dinner, and it seemed every woman in Chatham Square came to tea in the course of the week. Katherine was expected to attend these functions, for Millie unabashedly needed her assistance grasping the utensils and cutting her food. Katherine was also expected to take part in the conversation as if she were a guest, and she thought she did a fair job upholding her end of the discussions. The conversations held no satisfaction for her though. She wasn't familiar with the names being gossiped about, and the conversation often revolved around events and places she had no experience with. She reminded herself that her longings as she'd sat in the tea shop so many months ago were finally being fulfilled; she lived in a lovely place and was included in social circles with beautiful, interesting people—and she found it all rather overwhelming.

On her first Sunday, Katherine accompanied Millie to church. The elderly woman informed Katherine proudly that she had not missed a Sunday in fifteen years. Dressed in formidable lavender, with a garish hat trimmed with real sparrows perched on her white head like a nest atop a flagpole, she sat like Queen Victoria herself while Bob, the middle-aged stable hand and driver, manhandled her wheelchair up the removable ramp into the carriage and strapped it in place. The carriage had been modified to allow for Millie's wheelchair, with half of the seat removed and half remaining for Katherine to sit on. Once at the church, Bob had to roll her out again, but he remained with the carriage and didn't accompany the women inside.

"Bob doesn't care for preaching," Millie informed Katherine with a disapproving sniff. "If he prefers to stand outside rather than come in, it's his own fault if he gets cold."

"Yes, ma'am," Bob said cheerfully. "But you're always telling me if I don't go to church, I'll end up someplace very warm anyway, so I'm not too concerned about a little cold now."

Katherine's jaw dropped at his bold response, but Millie chortled with laughter as Katherine rolled her chair away.

Several people stopped to exchange pleasantries on their way to their pews. Katherine got the impression that everyone in Toronto must know Millicent Pendover. What was more, everyone who knew her sincerely liked her. Millie's genuine interest in the lives of those around her combined with her engaging humor made it impossible not to. She instructed Katherine where to park her chair, and then Katherine helped her into a pew and took a seat beside her, next to the aisle.

As the minister stood to begin the service, the door opened, and a young man in a flapping dark coat came striding swiftly down the aisle. Katherine craned to see who had caused the disturbance. To her astonishment, he stopped at their pew, pushed her lightly on the shoulder, and hissed, "Scoot over, please!"

Katherine slid closer to Millie, and the young man dropped onto the bench beside her. The cold flowed from his coat, his cheeks were ruddy, and his eyes were a bright-blue contrast. He removed his hat to expose mussed gold hair—not blond or yellow but shiny gold. He beamed at the minister as if giving his permission for him to go ahead with the service now. The minister cleared his throat and did so, but Katherine couldn't hear a word because the man leaned across her and whispered loudly to Millie, "Nearly missed it that time, didn't I?"

Millie responded with a light slap on the man's hand and a fond smile that took away any sting. "Behave," she ordered. Turning to Katherine, she whispered, "My grandson, Colby Pendover. This is my new assistant and friend, Miss Kate Porter."

"Hello, Kate," Colby whispered, bestowing a very nice smile on her.

It was odd to hear a man other than Alonzo call her Kate. She wasn't sure she liked it or this young man's casual familiarity. "Hello," she whispered back.

"Grandma, what happened to your last companion?"

"Shh. She married Jody Barnwell's youngest son, Winston."

"Winnie married Aggie?" Colby forgot to lower his voice, and the minister choked on his sermon and ground to a halt. Colby bared his teeth at him in an apologetic grin and placatingly held up his hands, palms out. The minister coughed and resumed. Colby leaned forward to speak around Kate in a stage whisper. "My word, Grandma! Are you serious?"

"It was all very sudden."

"I should say so! Well, no loss, I guess. At least you're prettier than Aggie, Kate. She was six feet tall with teeth like a horse, remember, Grandma? And—"

"Hush!" Millie replied, reaching to slap his hand again.

"Meant in the nicest way, of course. I have nothing against horses," he added swiftly.

"Colby . . ."

"Aggie had a generous heart," he went on, still in his stage whisper. He leaned confidentially against Katherine's shoulder as if they were old friends. A mischievous smile quirked his finely cut lips. "But she did enjoy the brandy, don't you agree, Gra—"

"You're in church!" Millie squeaked.

Several heads around them turned.

"I hope I haven't offended you, Kate," he said, eyes lowered contritely. She caught a gleam from under his lashes. "I merely meant to illustrate that you were prettier."

Bemused, Katherine shook her head. It was the second time a man had called her pretty. She didn't know what to make of it.

Colby smiled beatifically, as if in great relief, and sat back, arms folded. Slowly his lovely eyes glazed over. Katherine doubted he heard a single word of the service.

When church ended, the young man roused himself and helped Bob get Millie and her chair back into the carriage. He accompanied them home and stayed to dinner. Katherine correctly surmised from his manner that this was a Sunday tradition. He was unquestioningly placed at the head of the table, and when the maid served him his dinner, he gave her a grin and said, "Thank you, Dot."

Dot promptly turned a shade pinker and hurried out in such a rush that she slopped the soup.

Millie shook her head, but her eyes twinkled with amusement. "You're terrible, Colby."

"Is it my fault I've a distracting effect on females?" he asked cheerfully, reaching for his fork. "Kidney pie! My favorite!"

"You said the same thing last week about pork loin," Millie said, sniffing.

"So I did."

"And the week before that, your favorite was guinea hen."

"Whatever you serve is my favorite," Colby replied.

"Because it's free."

"Because your gracious presence sweetens everything around you."

Millie waved a hand at him. "Go on with you! What am I to do with you?"

Colby took a hefty swallow of wine and blinked at her. "Whatever do you mean, Grandmother?"

"Your parents have let you run wild. You have no sense of propriety or dignity. They should have insisted you return to school. I don't know why Samuel isn't firmer with you. He certainly wasn't raised so leniently!"

Colby turned his blue gaze on Katherine. "Have you nothing to say in my defense? Are you going to let her speak to me in such a fashion?"

Katherine eyed him narrowly. "I expect she knows the truth of it better than I."

Colby laughed delightedly. "I see I can expect no sympathy in that camp! She has better wit than Aggie did, at any rate."

"Be nice, Colby," his grandmother said.

Colby leaned forward and addressed Katherine conspiratorially. "She tippled, you know. Drank the cupboard dry regularly. That's why I told Grandma to get rid of her and hire someone else. Though it looks like that wasn't necessary in the end."

"Ha!" Millie snorted. "You told me *I* was being heartless when I suggested she go!"

"Well, she was a devoted sort of person." Colby sighed. "She used to follow me around with eyes like a spaniel."

Katherine played with her fork against her plate. "Eyes like a spaniel and teeth like a horse. What an unfortunate combination."

"Indeed it was," he said eagerly. "It wouldn't have been so bad if she'd also had a sweet disposition or a kindly heart or the figure of Ariadne."

"I believe you mean Aphrodite," Katherine said smoothly.

"So I do." He stared at her. "My word, beautiful *and* intelligent!"

Katherine was momentarily knocked off balance by this remark.

Millie jumped into the intervening pause. "Kate is very well read, Colby. She's had a sound classical education."

"It isn't fair," he mourned. "So much in one woman and so little for poor Aggie."

"You're impossible," Millie cried, closing her eyes.

"Still, Winnie must have seen something in her to throw everything over for her. At least, I assume the Barnwells disinherited him for running off with a servant. I do hope your health is improving, Grandma," Colby said now, polishing off his plate.

Millie's eyes snapped open and fixed on him suspiciously. "Why? I thought you'd be of the opposite mind, seeing as you're my sole heir."

"Why, what an awful thing to say! I'm wounded!" he cried. "No, I was merely wondering if you are in fit health to mind yourself for an hour this evening while I take Kate for a walk around the park."

Katherine jumped, and her fork hit her plate with a ping. She opened her mouth to protest, but Millie didn't look at her.

"I'm not a complete invalid. Take an hour. Take two," the woman said.

"Thank you. I think I shall."

"Is anyone going to consult me?" Katherine asked.

"No," Colby said shortly.

An hour later, they were strolling through the park adjacent to Chatham Square. There were pine trees planted in thickets, with snow lingering in their shadows, but the walkways were clear. The breeze had dropped, leaving the evening air cool and mellow. The park was deserted except for an old couple walking their dog. The old man's nose was red with cold. They hobbled with shoulders rounded and collars pulled to their ears. But Colby strode briskly along with his top coat button open and no scarf. Katherine practically had to jog to keep up.

"I've always felt a good walk after dinner was good for the digestion," he said, looping Katherine's arm comfortably through his. "I make a point of going out every evening. On the occasions when I'm dining at Grandma's, I do hope you'll agree to accompany me as you have this afternoon."

"I wasn't given much choice," Katherine replied. The quick pace was overheating her, and she pulled at the muffler around her throat.

"So what do you think of the old dear so far?"

"I think she's marvelous," Katherine replied sincerely.

"Getting along all right? No complaints?"

"None."

"She's not working you too hard?"

"Not at all. I enjoy working with her."

"Good. And what do you think of Chatham Square? Neighbors all right? Did you enjoy the church service this morning?"

"Yes." She laughed. "It's all very nice, thank you."

"And what do you think of me?" Colby went on happily. "Any reservations? Thoughts you'd care to share?"

"I withhold my opinion on that topic," she said.

He stopped short in the path and turned to face her. He stood a head taller than she. His cheeks were pink with cold and exercise, and his breath made a misty halo around his golden head. He was probably in his late twenties, but his boyish energy and eager expression made him appear younger. "Tell me," he said.

She resumed walking, and it was his turn to keep up with her. "I think you have a lot of nerve," she said tranquilly.

"It comes in handy at times."

"And I suspect you have an overly healthy opinion of yourself."

"Justly deserved, no doubt." He grinned.

Katherine tried to look disapproving, but his smile was too contagious. "I don't know what to think." She laughed. "I've never been assaulted by anyone like you before."

"Assaulted!" He looked startled.

"That's what it feels like. You're somewhat overwhelming."

He tipped his head to one side, studying her. "And yet you don't seem to be alarmed."

"If there were anything to fear, Millie wouldn't have let me come with you."

Colby threw back his head and laughed, an infectious, boyish sound. The old couple blinked at them in consternation and hurried on, their dog barking. "You're right there, anyway," Colby said. "Grandma's taken a great liking to you. She wouldn't put you in any dangerous or compromising situation."

Katherine wondered what Colby Pendover would think if he knew what a compromising situation she had just left in the woods of Springfield. She gazed across the park, watching the sun set in a bronze pool behind the trees. Alonzo's children would be getting ready for bed now, running out to the lavatory in the woods, shivering back to the train car where the golden heat of the stove waited for them. She could see Tony's eyes, luminous in the lamplight, Lilia's hair a dark spray across her pillow, and hear Alonzo's voice as he softly sang to them . . .

"Where did you go?" Colby's voice purred in her ear.

Katherine came back to the park with a jolt. "I'm sorry?"

"You went all soft-eyed and funny for a moment," he said. "Have I worn you out? Shall we go back?"

"Mm. Yes, please."

He put his hand on her elbow as they turned back, and they slowed to a peaceful walk. The old couple had disappeared, and a light snow was beginning to fall as clouds covered the sunset.

"Will you come with me again next Sunday?" he asked as they left the park and proceeded toward Millie's house. "See? I asked nicely this time."

"If it's all right with Millie," Katherine replied, smiling.

"It will be," he said.

Chapter Nineteen

MILLIE HAD NO OBJECTION, SO the following Sunday Katherine and Colby walked out again, this time taking the carriage down to Lake Ontario to walk along the shore. The air was chill, but the wind had dropped, and it was almost warm in the patches of sunlight between the trees. The path was graveled to reduce the mud, and their boots made a pleasant crunching sound as they sauntered, gloved hands in their coat pockets.

"Tell me more about yourself, Kate," Colby said. "It occurs to me I really don't know much about you. Grandma's been rather vague."

"There isn't much to tell," Katherine said, gazing out over the gray-blue expanse of the lake. There was a ship far out, a lavender smudge on the horizon, and she thought a flock of seagulls swirling farther along the shore toward the pier looked like confetti. It made her feel festive somehow. She did wish she had met Colby in a warmer season though. She burrowed her chin into her scarf.

"Come now, you strike me as a very interesting woman. I'm dying to hear how you ended up with Grandma. Where were you born?"

"Here in Toronto," she answered.

"And your parents?"

"David and Emily Porter. Both deceased."

"Brothers or sisters?"

"None."

"No relatives at all?"

"A cousin Martha, now Mrs. Hugh Fitzgerald, and—"

"Not the Hugh Fitzgerald who owns Nethercott Textiles!" Colby stopped walking and stared at her.

"The same. You've heard of him?" Katherine asked.

"All of Toronto has heard of him. That means you're related to Hugh's brother, Reginald."

"Only by marriage."

"What a coincidence! I went to school with Reg. He and I go way back."

"What a small world this is," Katherine murmured.

Colby's beautiful eyes narrowed. "But if you come from such a family, why on earth are you my grandmother's companion?"

"I like Millie very much."

"No, I mean, why are you working at all? Surely after your parents' death someone in your family would have, well, seen to your—"

"Let's keep walking. It's warmer when we walk," Katherine interrupted and strode off briskly.

Colby jogged to keep up. "Am I treading into areas I shouldn't?" he asked cheerfully.

"Well, yes, a little," she said. "I just felt the need to take up employment."

"What of your other options?"

"Other options?"

"Marriage, for one. Surely you could have gone that direction instead."

Katherine brushed her hair from her eyes and smoothed her hands down the front of her coat. She could hear Martha's voice in her ear. *Stop fidgeting. You're nervous as a hen. Do look me in the eye when I speak to you.* She pushed her hands back into her pockets and met his gaze. "That opportunity never seemed to arise." She said it lightly, but then her voice trailed away, and she turned to gaze at the water. It wasn't the truth, but she felt a deep reluctance to tell this man about Alonzo Colaco and his marriage offer. She suspected Colby would treat it lightly, as he did everything, and that would diminish its value. It was something precious she wanted to keep to herself.

Colby mistook her emotions. Reaching out his gloved hand, he pulled her hand from her pocket and wrapped his around it. Gently, he said, "I'm sure it will happen one day. I can't imagine why some chap hasn't jumped at the chance already."

"I imagine most chaps are practically minded," Katherine said, shrugging. "I don't come with any dowry or inheritance, no family to speak of except by marriage . . ." She flashed him a smile. "And very little income. Don't tell Millie I said that."

"But surely Hugh Fitzgerald would have set you up with something."

"He offered once, but I wasn't comfortable accepting it. I'm indebted to him enough as it is."

"Well, fair enough, I suppose, though that might be seen as a little prideful."

"Prideful!" She stared at him.

"Don't you think refusing charity is a sign of pride? Well, in any event," he went on briskly before she could respond, "I don't think you have to buy yourself a husband anyway, Kate. You can attract one all by yourself with your beauty and charm."

She shook her head. "My, you're laying it on thick, now, aren't you?"

"I have to make up for the pride remark." He grinned like a small boy. "Is it winning me any points?"

She tipped her head to one side and regarded him with twinkling eyes. "Perhaps a few. But we've talked only of me. What about you? What do you do?"

Colby laughed and shook his head. "Father wanted me to be a solicitor, so I studied law for a while, but I never finished. Too much to remember. Then for a while he took it into his head that I should be a soldier, but there was entirely too much effort required for that. Mother suggested I try being a schoolmaster, but that required that I interact with *children*, and that would never do."

"You don't like children?"

"In moderation, I suppose, but not an entire classroom of them at once." He shuddered theatrically.

"But what did *you* want to be?" Katherine asked.

"Hadn't given it much thought, really, when I was younger. I mean, if I may be frank, it isn't as if I really need to work for a living, is it? But Father felt every man should have something worthwhile to occupy his time. Reason to get up in the morning and all of that, you know. So in the end, I went to work for him. I sit in an office and help direct the *pater*'s business dealings. He's often away around the world, and I'm his eyes and ears, so to speak, in his absence."

"Oh. Do you enjoy that?"

He laughed. "Not at all. Boring as mud. But it will do until something else comes along. And it keeps me in coats and carriages, doesn't it?"

Katherine fell silent, thinking about this. She couldn't help but contrast it with the image of Alonzo, lovingly turning a tin cup in his hands, gently tapping out the dents and flaws. She thought of the friendly way he interacted with his customers and the way he had bowed his head next to hers, showing her how to use his small tools. She knew instinctively that Alonzo would never let himself waste a moment on a profession he felt no passion for and that whatever he did, it would not be because of someone else's idea of what he should do. And it would certainly not be for the purpose of coats and carriages.

* * *

Sundays fell into a routine. Colby continued to join them at church, slipping into his seat at the last moment and proceeding to whisper throughout the service. Dinner was always full of laughter, and Katherine could see Millie's energy increase whenever Colby came, as if she were a lamp and he were the kerosene. She burned brighter in his presence. And Katherine suspected she herself did too.

As the weather continued to improve, Katherine and Colby fell into a habit of walking out each Sunday afternoon, sometimes to the park and sometimes along the lake. On one of these occasions, when they returned to the house and joined Millie for tea, Colby asked if he could take both Millie and Katherine to the opera.

Katherine couldn't help clasping her hands together with delight, and she looked at Millie with hope written all over her face.

"I take it you want to go," Millie said dryly.

"If I may. I haven't been to an opera or the theater in ages. I do so enjoy music."

"There you are, then," Colby said, pleased. "I'll call for you both Saturday evening."

"Not I," Millie said firmly. "It's *Lohengrin*. I can't abide romantic operas. All the waving of one's arms about and throwing *leitmotifs* around as if one were scattering candy to the crowd."

"Oh, come now, Grandma, you can't turn your nose up at romance."

"I'm eighty-seven. I can do what I want. Besides, it would keep me out too far past my bedtime."

Katherine looked regretfully at Colby. She'd have loved to have gone, but perhaps it was too much to expect of Millie. She swallowed her disappointment and then heard Millie say, "Kate can tell me all about it when she gets back."

"But—Do you mean . . . I can't go without you!" she stammered, astonished.

"Of course you can. Colby can be trusted to bring you back in one piece, I should think. You can tuck me in bed with a good book for the evening and go have a good time."

Katherine didn't feel inclined to argue about it, and so it was decided.

By the time Saturday evening finally came, Katherine had worked herself into a dither. She wasn't convinced that even her best green velvet dress was good enough for the opera, her shoes were sadly worn, her hair would not cooperate, and her stomach was inexplicably jumpy. When she heard Colby's carriage roll up to the door, she gripped her small handbag and went to say good night to Millie.

"Have a lovely time," Millie told her, patting Katherine's hand. "I want to hear all about it tomorrow morning. And if Colby tries to hum along, you must stop him. He's incorrigible at operas. Try stamping on his foot. It's worked in the past."

Katherine couldn't help laughing, and the tension went out of her just like that. Impulsively, she bent down and kissed Millie's soft pale cheek. She supposed it wasn't what a servant should do, but she felt decidedly unservant-like tonight.

Millie seemed unfazed. "Hurry before he gets impatient."

"Thank you for letting me go," she said and scurried downstairs.

Colby's eyes lit up when he saw her, and he insisted on taking her coat from the maid and placing it around Katherine's shoulders himself.

"It won't be fair to the singers," he said, ushering her into the carriage. "All eyes in the audience will be on you instead of them."

"Oh hush. Don't overdo it," she said, but she was smiling.

When they arrived, there was only a five-minute wait for the doors to open. Colby checked their coats and helped her to her seat. Katherine gazed delightedly at the other patrons filtering into their places. She drank in the sight of the lavish gowns and jewels of the women. She could scarcely believe she was here, seated among them. She felt the expectant hush and murmur of the room as the lights dimmed and the curtain rose.

"It's like Christmas," she couldn't help whispering to Colby, and he laughed and reached to hold her hand. He held it for the entire first movement, but with the first opening strains of the orchestra, she forgot all about his hand around hers.

The opera was all she had hoped it would be and more. The music thrummed within her; the costumes and set were magical. She wanted to cry at the beauty and excitement of it all. She wasn't entirely sure she understood the story line, but it hardly mattered. Standing at intermission and sipping the drink Colby had brought her, she closed her eyes and savored every sense. This, she told herself, was precisely the life she had always wanted. She wanted to have this experience again and again. She wanted to belong to this world.

She opened her eyes to find Colby watching her fondly.

"Happy?" he asked.

"Very much so. Thank you for bringing me."

"Thank you for coming with me. For a while, I feared you would back out when Millie declined the invitation."

"Are you enjoying the music as much as I am?"

He reached to take her empty glass from her, and as he did so, his fingers brushed hers and lingered.

"I have never enjoyed *Lohengrin* so much before. I am seeing it through new eyes—yours."

"The lights are dimming. It's time to go back in."

"Have I told you how pretty you are tonight, Kate?"

"Everyone looks pretty in the dark," she replied cheerfully and then fell abruptly silent. It was what she had said to Alonzo that night in the woods. As she resumed her seat, she felt a shiver crawl over her arms. She imagined how she would feel if it were Alonzo sitting here beside her in the darkened theater, his arm brushing against hers in the seat. She imagined him in Colby's black suit, his curly hair brushing his collar. She imagined his face lapsing into stillness as the exalting music rushed over them. He would enjoy it as much as she, for she knew he appreciated the beauty of art and music . . . but no doubt he would have something to say about the flash and glitter of the patrons in their latest fashions, their desire to be seen by others, the pretence of it all. He would probably draw some parallel between the dressy show happening on stage and the one going on in the balcony. She frowned and forced the thought away. She would not let thoughts of Alonzo interfere tonight, not now, when she was enjoying herself so much.

* * *

The next morning Katherine awoke to find the house buried in two feet of snow. She lingered at the window, remembering the game of Fox and

Geese with the children and Alonzo's kiss afterward. Would she never get that moment out of her head? Was she going to relive it the rest of her life, every time she saw snow? She forced herself to think instead of the opera the evening before, of the beauty that had surrounded her. Colby had been an impeccable companion, and she had been proud to be seen on his arm. She forced herself to contrast this with the shame she had felt to be seen riding down the street on Alonzo's gypsy wagon, making herself look at her feelings unflinchingly in the cold light of morning. She couldn't deny the humiliation she'd felt, and she told herself again that if she really felt that way, it had been the right decision to leave. Alonzo deserved better.

If only she could feel better about leaving.

"You are impossible to please," she told her reflection in the mirror. "You are surrounded by everything you always wished for. Be happy about it." She turned away from her image and went down to breakfast.

Millie had guests for dinner that night—Reverend Cook and his wife, Maryse, a French-Canadian woman not much older than Katherine. She and Katherine fell to chatting enjoyably together, and Katherine didn't follow Millie's conversation with the minister until a word penetrated her ear and made her snap to attention.

"Gypsies."

She swung her head round to face them.

"Sorry, what was that you just said?"

The minister waved a dismissive hand, but Katherine saw Millie's blue eyes observing her thoughtfully.

"I was just telling Mrs. Pendover about the gypsies camped down by the Humber River," Reverend Cook said.

"Oh yes," Maryse said. "There are several families, and they're causing such a commotion in the area. People don't feel safe having them there."

Katherine felt her face grow warm, remembering she had told Millie about being mistaken for a gypsy herself. "Have they harmed anyone?"

"No, I can't say they have, and I don't really expect them to," Reverend Cook said. "They seem willing enough to keep to themselves. But still, it does bring an unfortunate element into an otherwise respectable neighborhood, doesn't it? I've done what I can to assist them, especially with it being winter—"

"Of course," Millie murmured, her eyes still on Katherine.

"But, really, you can't help people who won't help themselves."

"No, it only encourages them," Maryse agreed. "I hope they'll move on soon. Everyone would be quite relieved."

"Charity, my dear," her husband said gently. "I'm sure they'll move on in the spring."

Katherine looked down at her plate, her appetite gone. *In the spring.* Alonzo had said they'd move north in the spring. She swallowed hard and reached for her water glass, determined not to show her emotions, but in the end, she had to pretend a coughing fit and excuse herself briefly from the table.

* * *

The following Monday, Millie had a cold, and Katherine confined her to bed and administered chicken soup and hot rum. She was sitting beside the bed, ploughing through a Jane Austen story aloud while Millie drifted in and out of a doze, when a distant bell sounded. In a moment, feet pounded on the stairs. Katherine lowered the book as Colby burst into the room. He still wore his coat and hat, and his entrance brought a breath of cold air and the smell of cinnamon into the room. He produced a paper box with a flourish and deposited it on the bedcovers beside Millie.

"It isn't Sunday," Millie remarked.

"Hot cinnamon rolls," he announced, swooping to drop a kiss on her papery cheek. "A cure for whatever ails you, from influenza to heartache." He came over to Katherine. "I picked out a maple cruller especially for you," he said, handing her a smaller bag. Before she could move or react, he dropped a kiss on her cheek as well. She stared up at him, astonished.

Colby turned back to Millie. "As soon as I heard you were ill, I nipped out to the nearest bakery and rushed here to your side," he said, putting his hands in his pockets and rocking back and forth on his toes. He looked very pleased with himself. "Are you improving?"

"Yes, thank you," Millie said, attacking the pastries with the enthusiasm of a child. "A little common cold is not going to get me down. You'll have to wait awhile yet for your inheritance." She licked a bit of frosting off her fingers.

"Dear Grandmother, please don't jest," Colby protested. "Do you think I'm so thoughtless as that? No, if I thought you were dying, I wouldn't have spent the money on the pastries."

"Go on with you," Millie said, smiling. "Both of you leave me alone to enjoy my snack in peace."

"But . . ." Katherine began.

"I can handle finger food just fine on my own," Millie said. "Besides, you know perfectly well my grandson came to see you, not me."

"How astute you are, my wise relative," Colby said, and snatching Katherine's hand, he plucked her out of her chair. "We won't be long, and then you can have me all to yourself."

"Ha!" Millie said with her mouth full.

Katherine, in her coat and hat, found herself being bustled into the waiting carriage, with Colby following after. She realized she was still holding her pastry, and, breaking it in half, she shared it with him as they drove.

"Where are we going? Along the lake again?" she asked as the carriage moved deeper and deeper into the city.

"A quiet teahouse where we can sit and gaze into each other's eyes undisturbed," he said. "But don't worry. I'll have you home before *Grand-mère* can miss you."

Katherine finished her pastry and drew on her gloves. A small part of her worried about the confusion this charming man's company threw her into, but part of her was glad of it. It kept her too busy to dwell on anything else.

The carriage rolled to a stop, and Katherine saw with a twinge of relief that it was not the Duke of Paisley, where she had first met Alonzo months ago. She followed Colby inside and surrendered her coat. He led her to a private table in one corner.

"Tea and muffins," he told the waiter.

"Oh, I just had that cruller," Katherine protested, but he waved his hand.

"Half of your cruller won't do me, and I can't sit and eat in front of you, so you must have more."

He leaned back with arms folded and regarded her thoughtfully.

"I feel we're the best of friends now, Kate," he said, sounding slightly as if he had rehearsed what he was saying. "I mean, we've known each other—what now, six or seven weeks?"

"About that, I suppose. It's not really that long—"

"A lifetime. Long enough for me to know that each time I see you, I grow more fond of you. It seems to be growing rapidly beyond my control."

She stopped, eyes wide. Her mouth moved speechlessly a second before blurting, "Are you making fun of me?"

"Of course not!" Colby protested. "I mean it sincerely. You're beautiful and intelligent and, if I'm not mistaken, I think you like me too a little." His sandy eyebrows raised a fraction to meet the gold sheaf of his hair.

Katherine hesitated, then nodded.

"There, then," Colby said with satisfaction. "If that's the case, is there any reason why I shouldn't call on you formally? I'm not promising anything yet, it's early days, but I would like to pursue our friendship a little further to see where it leads. Have you any objections?"

Katherine's mouth had gone dry as dust, and her mind raced. "The first day I met you," she said slowly, "you were shocked and horrified to find out your acquaintance Winston Somebody had run away with Millie's last companion. Now here you are, speaking of doing the same . . . I mean, not *exactly* the same, but you understand what I'm saying. I'm your grandmother's employee. Doesn't that bother—Or rather, isn't that a bit hypocritical?" She paused, wondering if she had overstepped herself, but Colby's mouth curled up at one corner.

"It's not the same thing at all, and you mustn't think it is. You're an entirely different animal than your usual class of servant, and much different from Aggie." He popped the last of his muffin into his mouth.

"What do you mean?"

"You're educated, you're elegant, and you obviously come from a better sort of family than many. The longer you're with Millie, the more you fit in. No one would ever know you are from 'outside the circle,' so to speak."

Katherine wasn't sure she liked the way he had put that, but she couldn't quite formulate an appropriate response.

When she remained silent, he laughed. "I see my flattery has knocked you speechless. Have you finished mangling your muffin? Shall we go now?"

She had hardly touched her tea and hadn't tasted her muffin, only broken it into pieces. She allowed him to help her on with her coat and followed him out to the carriage. He took her hand to help her up and sat beside her, still holding it. His palm was smooth, not roughened by work. His nails were cleanly trimmed. She couldn't help comparing his hand to Alonzo's and thought it looked less capable, less strong. But then it would if he spent all his time indoors in an office. She remained still and didn't pull her hand away.

When they arrived home, Colby went upstairs to take his leave of Millie, and Katherine went to her bedroom to change her boots. The sun was dipping lower in the sky, turning the clouds a salmon pink, and she went to the window to look out.

Questions whirled in her mind. She'd come to Millie's house to try to sort out her thoughts about Alonzo only to be thrown into turmoil once more. She had difficulty grasping the idea that Colby was interested in courting her. It was flattering but alarming at the same time. Was he serious? What did she really think of him? She'd known him only a short time, but she did like him. He was handsome, and he certainly stood to inherit well. Marriage to him would plunge her right into the circle she'd sought so long to join. Only in her most impractical daydreams had she ever hoped to hit quite so heady a target. Realistically, no other man of his caliber or social standing would ever likely be so willing to overlook her disadvantages, and she would be a fool not to jump at this chance to gain all she had longed for.

And yet her head warred with her heart. She kept hearing the way he had phrased it: "No one would ever know you were from outside the circle." Did he see her as permanently outside that circle himself? Would he ever truly see her as within it, belonging to it? Would she feel she had to forever hide her background if she became his wife? Alonzo would never expect such a thing. He never judged other people or thought himself better than someone else. Look at how he had befriended Jin. Alonzo was probably unaware there even *was* a circle . . .

"Nothing's certain," she told herself. "Colby hasn't proposed marriage. Don't get ahead of yourself, Katherine. He said only that he wanted to get to know me better. There's nothing wrong with that, and it isn't as if I've promised anything." But still, it was flattering. The more she thought about it, the more excited she became. She eyed her reflection in the mirror over her dressing table, observing the high color in her cheeks, her shining eyes. She could almost overlook the fraying hem, the sturdy but unstylish shoes. He'd said she was beautiful. Seeing her own expression, the suppressed excitement lighting her face, she could, for a moment, believe him.

When she went to Millie's room, she wore a straight expression, but Millie missed nothing. Perhaps Colby had even told her of their conversation. Her glittering eyes looked Katherine over once shrewdly, and she remarked, "I see you aren't adverse to my grandson's company."

Katherine tried to look indignant but failed. Breaking into a smile, she said, keeping her voice casual, "He's very charming."

Millie reached out a crabbed hand, and Katherine went to take it.

"He's always been charming, even as a child. But with you, he outdoes himself. I'm not feebleminded. I see a lot from this bed. I can see your expression now, all hesitation and happiness."

"Do you mind very much?"

"That he's interested in you? I want you to know, Kate, that I haven't seen Colby quite like this before. He's always very jolly on the outside, but there's a sensitive streak in him. I can tell he's in earnest. With you, it isn't merely a charming act. He's never quite been like this before." She patted Katherine's hand with her fingers, her heavy silver ring flashing in the lamp light. "I'm not one to hold your background against you, dear. What makes my grandson happy makes *me* happy. And it appears he thinks you make him happy."

Katherine didn't know what to say to that. "I've only just met him," she protested.

Millie patted her hand. "Well, we shall see. But don't you two take too long to reach any decisions. I'm not getting any younger."

"You're going to outlive us all," Katherine said firmly. "Now, enough excitement. Where did we leave poor Jane Austen?"

Chapter Twenty

So COLBY BEGAN TO CALL regularly, not under pretence of visiting Millie but to see Katherine. She looked forward to his visits with both happiness and worry. She knew at some point he was going to make a decision and then he'd ask her to make her decision. She wanted to put off that time for as long as possible and just enjoy his company. Now that it seemed her former dreams may become a reality, she was anxious. Her happiness seemed to her to be perilously balanced on thin supports. Suppose she didn't fit into the role of Colby Pendover's socialite wife? What if Martha's cutting remarks had been true all along, and she would not, at the end of it all, truly belong? Suppose—and this thought chilled her more than the others—suppose she attained everything she'd thought she'd wanted and it turned out not to be what she'd anticipated at all?

Part of her wished Colby had not spoken at all so that she could have just enjoyed herself and the luxuries she was experiencing a little while longer. So that there was no decision to make. And yet she feared if she didn't make the decision at some point, it would be made for her. She knew Colby had more than enough energy and enthusiasm to sweep her along before him in any direction he chose, like a toy boat on the ocean. A small voice in her head warned her that unless she knew her own mind thoroughly and stated it firmly, she could easily find herself lost, swept up in his wake. She was just on the verge of figuring out who she was and what she valued, and she didn't want to lose that emerging sense of self in the tidal wave of Colby's personality. At the same time, she knew it would be an easy thing to do, to just let go and let him carry her along for the admittedly enjoyable ride.

* * *

Some days later, Colby invited her to a concert featuring a visiting orchestra from Vienna. It sounded like a splendid affair, even more so than the opera had been, and Katherine debated only a few minutes before deciding to splurge a great portion of her wages on a new dress. She wanted to make Colby proud to be seen with her. She didn't want to be the meek, colorless duckling Martha had made her feel for so long. She obtained Millie's advice about where to go for the dress, but she went alone to select the fabric, choosing a deep burgundy that would complement her coloring and opting for a simple but elegant pattern. As she surveyed herself in the dressmaker's mirror, she was quite pleased with the picture she made.

As she left the shop after the final fitting, Katherine fingered her purse, debating, and then turned left toward the shops instead of right. Surely she had to purchase appropriate shoes to go with the dress. It would quite spoil the effect if she were to wear her old ones. And her old handbag would need to be replaced, and she probably needed a new shawl or wrap because the evening air was still cold and her old coat would never do. The thought crossed her mind that Colby's courting had better not be too drawn out; her pocketbook could never sustain a long courtship.

Colby was the perfect gentleman the night of the concert, attentive and kind and wildly handsome in his evening suit. After an initial moment of nervousness, Katherine let herself get swept up in the excitement of the night. Every detail was flawless, right down to the matched black horses pulling the carriage and the grand vases of deep red roses flanking the concert-hall entrance. Her new skirt swept gratifyingly as she mounted the stairs to their balcony seat, her arm through Colby's. She felt inordinately proud that he was her escort.

Several times they paused on the staircase to greet people Colby knew, and Colby murmured the introductions. "Mr. and Mrs. Patrick Ryerson, Miss Katherine Porter." "Mr. and Mrs. William Massey, Miss Katherine Porter." "Mr. and Mrs. Timothy Eaton, Miss Katherine Porter." The names dazzled her, for she had read of these families in the newspaper and listened to Millie and her friends gossip about them. The last introduction made her gape, in spite of herself, at the white-bearded gentleman executing a short bow before her. She had shopped in Timothy Eaton's department store, for goodness sake! Now here she was, meeting him in person. Colby seemed to know everyone worth knowing in Toronto, and the way he spoke her name to them implied that they should all know her too. As if she unquestioningly fit among them.

Soon after that evening, Colby brought two heavy off-white envelopes to Millie's house and set them on the parlor mantel, where they fairly glowed in the firelight. "Dinner invitations," he said. "You and me, Kate."

"Oh! From whom?" It felt rather odd to think that someone would assume she and Colby were one unit to be invited together. They had been seen in public alone together really only two or three times. But then, she supposed, that was what they were: a couple . . .

A strange sick sort of feeling began in the pit of her stomach, but before she could really register it, Colby said casually, "The Masseys and the Eatons."

Katherine was stunned to think that such important people would invite her to their homes, but before she could say anything, Colby waved a hand.

"But don't worry about it at all," Colby told her, dropping a kiss on her forehead. "I only wanted to show you you're making a splash in Toronto already. Of course I've already declined both invitations."

Katherine blinked at him, aware that her face was awash with disappointment. "But why?" she asked, hating the dismay in her tone. "Why would you decline?"

"Oh, I didn't think you were quite ready for that," Colby said airily, turning to help himself to the brandy on the side table.

"Quite right," Millie chimed in from her armchair. "Time enough for all that. And it would mean having to purchase two more dresses, my dear. You can't wear the same thing to every event."

Katherine was taken aback, not just by the blunt words but by the fact that Millie had spoken them so lightly in front of Colby. She felt as if she had been abruptly brought down out of a fairy tale and returned to reality with a bang. Millie was right, of course. She didn't have the wardrobe for extensive socializing. But what had Colby meant—that she didn't know proper etiquette? That she couldn't be counted on to behave appropriately at the Eatons' table? She tried to tell what he was thinking, but his face was bland as he held his brandy up to the firelight and admired its mellow color. She swallowed down her disappointment. "Still, I would have enjoyed going. It was very kind of them to ask us," she said wistfully. "Have you been to their home before?"

"Loads of times. They'll ask again, I'm sure," Colby replied. "And by then you'll be ready. All in good time." He dropped another kiss on her forehead as he passed by on the way to his chair by the fireplace. "But I do have another treat for you, Kate. There's to be a poetry reading by some famous female poet or other—I forget the name. I thought you might like to go to that with me. It's Thursday next."

The rest of the evening passed pleasantly, but that night as Katherine lay in bed, staring up at the high, dark ceiling, she played the conversation over again in her mind. She wasn't sure what Colby had meant by "By then you'll be ready." Did he see her as a pet project, someone to train and mold to fit into his world? It was a condescending thing to have said, even cutting. And yet he had been so charming the rest of the evening that Katherine couldn't hold it against him. Surely he hadn't meant to hurt her feelings. He was so kind to her in every other way. Really, if she looked at it from another angle, he was trying to *spare* her feelings by not rushing her into social situations she was not prepared for. Perhaps she was being overly sensitive. She would forgive and forget his remark. After all, she did have the poetry reading to look forward to.

* * *

As spring returned to the city, Katherine remembered her promise to Lilia to visit. She had told Alonzo she would let him know her decision, and he had said he'd known it already. Should she go anyway? She told herself it would be better not to. It was better not to upset the children by visiting and getting their hopes up and then leaving again. She told herself it would be kinder to just let it go and that visiting wouldn't accomplish anything. She should let them go back to Collingwood and forget her. But she knew she wasn't being honest with herself. The real reason she didn't want to go was because she was a coward, pure and simple. She didn't want to see the disappointment on Alonzo's face. She knew he deserved more than she could give. It wouldn't be kind to saddle him with a wife who couldn't wholly accept him and his way of being. Unless she was honestly able to look him in the eye and say she had no reservations, it was better not to go.

But even that wasn't entirely the truth, she thought, catching sight of herself in Millie's dressing table mirror. She paused, taking in her pale complexion and bleak expression. She was afraid that once she looked into his indigo eyes again, she would not be strong enough to stick with her resolve.

She wasn't given much time to dwell on the dilemma, however, and couldn't have found time to make the visit even if she'd dared. She discovered her calendar was stuffed with appointments every day. There were teas and dramas and musical soirées to accompany Millie to. She attended the

Women's Literary Club, for Millie was, like the club, a supporter of the suffragist movement. There she heard Dr. Emily Stowe, the second female physician licensed in Canada, give a moving speech. Once, she even accompanied Millie to hear Prime Minister John A. Macdonald speak, though it was something about the Canadian Pacific Railway and was admittedly numbingly boring.

There seemed to be no end to the entertainment, stimulating conversation, and new acquaintances. The hostesses at the various venues treated her as an equal when she was with Millie, and she let herself join in the light conversation and felt she was beginning to extend her circle of friends outside the Pendover home. She no longer felt overwhelmed or out of her depth in conversation, and she genuinely liked the women she met, especially Maryse Cook. When she remarked to Millie one day about how much of her time this was absorbing, Millie merely waved it away.

"I love watching you unfold and blossom," the old woman told her. "I relive my own youth vicariously through you, you know."

"Still, it hardly seems fair that you are paying me to attend suffragist meetings with you when I enjoy it so much," Katherine said.

Millie chuckled. "And can you only be paid for work which you *don't* enjoy?"

"I suppose when you put it like that . . ."

"I'm enjoying your company," Millie assured her, reaching out to place her gnarled hand on Katherine's.

"And I'm enjoying yours," Katherine assured her.

"There you are, then. No complaints?"

"None at all," Katherine said.

"Me neither. And no regrets?"

Katherine frowned. "I just said—"

"No, complaints and regrets are very different things, Kate. Complaints are about the present. Regrets are about the past."

Katherine thought about this. Millie seemed to be watching her closely, waiting for her response, but she wasn't at all sure what it should be. Finally, she said sincerely, "I don't regret meeting you."

Millie patted her arm. "You are a dear girl. I'm glad you're here. And perhaps we'll win you over to the suffragist cause so it won't have been in vain! Now fetch me my wrap, and ask Bob for the carriage to be brought round."

After that conversation, Katherine tried to relax and simply enjoy what she was offered. If Millie wanted to pay her to socialize, then she would. She splurged on another dress, this one a pale blue cotton appropriate for afternoon social teas, with a modern hat to match, and told herself it was about time her fortune changed after her past years of struggle and slim income. If it was not all quite as fulfilling as she'd dreamt it would be, well, that was the nature of dreams. Reality never quite lived up to them, but she supposed that was a lesson to be learned on her way to mature adulthood. She would just be grateful for what she was given.

Early spring was unusually dry compared to December, with only occasional snowfall, and the temperature stayed below freezing for days at a time, minimizing the slush in the streets. The dry weather made it easier to be out and about, even with Millie's wheelchair, and Katherine could still enjoy outings in the park with Colby, swathed in muffler and mittens. Sometimes they took Millie with them, pushing her chair around Queen's Park under the bare trees, the elderly woman so wrapped against the cold that she was difficult to discern beneath the layers.

The cold made Katherine wonder how the Colaco children were faring, and she pictured them curled up near the woodstove with their books or tramping through the woods in their coats and boots with Bo. Alonzo would have moved back into the train car with them in her absence. She imagined them all together in the cozy, fire-lit train car and then scolded herself for thinking of it. She was foolish to miss the warmth of the tiny house when she had so much luxury around her at Millie's. It would never do to dwell on it, and she tried to keep those thoughts at bay. Still, there were times when something would catch her off guard and bring her up short—a chance word, the sight of a piebald horse, a glimpse of something as simple as a tin cup—and she would be unable to stop the flood of memories of Alonzo and his children. She fought against the aching sensation of loss, telling herself it had been her own decision. Surely it would ease in time.

When she wasn't accompanying Millie, Katherine often went with Colby to musical evenings or dramas. She genuinely enjoyed his company. Colby was an attentive escort, making sure everything went smoothly for her. Under his gentle, cheerful kindness and subtle tutoring, it was possible to feel as if she'd always been a part of this life. Millie didn't question her about the growing friendship between her and Colby, but Katherine often looked up from her book or a letter she was writing to find the old woman's sharp eye sagely studying her. But it was the prerogative of the old to look that way, and Katherine tried not to blush under the appraising stare.

* * *

One Friday in early April, Kate and Millie were just finishing lunch when Colby appeared at the dining room door.

"You're not usually here on a Friday," Kate observed, watching him plop into a chair and help himself cheerfully to the rest of the roast chicken.

"Nothing was happening at the office, and I decided to give myself the afternoon off. Anything exciting happening around here?"

"Sorry to disappoint you. We're just shopping this afternoon," Millie said. "For boring things like a silk scarf to go with my new hat."

"I could accompany you," Colby offered. "Where are you going? Yonge Street?"

"Most likely."

"Splendid. I want to visit my tailor."

"You can drive us, then, and I'll tell Bob he has the afternoon off once I'm aboard," Millie said.

Once Millie was strapped into the carriage and Katherine was seated beside her, Colby took the reins, and they started off. The day was brisk and cool, with a steady breeze coming off the lake, and few other carriages were on the road. It didn't take long to reach their destination. Colby wheeled Millie out of the carriage and into the shop, then took one of the seats by the window reserved for waiting husbands and let the women conduct their business while he read a newspaper.

"A saffron yellow silk would be best," Millie said, directing Katherine where to push her chair. "I have in mind just the thing I want. Darker than that one there. Not so green as that one."

But the shop did not have what she wanted. The assistant brought out several scarves and lengths of silk, but none of them pleased Millie.

"It must be saffron yellow to complement the silk roses on my new hat," she said firmly. "We shall have to go to another shop."

The flustered-looking assistant stood with her hand on the pile of scarves she had displayed and glanced at Katherine. Katherine smiled and lifted her shoulder in a "What can you do?" gesture. The assistant nodded.

"You might try the Chinese district. They sometimes import silks we generally don't stock."

"Thank you, we'll try that," Millie said. She waved her hand at Colby, beckoning him over. "Back into the carriage, my boy."

The tailor Colby wanted to visit was near the Chinese district, so they stopped there on their way. The women waited in the carriage while he went into the shop, and Millie shot Katherine a wry smile.

"May as well make yourself comfortable, my dear. He will be awhile. Colby is in his element among clothes."

Katherine thought about this a moment. "Perhaps he would be happier working in the clothing industry somehow," she said. "I know he isn't overly fond of the work he does for his father. Maybe he should try being a tailor or having his own clothing shop."

Millie's mouth fell open, and she made a choking sound Katherine wasn't sure was a laugh.

"I would love to see my son's face if Colby announced he was going to be a tailor!" Millie chortled. "Wouldn't that be a scene though! My late husband would rise from his grave."

"I only meant . . . well, I'd like to see Colby happy," Katherine stammered, her ears hot with embarrassment.

"That's commendable, but my dear, the Pendover family has a certain position to uphold. Samuel would never allow it. Even owning such a shop would be considered too vulgar."

"But there isn't anything dishonorable about being a tailor," Katherine protested weakly. "And doesn't your son own several businesses himself?"

"Businesses. Factories. Worldwide enterprises. Not tailor shops," Millie said gently. "It's true Colby enjoys dabbling in clothing as a hobby. But certainly not as a career. Though perhaps you are onto something after all. Now that I think about it, he might like to become involved in the textile industry. Perhaps your cousin Hugh Fitzgerald is in need of a foreman at Nethercott or something. Colby knows Reginald. He could speak to him, I suppose. Maybe I'll drop the suggestion in his ear."

Katherine was about to remark on this when she caught sight of a small figure in a tan coat moving along the street, carrying a basket. Before she even realized she had moved, she was out of the carriage. "Ah Lam!"

The figure stopped, startled, and then her face broke into a broad smile, and she hurried over to Katherine, exclaiming in Cantonese. The two women exchanged a brief hug, and Katherine couldn't help laughing at Ah Lam's surprise.

"It's so good to see you! What are you doing here?" Katherine asked.

Ah Lam held up the basket she carried over her arm. "Jin lunch," she said and nodded toward the tailor shop Colby had entered.

"Oh! This is where Jin works?" Katherine cried. "I'm so pleased to know! But I thought you were living above the shop, weren't you?"

Ah Lam puzzled over this a moment, then seemed to understand what Katherine was asking. "Yes, yes, live here," she said. "Huang Fu school. Jin work. I . . ." She paused, searching for the correct words, then pointed down the road. "I work there. Come lunch for Jin."

"Oh, you have employment too," Katherine said. "I'm very happy. It all seems to have worked out for you. Your English is improving. And you are looking very well."

"Very well, yes, thank you." Ah Lam's eyes turned toward the carriage. "Mr. Alonzo?"

"No, I no longer live there," Katherine said, feeling the familiar stab at her heart. "I work for this woman now." She turned to gesture toward the carriage and caught sight of Millie's astonished face peering out the window. She took Ah Lam's arm and gently pulled her forward to make introductions. "Millie, this is Ah Lam, a dear friend of mine. Ah Lam, this is Mrs. Pendover."

Ah Lam gave a small bow, her lovely porcelain face friendly, but Millie remained absolutely still, not acknowledging the greeting, her face seeming to have turned to stone.

"Ah Lam's husband works for the tailor. Isn't that a coincidence? I had no idea I'd ever see her again." Katherine gave Ah Lam's arm a squeeze. "I'm so glad I ran into you. Please tell Jin hello for me. And Huang Fu."

"Thank you, yes. Huang Fu miss the children," Ah Lam said with another quick bow. "Mr. Alonzo very good to us. You very good to us. You are always here," she added, and she placed a hand on her heart.

As she turned to go, Colby came out of the shop. His eyes fell on Katherine's hand, still wrapped warmly around Ah Lam's arm, and he stopped dead on the walk. "Is there some trouble here?" he asked quickly. "Did this person bother you, Kate?"

"Not at all. It's such a coincidence! She's a good friend of mine, and her husband works for the tailor you just visited. I haven't seen her in weeks and weeks. She was coming to bring her husband his lunch, and I saw her."

"She—This is a friend?" Colby looked taken aback. "But . . ."

Ah Lam made him a polite bow. Katherine gave her another brief hug, and Ah Lam hurried away down the alley toward the back door of the shop. She waved as she disappeared inside. Katherine turned happily back to Colby, but his expression made her pause. His eyebrows were lowered, his lip turned up in what she thought was almost a sneer.

"Where on earth would you have met a Chinese woman?" he asked her. "And what possessed you to call her your friend?"

"That's what she is," Katherine said, puzzled. "She's sweet and kind."

"I'm surprised at you. And embracing her out here on the street, where anyone could see! Please don't do that again," Colby said shortly and swung up into the carriage seat without assisting her back inside. Katherine looked at Millie, whose face remained frozen in the window in astonishment, and suddenly it hit her. This wasn't the secluded clearing in the woods. This was Toronto, where the line between the Chinese and their non-Asian neighbors was not crossed. Somehow in her happiness at seeing Ah Lam, she had forgotten. She had assumed that suffragist, unconventional Millie's broadmindedness encompassed more than it apparently did. And it came home to her just how much she herself had changed while she'd lived with the Colacos.

As she climbed meekly back into the carriage, Millie shook her head and murmured, "You astound me, Kate. I see we still have a ways to go."

* * *

The incident was not mentioned again, and Katherine was careful to do nothing to upset Millie or her grandson, but her heart was unhappy. Part of her wanted to protest, to explain how their prejudices were unfounded, and the other part of her was afraid to press the issue. Millie was so kind to her in all respects and seemed so reasonable and down to earth. If there were social boundaries even she would not cross, then perhaps Katherine had become *too* liberal and had lost all sense of perspective back at the clearing in the woods. She doubted herself one day and defended herself the next. But she kept this battle private, playing it out only in her own mind, and was careful not to let her employer see it.

The rest of April spun by, and then in the first week of May, Colby announced that his parents were coming back to Toronto, having arrived home from their recent travels, and would soon be on their way to their summer home in Ottawa.

"We'll have them to dinner a week Sunday," Millie said, looking excited as a little girl at a party. "They can meet Kate. I think she's ready."

Katherine looked up at this. She'd been embroidering, sitting on a settee near Millie's wheelchair. Now the needle slipped from her fingers and dangled, twisting on its silk thread.

Colby, standing before the fireplace with his hands behind his back, returned her look, his broad smile creeping over his attractive face. "I believe she is. Don't look so stricken, Kate." He chuckled. "They really are nice people. They'll approve of you."

She didn't know what to reply. There was the fact that she was now considered "ready" for a formal dinner party. There was the immediate problem of once again coming up with something to wear. And most importantly, there was the fact that Colby wanted to introduce her to his parents, which seemed monumental. The surreal quality of the past weeks had come to an abrupt end, and she knew she'd soon have to face an unknown future, a future of her own making. His gaze upon her was unnerving. She stood and pulled the bell for the maid to bring them their tea.

When he left that evening, Colby took her hand, and she accompanied him to the hall. At the door, he kissed her for the first time. It was a gentle kiss, lasting only as long as was proper and polite, and he held her lightly, his hands on her upper arms. It was different from Alonzo's kisses, pleasant but . . . well, frankly, rather dull. Katherine realized what she was thinking and stiffened with embarrassment. Misinterpreting her sudden withdrawal, Colby let her go and held her away from him. There was a question in his eyes, and Katherine dropped her gaze, hoping her own thoughts weren't so easily read.

He cleared his throat. "Kate, I've made my decision. I want to ask you to marry me."

Katherine opened her mouth to say yes, but no sound came out. She swallowed and tried again and heard herself say, "I will give you my answer soon, Colby, but not yet. Please give me just a little more time."

His face darkened slightly with disappointment, but he nodded. "Of course, darling. You can give me your answer next week when I come with my parents."

"All right."

"If Hugh Fitzgerald is your guardian, perhaps it would be more proper for me to speak to him first?"

"No, no," Katherine said quickly. "I mean, it's not necessary. I haven't been his ward for several years."

He kissed her again, lingering a little longer this time, then pushed her gently away and put on his hat.

"My parents will love you as I do," he said. "And, Kate, do wear your burgundy dress with the millions of tiny buttons. You look smashing in that."

"All right," she said again and watched from the doorway until his carriage had disappeared.

She lay awake that night, listening to the creaks and sighs of the house. The grate gave out delicious heat. In the morning the maid would bring breakfast to the morning room where she sat with Millie, basking in the heat of the fire someone else made. She would be brought warm water for washing, and she would put on clothing someone else had freshly laundered. She'd spend the morning going over Sunday's menu with Millie. She'd eat a light lunch, prepared by someone else. She would read for a while or take down a letter to Lady Haverlock or Mrs. Shrillsbury. Later, an elegant dinner would magically appear on the table, the used dishes deftly whisked out of sight. Perhaps some entertainment in the evening . . . All this was hers to enjoy and always would be if she married Colby Pendover.

Was that a legitimate reason to marry someone? She sat up in bed, arms around her knees. Women married for such reasons all the time. Colby was handsome, considerate, and funny. She could picture herself being quite happy with him. He certainly cared for her. His embrace had been brief and a bit self-conscious. It hadn't reduced her to a puddle of lava like Alonzo's kisses had, but perhaps that was appropriate. She had found it pleasant all in all. Colby would take care of her. He would establish her in the circle of his acquaintances, dress her in elegant clothing, and—she was sure soon—would take her to dine at the Eaton home. Her financial worries would be over. She need never seek an interview with a prospective employer again, never worry over a salary. He would fill her life with ease and laughter. With such a husband, her family would surely approve of her and be impressed, not ashamed. All things considered, it would be prudent to accept Colby's proposal.

She winced at the coolness of the voice of reason speaking in her head. Quite inexplicably, she suddenly found she was weeping. She buried her face in her knees and gave herself over to it.

* * *

The week passed, and the following Sunday came all too soon. The house-keeper arranged great mounds of glasshouse flowers in strategic locations throughout the house. The crystal sparkled like ice on the lace tablecloth. Wonderful warm smells seeped from the kitchen. Millie, with Katherine's help, struggled into a formidable pink gown with fifty jet bead buttons marching down the back, and Katherine teased the thin white hair into a pile with dangling curly wisps.

"You'll like my son and daughter-in-law," Millie assured Katherine. "Julia is fluff-brained, but Samuel's a wonderful man. He is much like Colby—you'll see. It seems so long since I saw them last!"

"You look marvelous," Katherine told her and hurried to her own room to don the burgundy dress. She added her one simple gold necklace and was dabbing on a touch of scent when she heard voices downstairs.

Jergens had carried Millie downstairs and transferred her to the sofa, and she and the guests were already in animated conversation when Katherine entered. Colby, splendid in black, hurried to bring her in.

"Kate, this is my mother, Julia Pendover, and my father, Samuel. This is Kate—Katherine Porter."

Colby's mother was an elegant woman in a cream-colored gown, and Katherine saw that Colby got his fair coloring from her. Her golden hair was piled artfully on her head, with a delicate touch of pearls at her throat, pale as her gown. She looked delicate and perfect as a meringue. She took Katherine's hand and greeted her warmly. Samuel Pendover was a balding man with Colby's face in an older, less-expressive rendition. She imagined Colby would look just like this one day, and the thought made her smile.

"So you're the charming young lady Colby has told us about. Delighted to meet you. I've heard of your family, of course. How is Hugh? I've met him on occasion. Fine fellow, fine fellow."

Katherine's opinion of Colby's father dipped at this, but she smiled again and made agreeable noises. The next half hour was spent swapping news and hearing about their recent trip to Andalusia, particularly Cordova, which Julia insisted was just divine, and then dinner was announced.

As they moved into the dining room, Colby leaned close and whispered in Katherine's ear, "Dot will help Grandma with her food tonight. You can just enjoy the meal with my parents."

"Thank you. That's very considerate," Katherine said, but he had already moved forward to pull out her chair.

The food was superb, the lighting mellow, and the weather against the window gray, giving the dining room the feeling of a cozy cave. It was rather nice to be off duty, Katherine thought, and have Dot help Millie so Katherine could attend to her own meal before it grew cold. She relaxed and was savoring the combination of lovely smells, tastes, and sights when Samuel set down his wine glass, looked at her, and said, "So how *is* old Hugh these days?"

"Fine, thank you," Katherine said, though she had no idea if Hugh was well or not.

"I'll have to have them to the house," he said. "We could all make a weekend of it."

Katherine felt a shock of anxiety run through her. The last time she'd seen Hugh, she had all but announced her feelings for Alonzo and thrown Hugh's hatred of Catholics in his face. She did not want to contemplate what would happen if they were all to meet again in Samuel Pendover's home in honor of her engagement to Colby. It didn't bear thinking about. "That would be nice," she said faintly.

"You can't invite anyone until I get in a new cook," Colby's mother said, sounding put out.

"What happened to the last one?" Colby asked.

"She got married and left without a week's notice. They'd been seeing each other behind my back. I didn't know a thing about it, and Mrs. Partridge—that's our housekeeper—she didn't see fit to inform me. That's just what she said—she didn't see fit to inform me! But of course she wouldn't tell me because she knew I would send the chit packing. They stick together, let me tell you. It's no good hoping they'll be disloyal to one of their own kind."

"Own kind?" Katherine murmured without realizing she'd said it aloud.

Julia smirked at her. "Yes. They stick together, that sort." When Katherine still looked blank, Julia added, "You know. Servants. Hired help. They'll never tell on each other. They're thick as thieves. Though of course a cook isn't quite of the same plane as a maid, but you know how it is. You must never trust the lower classes entirely, and the Irish not at all."

Samuel chuckled and said, "Now, dear, remember Miss Porter is related to the Fitzgeralds, and that's an Irish name if ever there was one."

"Well, of course I don't mean *them*."

Katherine shifted her eyes to Colby. He had gone distinctly pink and was busying himself with his food. Katherine transferred her look to Millie and saw a funny expression on her face. It was a look of regret, but a challenge lurked behind it. The shrewd eyes gazed into her own, daring her to speak.

Katherine didn't rise to the challenge. She took another bite of bread and said nothing. She felt a tightness in her throat that made swallowing difficult. They hadn't told Colby's parents that she was Millie's hired companion. They thought she was just a guest, a friend. No doubt he had told them only that she was related to the Fitzgeralds and nothing more. It was all there under the surface—the nervousness, the embarrassment. No wonder Dot was playing her role in helping Millie tonight! Colby was ashamed to say who Katherine really was. It was her family all over again, and Millie's involvement felt like a betrayal. How did Colby think he could get away with marrying her without his parents learning she worked for Samuel's mother?

She was so wrapped in her own thoughts that she missed what Julia was saying, and so was startled by the sudden gasps and exclamations that went round the table. She looked up, confused, to find everyone looking distressed.

"What?" she asked. "I mean, pardon? I'm sorry . . ."

"The *Victoria*," Millie said. "We hadn't heard, Samuel. That's dreadful news. I'm surprised you didn't mention it the moment you arrived."

"Too painful, Mother, too painful," Samuel muttered, a hand to his forehead.

When Katherine continued to frown, Colby leaned closer and said in a low voice, "The steamer. It capsized on Tuesday, and 182 people were drowned."

"Oh, but that's terrible!" Katherine exclaimed, stricken.

"They allege it was overcrowded," Julia said. "But you know how newspapermen exaggerate. I'm sure there was no fault on the company's part."

"Out holidaying on the Thames for the queen's birthday, no less," Colby said.

"I've never heard anything so awful," Katherine said, feeling sick. Such a loss of life all at once!

"Thank you, my dear. Yes, it's a terrible blow," Samuel said. "It will take a lot to recover from the loss."

Colby leaned close again. "Father owned half shares in the Victoria," he explained.

And suddenly it became crystal clear to Katherine that the Pendovers were lamenting the financial blow, not the loss of life. It was the legal liability that made Samuel look so dismayed. She sat back in her chair, her cheeks aflame, feeling as if she'd been struck in the face.

Distantly she heard the doorbell ring. The room felt too hot. She lost track of the rest of the conversation, and when Julia directed a question at her, she could only stare at her blankly without responding. Julia waited, an uncertain smile coming and going on her lips.

The butler entered, followed by a maid bearing a tray of puddings. Deftly they began to deal them out. Katherine couldn't bring herself to taste the gelatinous mass. Her eyes were stinging.

"Who was at the door?" Millie asked Jergens as she was served.

"Only a tinker, mum. I sent him round to the kitchens for a bite to eat."

Julia sniffed. "Imagine! Coming to the front door like that! As if he were somebody!"

Katherine didn't hear her. She had stiffened as the housekeeper spoke, and now, without thinking, she dropped her serviette and stood. "Excuse me, please."

Colby and his father blinked at her, then heaved quickly to their feet.

"Certainly, my dear," Colby said. "Everything all right?"

Katherine didn't reply, only stumbled for the door. She felt Millie's gaze follow her out of the room.

Chapter Twenty-One

SHE FLED DOWN THE HALL, through the corridors, heart pounding. The kitchen was ridiculously far from the dining room. She swung around the last corner and hurled herself at the kitchen door.

Two astonished faces looked up at her, the cook with her ladle poised over the bowl she was filling, and a gray-haired, rumpled man sitting at the table. His face was weather-beaten and unshaven, his clothes disgraceful. He blinked his rheumy dark eyes.

Katherine stopped cold, as if she'd been blocked, unable even to stammer an excuse. The cook frowned and resumed filling the bowl. Katherine closed the door quietly and turned away.

Her stomach was hollow, as if someone had punched her, and she was shaken to realize how much she had hoped the bold tinker was Alonzo. She felt drained and empty. She climbed the stairs to her room, thinking fiercely that Dot could spoon up Millie's pudding for the rest of her life for all she cared. She couldn't go back in that dining room with Colby's parents, with Colby.

Once in her room, she flung herself across the bed and let her emotions take over, sobbing into her quilt without restraint. All those people dead in the river, and the Pendovers seemed to care more about the financial cost! Life snuffed out so quickly in the midst of merrymaking, gone just like that. And when it was gone, there was no fixing anything that had been left undone or broken.

If life was that tenuous and fragile, if it could be cut so short so suddenly, what was she doing with hers? She sat up and scrubbed at her eyes, dashing away the tears. She had spent months in this house, with these people, and she'd immersed herself in their bright, busy world, but it was all empty; she could see that now. None of it nourished her. What did any of it matter, really? She was ashamed of the kind of person Colby was and ashamed that he had nearly succeeded in molding her to fit his world. And to think she had ever been ashamed of Alonzo and his way of life!

She had never felt so unutterably lonely. She missed all of the Colacos, but especially Alonzo. She missed his voice, his laugh, his hands—hands so much more capable and comforting in their roughness than Colby's soft ones could ever be.

Colby! Her sorrow turned to anger, and she brought her fists down on her mattress. He hadn't told his family her position in the house. How could she have so misjudged him? She didn't know him at all. She'd forgiven his slights and overlooked his occasional cutting remarks, letting herself be swept up by his charm and telling herself he didn't really mean them, but really he was just a thinner, more handsome Hugh. And that mother of his was just another Martha. If Julia and Samuel knew her background, they would always consider her outside the circle, but finally she saw clearly that she didn't want to be in the circle anyway. Money and social standing was all well and good to have, but it was wrong to judge a person's worth by how much of it they had. She shouldn't have to dress like a doll and hide who she was in order to be accepted. To be *valued*.

"All I want is for someone to love me for who I am, without thought to what I do or have," she mourned. Then she stopped cold as a voice in her brain responded tartly, *That's all Alonzo asked too.*

She sat up, hiccupping into silence. How could she be angry with Colby when she herself had treated Alonzo the same way? He'd treated her as an equal from the beginning, just as he had with Jin and Ah Lam. He hadn't expected her to be anything but what she was and would never be ashamed of her, whatever the situation. He'd loved her without condition. That was all that mattered, she saw now. Nothing else was important—not a grand house or a gypsy wagon, not gowns and carriages, or the scorn of strangers. None of it mattered if there was unconditional love.

She saw, with a rising sense of panic, that she'd been very, very foolish.

She went to the window, gripping the curtains on each side. Out in the dusk, the early green leaves on the trees were unfurled, the last of the daffodils were in bloom, and mud lay in the shady corners of the yard. It was late May. Was it too late? Had he gone north without her?

"Oh, please, oh, please!" She chanted it to herself like a prayer as she randomly threw belongings into her trunk, wadding up her dresses, crushing her new hat after them. She finally knew her own mind, knew what was truly important to her heart, but had she come to her senses too late? She doused the lamp and struggled into her old coat. She thumped her trunk heavily down the stairs and left it outside the dining room. Four pairs of eyes turned toward her as she entered. Colby's mouth dropped open on seeing her coat, but Millie's face registered—what was it? Triumph. Satisfaction. As if she'd just won a prize in a contest. Her smile fairly glowed across the room.

"I'm sorry. May I speak with you?" Katherine said formally.

The old woman jerked her head. "Was it he?"

"No, but—"

"There's no need to explain, Kate."

"But I want to."

"There is no need," Millie repeated, her voice softening. "I knew from the start you would go back eventually, as soon as you realized the worth of what you had."

"You knew?" Katherine said quietly, her cheeks growing warm. "You always knew."

"Better than you did, I wager." Millie smiled gently. "I was looking out the window the day I interviewed you. You were still under examination, you know. And I watched you say good-bye to your former employer. I saw the *whole* good-bye, mind you. And it was then I knew I wouldn't have you long, but I'd make do with the time you gave me. I'm just surprised you let this go on as long as you did."

"It did take me awhile to figure it out," Katherine said, giving Millie a trembling smile. "But I finally got it in the end."

"Yes, and that's what matters. But you had to come to that conclusion yourself."

Kate wiped her eyes with her fingers, abolishing the last of her tears. "Thank you for everything, Millie. I've truly loved it here."

Dot gaped at her, Millie's spoon forgotten in her hand. Colby started to his feet.

"Sit down, boy!" Millie barked without looking at him.

Colby sat, his face blank with surprise. His parents looked from one to the other, baffled.

Millie smiled, her face folding into a thousand crinkles. "I'll miss you, dear. You must all come visit."

"We will," Katherine said and added sincerely, "I'll miss you too."

"The carriage is at your disposal. Bob will drive you wherever you want to go."

"Thank you." She looked at Colby's astonished face. "I'm sorry. You've been very kind." Katherine turned toward the door.

Behind her, Millie added, "Tell him *buona notte* for me," and began to giggle.

Without another glance at the people at the table, Katherine fled from yet another dinner party.

* * *

The carriage rattled as slowly as a donkey cart. The roads were empty, but the evening was dark, and Bob didn't want to risk injury or disaster. Katherine leaned forward in her seat as if by doing so she could urge the carriage to travel faster. It was ten o'clock by the time they left Springfield behind and neared the turnoff for the clearing. Katherine gripped her hands together in her lap and chewed her lower lip in her anxiety. What if he had gone already? Where was it they spent the summer? Collingwood, that was it. She'd follow him.

"This is it! Stop here, please, Bob," she cried, pounding on the ceiling.

He pulled the horse to a stop. "There's naught here but trees," he said. "I don't think—"

Katherine jumped out onto the ground without waiting for help. "It's all right. This is the place. It's just along that path. If you can fetch out my things, please."

"Of course, miss. I'll carry your trunk for you, if you tell me where . . ."

"It's all right, you can just leave it here, and Alon—I will fetch it later. Just under the tree there will do, thank you."

"I'll wait here," Bob said firmly. "You come back and tell me it's all right before I go."

"Yes, good idea. Thank you. I will."

Picking up her skirts with both hands, Katherine hurried along the dark trail, stumbling over the winter's accumulation of branches and debris. She was shivering, more from fear than chill. She stepped into the clearing, already cursing herself for her stupidity—but it was not empty. The cart stood beneath a tree, its empty shafts resting on the ground. The train car still huddled cozily in its place, a dim glow in its window. The dark shape of the horse moved edgily, then settled. Bo began to bark.

The tightness that had encircled her heart began to unwind and ease, and she found she could breathe properly again. She hurried back to dismiss Bob with a nod and a wave. "It's all right! They're here!" Then she strode quickly back down the path toward the train car.

"Hush, darling Bo, it's Kate," Katherine called. The dog recognized her, his bark turning to a gleeful whine, and he rushed to meet her. Katherine caressed his head, murmuring loving words, but didn't break her stride. Bo fawned in ecstasy around her ankles when she neared the train car, tripping her up, and she bent to shush him.

The door above them opened.

Katherine straightened, her hands falling to her sides, her breath catching in her throat. Light spilled around Alonzo's form in the doorway, slanting across the smooth plane of his jaw, dancing in his dark curls. They stood facing each other, and then Alonzo came down the steps, closing the door behind him.

"I've come back."

"Yes."

"I love you," she said simply.

She held her breath and waited for him to echo her, to hold out his arms so she could fit herself into them as she longed to do. To cover her face with kisses.

He didn't move. "Why are you here?" he asked.

Katherine felt as if he'd thrown ice water in her face. "I told you. I-I love you. I know that now."

"I've always known it. I could tell that the first time I held you. The children knew that even before I did. But that doesn't answer my question, Kate. Why are you here?"

"Isn't that enough of a reason?"

"No."

"I've made my decision, Alonzo. I . . ." Her voice failed, and she felt the blood rush to her cheeks. She had been in such a hurry to get here, so afraid he would have given up and gone to Collingwood without her, it had never occurred to her that he might not want her back. She swallowed hard and said what she knew had to be said. "I've been a complete idiot and a hypocritical fool, Alonzo. Please forgive me. I was too stupid and shallow to see it before. I understand what's really important to me now. I want to be here with you. Nothing else matters."

He struggled for a moment to find his own voice, and then he blurted, "You have no idea how much it hurt me when you left. How much it hurt the children."

"I know—"

"No, you don't know." He took a step toward her, his voice tight with emotion. She was suddenly glad she couldn't see his face in the dark. "We lost one woman we loved—Ruth—because she didn't have a choice. She died. But, Kate, you had a choice, and you left anyway. You broke my children's hearts. And now you just walk back in here and expect me to trust you instantly?"

Katherine stared at him and felt her heart stop in her chest. She was shaken to realize the depth of the pain she had caused. "I'm so sorry," she said. "I don't know what else to say. But, Alonzo, I had to be sure. You can see that, can't you? I told you I had to be sure I loved you enough."

"And are you sure now? Because I can't let you back into Tony's and Lilia's lives if there's a chance you're going to go away again."

"I promise you I won't. Please believe me. I'm here to stay. Everything I want is right here in this train car." Katherine gripped her hands tightly behind her back to keep from grasping at him. He was so close and yet felt so far away from her. She took a deep breath, but her voice came out as a whisper. "Please let me stay." She stepped closer, closing the gap between them.

There was a pause, and then Alonzo reached out and took her face between his warm hands. He ran his thumbs gently over her cheekbones.

When he didn't speak, she repeated, "I love you. Please believe me. I've made my decision. Is it too late?"

He shook his head then. "Don't go away again," he said hoarsely.

Tears began to course down her cheeks. She only shook her head and put her arms around him.

He held her, his voice muffled in her hair. "Oh, Kate. I was lost after you left. I feared you wouldn't come."

"I thought you might not wait."

"I would wait a lifetime for you," he replied. Then at last he lowered his head and kissed her lingeringly.

It was at once familiar and new, and Katherine clung to him, joy beginning to spread in her heart. "I'm so sorry I ever doubted," she said again.

He put a finger to her lips. "Me too. But you're here now. That's all that matters. We won't look back."

"No."

He smoothed the hair from her face, holding her as if she were spun sugar and might melt away any moment. As if he would memorize her face with his fingertips. "Marry me, Kate. Share my life with me."

"I will. All of it. The cold water, the smoky fire, even the bush," she declared, beginning to smile.

"Actually, I built an improved lavatory while you were away. I'll admit it's very comfortable." He laughed suddenly. "Maybe you're domesticating me."

"Impossible. You'll always be half wild. And I love you for it."

He kissed her again, and she pressed her cheek to his. Then he straightened. "No more until we're properly married," he said seriously, "or I can't answer for the consequences."

"Then I'd advise you to find a minister immediately," she declared. "The sooner, the better."

He grinned. "Yes, I better had."

The door behind them flew open, and Lilia and Tony spilled out, shrieking, to launch themselves at Katherine. Laughing, Katherine tried to catch them both and ended up sitting on the damp ground with them tumbled on top of her. She knew her burgundy dress would be stained, but she didn't care. Lilia covered her face with kisses, and Tony clung around her neck and buried his face with no intention of ever letting go. Katherine caressed his curly head, letting the tears spill down her cheeks without trying to staunch them.

"I woked up and heard you," Tony murmured.

"You came to visit," Lilia cheered. "Just like you said."

"I came to stay," Katherine told her. She put her hand up for Alonzo to help her to her feet, but instead he dropped to his knees in the mud beside her and gathered all three of them into his arms.

He kissed each forehead solemnly. "Let's go get Michael," he said, "and make this family complete."

* * *

Alonzo moved back out to the cart without a murmur of complaint. That night, in the cot with Lilia curled warmly against her side, Katherine drank in the small, comforting things she hadn't realized she'd missed and sent prayers of gratitude heavenward that she had come to herself in time. He had waited for her. He had let her back in. The stove snapped and popped gently in the corner. The train car smelled faintly of onions from supper. Tony's breathing came deep and steady from above her head. She pulled the itchy wool blanket up to her chin and smiled to herself in the dark. It wasn't elegant or spacious. There was no servant to produce warm water and breakfast. She would likely never be invited to dine at a high-society table again. But none of it seemed of any importance at all anymore. Mr. and Mrs. Timothy Eaton would have to muddle along without her.

* * *

She told Alonzo everything over the next couple of days, everything emptying out in a painful trickle at first and then finally in a deluge. She told him about the awe-filled night at the opera and the awkward readjustment she'd experienced to living in a proper house. About forgetting herself and trying to carry her own dishes into the kitchen, scandalizing Millie's kitchen maid. About seeing Ah Lam again and the Pendovers' reaction to her friendship with a Chinese woman. She told him about the sinking of the *Victoria*, and she unburdened herself of the struggle that had gone on between her heart and her head.

"I couldn't admit to myself that everything I'd ever wanted turned out not to be right for me," she told him. "But after that conversation at dinner with Colby's parents, I finally knew who I was and what I valued. I could see what Colby valued too and how the sort of life he offered wouldn't reflect what was truly important to me. I couldn't live like that and be true to myself. But then I thought about how your way of being, the way you treat people, really reflects what you value, Alonzo. I saw what a wonderful thing that was and what I was in danger of losing. I will never, never look down on who you are again. You're the best, kindest man I've ever met, and I would be proud to be your wife."

"If that's your decision, if you really know what your heart wants . . ."

"It is."

"Then there's no sense in holding off. We'll get married on Friday and head for Collingwood as soon as I get everything settled. Will that suit you?"

"Immensely."

The children gave their wholehearted approval, delighted that Kate would not be going away again.

Katherine felt a deep sense of peace settle over her, and she knew beyond doubt that this time she had truly made the right decision. She wasn't just telling herself that to soothe her conscience; she knew it in her very bones.

* * *

The Catholic Church would not marry them because Katherine was Church of England, so they were married by special license by a judge at the courthouse. Katherine wore her next-best dress, the muddied burgundy being beyond hope, and carried a fistful of spring daffodils Lilia had gathered for her. It was difficult to keep the children from jigging and singing around her during the brief ceremony. The marriage was witnessed by the judge's clerk and secretary, and then it was finished, and Kate was signing the registry before she knew it. After such a momentous decision and all the difficulty of reaching it, it seemed that the wedding itself should surely have taken much longer. But it was done, and to celebrate afterward, Alonzo took them all to the Duke of Paisley Teahouse, where he and Katherine had first met.

"What's next?" Katherine asked, watching him over the rim of her cup as he buttered a scone for Tony.

"Next we take the train north, as soon as I sell up."

"Sell. You mean the horse and train car and everything?"

"Horse, train car, cart, and all. We can't haul them with us."

"I suppose not. It just seems so—*final*."

He grinned. "You'll like Collingwood. It's right on the bay and very pretty."

"What do you do there all summer?" Katherine asked. "Where do you live?"

"I can support you, if that's what you're concerned about," he said. "I have a home. You look very fierce, *bella*. Be patient. It'll all become clear."

"Why do I have the strange feeling you're being evasive?"

He grinned at her. "I'm afraid I don't know that word, Kate. Will you teach me?"

"Why is it your English is excellent until I ask something you don't want to answer?" she grumbled.

They spent the day showing the children the sights in the city and bought them fruit ices in the park, even though the weather was not yet summery. But they were in a celebratory mood, and only ices would do. They arrived back at the train car as night fell, and as soon as supper was finished, the exhausted children fell into bed, sticky and happy. Alonzo went outside to see to the horse, and Katherine moved quietly about the kitchen—her kitchen, she thought with a happy shiver, even if only for a while longer—clearing away the dishes, wrapping the leftover bread in a cloth, wiping the table. The familiar work was comforting, and the quiet of the train car settled around her soothingly, like a shawl.

When she'd finished, she changed into her nightgown and settled down beside the lamp to do some sewing. Alonzo still hadn't returned. She watched her needle flash in and out in the lamplight, steadily at first, then with growing agitation. Where was he? What could possibly be keeping him from her on their wedding night? She glanced at her watch and saw with some embarrassment that it was only eight thirty.

"A little anxious, are we, dear?" she murmured wryly to herself.

At last the train car door opened, and Alonzo poked his dark head in. His eyes twinkled with a light she recognized too well. He was a little boy bent on mischief.

"Are they asleep?"

"Yes."

"Come with me, then."

"What, outside? In my nightgown?"

He pursed his lips. "It's not as if the neighbors will see. The nearest ones are miles away."

So she slipped on her shoes, took her shawl, and followed him out.

The moon was a curved, three-dimensional pearl above the black trees. Looking at it, Katherine felt she could reach up and catch it with her hand. Alonzo took her elbow and guided her through the dark into the woods.

"You want me to inspect your new and improved lavatory again? I told you just this morning it was grand."

"Not that," Alonzo whispered in her ear. "This."

They had paused in the clearing beside the stream where she used to bathe. The water ran smoothly over black stones, hollow and cold sounding. At the edge of the trees, ten feet from the river, there was a sort of shack or lean-to built of maple and birch branches. It had three walls and a roof, and the opening faced the water.

Wondering, Katherine let Alonzo lead her inside, and she found to her astonishment a comfortable room. Long dry grass like hay had been spread on the ground, and thick wool blankets were spread over it. A small oil lamp burned cozily on a rock in a corner, and the air was warm with the smell of freshly cut wood. A single red hothouse rose lay across one of the white pillows. How had he managed to find a rose in the city without her noticing? She stared, open-mouthed, at the bower he had built for her, then removed her shoes and stepped farther inside.

Alonzo moved to stand close behind her.

When he put his hands on her shoulders, she leaned back against him and shook her head slowly. "You're amazing," she said at last. "I never expected this."

He gave a low chuckle that vibrated through his chest beneath her ear. "Did you expect me to spend my wedding night in that cot with my children two feet away?"

"It would have been a trifle awkward," she agreed, smiling.

"We'll hear them if they wake up and call us."

He turned her toward him then and trailed a finger slowly down her cheek to her chin, tipping her face up toward his. His eyes smiled down into hers. "Mrs. Colaco. I like the sound of that."

"I do too," she whispered.

Alonzo removed her shawl. Then his hands moved to her hair, taking out the pins, loosening the heavy length of it, and spreading it over her shoulders. The dark strands poured through his fingers like syrup, shining in the lamplight.

A funny little tingle of joy ran through her, and she felt unbearably self-conscious. She tried to cover it by being brisk. "Don't lose any of those pins. Here, I'll put them in my shoe so they don't get lost."

Alonzo tossed the handful of pins in the general direction of her shoes, and they scattered into the hay.

When she moved automatically toward them, he stopped her and took her face between his palms. "I have more important matters to think about than pins," he said softly. "This time I don't have to hold my feelings back. This time you're my wife."

Katherine mimicked his accent playfully. "*Wife*. Hmm. I don't know that word. You will have to teach me."

So he did.

Chapter Twenty-Two

IT SEEMED A SIMPLE THING to slip back into life in the clearing. Katherine hardly had to think about it as she hauled water, cooked on the minuscule stove, and gleefully abandoned her bustle once more. She resumed the children's lessons around the table each morning while Alonzo traveled to the city, and it felt as if she had never been gone.

And yet there were subtle differences. Bo seemed to be particularly clingy and settled himself across her feet every time she stood still or sat. The children, especially Tony, became anxious if she left their sight, and he kept asking her if she was happy.

"Of course I am," she assured him for the twentieth time. When he remained unconvinced, she sat and took him onto her lap, smoothing his hair with her hand. "I know it upset you when I went away," she told him. "I went to take care of Mrs. Pendover for a while. But I'm back now, and I'm not going to leave you again. I'm very glad to be part of your family now."

"And you're going to Collingwood with us?" he asked once more.

"Yes. Next week, on the train. We're all going together."

"Can I sit by you on the train?"

"Yes, you can. I'll even let you hold my hand if you like. Are you excited to be going back to Collingwood?"

"Yes. I liked living in the train car, but going home is better."

Home. The thought touched Katherine's heart. What was home? What lay ahead? Alonzo had been quite vague every time she'd pressed him, only smiling and telling her she would find out soon enough. She felt like a child on Christmas, waiting to see what would emerge from her stocking.

"I want to see Michael too," Katherine said now. "Will it be fun to have a little brother?"

"Maybe," Tony said noncommittally. "Lilia says it isn't always much fun having a little brother."

Katherine laughed aloud at this. "She does, does she? Well, I think you'll make a fine big brother. I think you'll love Michael very much, and he'll love you too. I think it will be wonderful."

Tony leaned his head on her shoulder. "Me too." He sighed contentedly.

* * *

It took only a few days for Alonzo to sell the cart and train car and the rest of his wares, though he retained his tools. Katherine helped him to pack up, all that they possessed fitting into three trunks. Katherine stood that last morning gazing at the train car already looking empty and lonely in its little clearing. She felt a genuine regret at leaving it. The trees. The river. The lavatory. She laughed aloud now and turned toward the cart, where the others waited for her. They would deliver the horse and cart to their new owner and board the northbound train that afternoon. Katherine took Alonzo's hand, and he helped her up onto the high seat.

"Are you sure we should spend the money on the train?" she asked for the fifth time as they pulled onto the road. "We could take the coach."

"I told you I have the money, and it will be easier on the children. Besides, I've promised them a train ride. They're all excited about it. Stop worrying." He softened the reproach with a reassuring smile. "Let me take care of my family."

"Do you think we'll come back to Toronto someday? I promised Millie we would visit."

"No doubt. We're free to go wherever we wish."

"I wrote to tell Martha we were married, but somehow I don't think she'd welcome a visit from us just yet."

"I don't imagine so," Alonzo agreed, chuckling.

She sighed and glanced back over her shoulder. Already the turnoff into the trees leading to the train car was lost behind them. She faced forward, remembering the first time she had ridden in his gypsy cart, feeling like the Harvest Queen on parade. Even though he had been about to sell it, he had painted the cart light blue two days ago, in deference to Lilia, and Katherine felt as if she were skimming along like a bird on a bit of the sky.

She watched Alonzo's gloved hands moving gently with the tug and give of the reins. His leg lay warm against hers, and she found herself anticipating reaching Collingwood, collecting Michael, and settling wherever it was they were to settle.

"It will take time to get used to someone taking care of me," she said. "For so long I've only had myself—well, and my cousins. And you know how I felt about their help."

"I'm not them," he said firmly. "I don't provide for you out of duty but out of love. That makes all the difference. Now sit back and enjoy the ride."

They caught the train at the Streetsville Station after dropping off the horse and cart with their new owners. It seemed so long ago that Katherine had passed through Streetsville on her way to Toronto from her disastrous job at the Colworthys'. So much had happened in the months since then that she could hardly believe it. She felt as if she were a different person . . . as perhaps she was.

The train passed through rolling fields and thick, dense forest, wending its way steadily north, but Katherine saw little of it before night fell. She pulled Tony onto her lap and cradled Lilia's nodding head against her shoulder, not caring how uncomfortable she was. They were together, and she could scarcely believe it. Her circumstances had reversed in an instant, in the nick of time, and now Alonzo slept peacefully on the seat opposite her, his dark curls shifting shadows as the lantern swayed with the train's movement. Watching him, she felt deeply, deliciously happy. All of life lay ahead of them, and together they could make of it whatever they wanted. She thought she could understand a little better now what the word *blessed* meant.

It struck her that she was now the mother of three, and the thought seemed both glorious and unbelievable. When she'd left the Colworthys last fall, she'd been depressed at the unlikelihood of her ever marrying, much less marrying well. She'd begun to believe Martha and Elizabeth were right and she would never have her own family and all the joy that went with it. How quickly life turned around! And glancing at Alonzo, she knew she had indeed married well.

They reached Collingwood in the gray of early morning. They and their belongings were deposited unceremoniously on the platform, along with Bo, who was miffed at having had to ride in the baggage compartment. Katherine squinted around her. It looked much the same as the platform in Toronto, though she knew Collingwood was a small town in comparison and that it sat on the shores of Georgian Bay, not Lake Ontario. She was too tired to take much in about her surroundings. She felt wrinkled, her mouth sour, her eyes gritty.

Lilia leaned against her legs, and Tony looked on the verge of a pout.

Alonzo, on the other hand, looked fresh as if he'd just started out, and his smile was optimistic. "Almost home."

"Wherever that is," she replied. The biscuits she had eaten on the train were rocks in her stomach. "We'll wait here while you find a cab."

"No need. John should be waiting for us with the carriage. I wired him when he could expect us. I told him about you too, of course."

"John?" she asked muzzily.

"O'Riley. Let's see if we can find him."

He took her arm and escorted her up the platform with the two children jogging behind. Outside the station, they found a line of carriages waiting for their passengers. One of them, polished to a high black gloss, sported a white bridal wreath. It was drawn by two beautiful bays.

A weather-withered man with gray hair stood beaming beside the horses' heads. When he saw them, he swept off his hat and made a half bow. "Mrs. Colaco. Welcome home, ma'am."

Katherine blinked at him.

"I'm John O'Riley." His blue eyes slid beyond her to the children, and his face creased into a hundred wrinkles. He stooped and held out his arms, and Tony and Lilia bounded into them with shouts of greeting, their energy having returned with their excitement. Lilia planted a kiss on the aged cheek.

"We've missed you, dears," John crooned like a doting grandfather. "Mrs. O'Riley has baked herself silly for you. My, how tall you are now! I can't believe it!"

"We have a lot to tell you," Lilia informed him. "We had a—a adventure, just like Papa said we would."

"I'm sure you did. I'll have to hear all about it. And it sounds as if your English has improved."

"I can read now," Tony informed him proudly.

"I never! Can you really, now?"

"In English!"

"There are three trunks, John. I'll help you with them," Alonzo said. He nudged Katherine. "Can you help the children in, *bella*?"

Bemused, Katherine clambered into the carriage and settled the children on the leather seats. Bo crouched down on the carriage floor and rolled his eyes.

"Mrs. O'Riley makes the best cookies," Lilia rattled. "Michael will be big. Maybe he can walk. Papa says he won't remember us, but we'll teach him."

When the trunks were installed, Alonzo swung into the carriage beside them, and they were off. They went so fast Katherine hardly had a chance to get an impression of the town, registering only neat clapboard houses and wide dirt streets lined with trees. There were few people about at this hour, and it wasn't long before they were out of the center of town and trotting along a road lined with poplars. Through the gaps, Katherine saw open fields, emerald green combed in neat rows emerging from the gray as the sun rose higher. There was the refreshing damp scent of crushed grass. Once, they passed a field of cows, and the children hung out the windows, calling to them and making cow sounds. Alonzo laughed and pulled them safely back inside.

"They're as excited as I am," he remarked.

"I don't understand. You've mentioned the O'Rileys, and I know they've been taking care of Michael, but who exactly are they?" Katherine asked. "Are they neighbors or—"

"I've known them since I first came to Collingwood from Italy," Alonzo said, waving a hand. "John has become a good friend."

"There it is!" Tony cried, back at the window. Katherine clutched his coattail to keep him from going out headfirst. "There's the house!"

The carriage stopped, and Katherine followed the children out onto the gravel drive. Tall maple trees frothy with bloom marched up to the house, which was bigger than she'd expected. Two stories high and built of red brick, it was snuggled beneath the trees like an egg in a nest and appeared solid and cozy. Clematis sprawled in pink profusion on each side of the green door and up to the roof. As she stood wondering, the door opened, and a woman who was the perfect counterpart to John O'Riley came out onto the steps. Katherine had never seen an old woman run before, but run she did, sprinting down the drive toward them, her skirts hiked to her black-stockinged knees like a girl. Her round face was beaming.

The children exploded in shrieks of joy and ran to meet her. She swept them into her ample bosom and bestowed kisses and endearments, crooning and laughing in delight. Then she set them on the ground, threw out her arms, and pulled Alonzo down into her embrace as if he were one of the children. Katherine had just enough time to see his laughing expression before it was buried under the old woman's kisses.

After awhile, Alonzo straightened and held her off, grinning. "I'm happy to see you too, Lucy. I want you to meet someone. Look who I've brought."

The old woman beamed at Katherine, her face a maze of wrinkles, eyes swimming with happy tears. Katherine grinned back, the affection contagious.

"This is my wife. Kate, Lucy O'Riley."

"What a charming girl!" Lucy gushed, coming to give Katherine a strong squeeze. She was shorter than Katherine, but she was a heavy woman, and Katherine felt her own corset creak under the pressure.

"Come in, have something to eat. I've just put the kettle on. Of course you'll want to see Michael, Alonzo. He's right here."

They traipsed into the house. It was spacious and meticulously clean, with gleaming wood floors spattered with colorful rugs. Katherine caught a glimpse of a cheerful parlor through a doorway on her left. The rising sun poured through its windows and spilled out into the entryway, splashing across their feet. It felt as if the house itself were welcoming them.

"Wait here." Mrs. O'Riley went up the wide staircase at a jog.

The children danced in their eagerness, and Lilia came to take Katherine's hand. "You will like him," she said anxiously. "I'm sure he's a good baby."

"I'm sure I'll love him just as I love you," Katherine assured her.

Alonzo stood with his face turned toward the ceiling, his breath coming in swift gulps. He looked on the verge of tears, and for a moment, it alarmed her. But then she understood. He hadn't seen his son since the previous spring—the son Ruth had died giving him. She felt her own throat tighten.

Mrs. O'Riley came down the stairs. She carried a little boy about a year old, dressed in light blue to match his wide, long-lashed eyes. His curly hair was jet black. He put one chubby finger in his mouth. Alonzo stood utterly still with his hands dangling. They exchanged a long, solemn look.

Mrs. O'Riley looked from one to the other. No one moved. Even Tony and Lilia were subdued, watching.

Then Mrs. O'Riley bent and placed Michael on his sturdy legs. "There you go, love. Show your papa how you can walk."

Alonzo stirred, knelt, and held out his arms. Michael hesitated, not quite trusting this stranger, but his balance was not good enough to remain standing for long. Necessity won out over inhibition. He staggered three steps and fell into Alonzo's arms. Alonzo swept him up and stood, laughing.

Everyone resumed breathing. Lilia and Tony danced around their father, demanding to hold Michael. Katherine found tears on her cheeks and wiped them off on her sleeve. Mrs. O'Riley patted her arm.

"Everything is all right again. We're all together again as it should be. It will all be fine now. You probably want a wash and a rest. Come upstairs, and I'll show you your room. Oh, it's good to have you all here. It's been too quiet all winter."

Katherine shook her head. "Wait. My room? What do you mean?"

"At the top of the stairs. As soon as we got Alonzo's wire, I fixed the master room up all nice. I'll bring hot water directly."

"But . . . we don't live here. Do we?" Katherine looked at Alonzo and found him watching her with shimmering eyes over Michael's dark curls. His lips twitched as he watched her reaction.

"We *do* live here," Katherine murmured, staring at him. "Do—Is—This is *your* house?"

"Welcome home," he replied, grinning.

"But you're a tinker. You live in—I thought . . ." She stopped, her head beginning to hurt.

Mrs. O'Riley gripped her elbow. "It's been a long trip. Come and lie down before lunch," she advised kindly.

Meekly Katherine followed her.

* * *

The master bedroom was twice the size the entire train car had been. The gleaming floor was half covered by a thick blue-and-white Oriental carpet. The maple bedstead was freshly made up with a milk-white comforter and lace-edged pillows. Under the window stood a bookshelf with a silver vase of pale-pink peonies. They reflected the flowered pattern of the china basin and pitcher on the washstand. And flanking the fireplace like a friendly old couple stood two matching jacquard armchairs with crocheted doilies on their backs.

Katherine heard the door close behind her as Mrs. O'Riley went to fetch water. She couldn't move. She could only stand staring at this lovely, elegant room and feeling as if she were in a dream. An unreasonable irritation started to rise within her chest. She heard the door open and close again and knew without looking that Alonzo stood behind her.

"Do you have gold-plated flatware too?" she asked and heard a bitterness in her tone she hadn't intended.

"We only use it on holidays."

She squeezed her fists so tightly they trembled. "You made fun of my dream when I told you I wanted all this. Yet you had it yourself all the time."

"I didn't make fun of your dream," he said. "As I recall, I only said material things didn't matter so long as you were happy with who you were."

"Why?" she whispered. "Why didn't you tell me who *you* were? You lied to me!"

He put his hands on her shoulders. "I'm still me. I've never lied about that."

She spun away from him. Her heart thudded painfully. "You let me believe you had nothing. I lived in that train car. I-I bathed in an ice-cold river. I dried my underwear on a tree, for heaven's sake! People thought we were gypsies. And all this time you've had all this waiting here for you!" She waved her arms to encompass the room, the house, the O'Rileys. "You let me marry you thinking you were a tinker!"

Alonzo put his hands in his pockets and looked down at his shoes. When he spoke, his voice was subdued.

"I *was* a tinker at the time."

"And what are you now? Here?" she demanded.

"I told your family the truth. I do buy and sell minerals. I'm a broker. I'm also part owner of a shipping company on Georgian Bay."

"But then why were you living in that tiny train car?"

"I can explain, and I will, but it will take a little time. I thought you would be pleased to find out I had this house."

"I-I guess I am. I mean, it's very nice. But why didn't you tell me right from the start?"

"Because when I first met you, it didn't matter. It had no bearing on how I was living. And by the time I knew I loved you . . . well, after some of the things you'd said, I wanted to be certain you were marrying me for myself, not for what I did or what I owned. I needed to know you married me because you loved *me*."

"But of course I did!"

"You very nearly didn't!"

Katherine felt her face begin to burn. He was right, of course. She very nearly hadn't accepted him because of what he did and how he lived. She had nearly married Colby instead because he had had all the right social connections, a wealthy family, and good prospects. Alonzo was right—and it made her furious. "Well, I'm pleased to know I passed your test!" she said.

"There have been so many times I've wanted to tell you," he said in a low voice. "When you went away, I nearly came after you a dozen times. Once, I got as far as Chatham Square and stood there staring at the house. But I couldn't do it. I had to know you loved me as much as I loved you."

She swallowed hard, at a loss for words.

He moved closer, his eyes on hers. "So much that you'd be willing to give up everything for me, as I would for you. You did in the end. And I would too, all of it, in a minute. If you want me to go back to being a tinker in a gypsy cart, I will."

She shook her head, feeling as if it were swimming. "If nothing else, I hope I've learned to value people for themselves and not for how they live, rich *or* poor. I just want you to be honest with me. I'm sorry I snapped at you, Alonzo, but I was caught by surprise."

"I don't blame you for being upset. You think I deceived you. It wasn't my intention. I thought finding out I wasn't penniless after all would come as a happy surprise."

"I feel as if I don't know quite who I married."

"Kate, I'm still me. I still value my family above anything else. My life as a tinker reflected that, and I hope that my life here with you will continue to reflect that. That hasn't changed."

She glanced around the room again and shook her head. "No wonder you didn't bat an eyelash when your cart was destroyed! You didn't have to rely on it. And the money you gave Jin . . . I wondered how you could afford it. Well, there's time to tell me now. How *did* you end up in that train car?"

He pressed his lips together before answering. "After Ruth died, I couldn't stand this house. I tried for several weeks, but it was empty without her. The children couldn't fill the space. I needed to get away, to breathe. As I told you, before I came to Canada, I was a tinsmith in Italy, like my father and grandfather, and I decided to become one again. It seemed easy to turn the management of my business over to my partners, acquire a cart, and go. I couldn't bear to part with Tony and Lilia, and I knew they needed me after they had lost their mother so recently, so I took them with me. I had to leave Michael. He had to have a wet nurse, and I couldn't care for him. And—you asked me to be honest—he was a constant reminder of what I had lost."

Katherine swallowed against the knot in her throat, fighting tears. She could easily picture the newly bereft father taking his children and fleeing the site of so much sadness. Her heart ached for him.

He took a deep breath and let it out slowly. "I told myself I'd come back home in the spring, one year from Ruth's death. I would see if I could stand living here in this house again. If not, I'd sell everything and move away, find another home away from the memories. But, Kate, I've felt only joy and excitement at coming back here, not sadness at all. I've felt happiness at the idea of living here with you. I didn't know how I'd feel until I arrived. I didn't know if I could stay, and I didn't want to get your hopes up until I was sure. But because of you, I feel I can come home again." He held a hand out to her, palm up, waiting, his eyes burning steadily into hers. "Will you live here with me, Kate? Will you do what you did before and take me as I am?"

She knew there could be no hesitation, no doubts at all. Whatever the circumstances, he was still the gentle and compassionate man she had fallen in love with. The trappings of life, the particulars of their home together—they could figure that out. Together.

She reached out and placed her hand in his. He drew her to him, holding her gently, and Katherine rested her cheek on his chest and closed her eyes. She *was* home; she felt it. Wherever he was, was home. And she knew she had found the circle where at last she truly belonged.

About the Author

KRISTEN GARNER MCKENDRY BEGAN WRITING in her teens, and her work has been published in both Canada and the US. She received a Mississauga Arts Council MARTY Award in Established Literary Arts in 2012, and her book *Garden Plot* was nominated in 2011 for a Whitney Award for excellence in LDS literature.

Kristen received a bachelor's degree in linguistics from Brigham Young University and has always been a voracious reader. She has a strong interest in urban agriculture and environmental issues. She enjoys playing the bagpipes, learning obscure languages, growing wheat in the backyard, and making cheese. A native of Utah and mother of three, she now resides with her family in Canada.

For more information on Kristen and her books, check out her website at www.kristenmckendry.webs.com, where you will also find a link to her blog, *My Daily Slog Blog*.